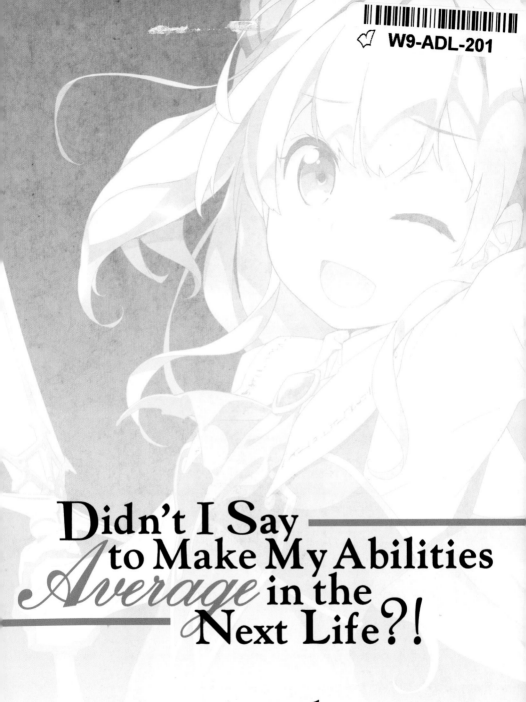

Didn't I Say
to Make My Abilities
Average in the
Next Life?!

VOLUME 1

Monika

Aureana

Didn't I Say to Make My Abilities *Average* in the Next Life?!

VOLUME 1

Seven Seas

DIDN'T I SAY TO MAKE MY ABILITIES AVERAGE
IN THE NEXT LIFE?! VOLUME 1

© FUNA / Itsuki Akata 2016

Originally published in Japan in 2016 by EARTH STAR
Entertainment, Tokyo. English translation rights arranged
with EARTH STAR Entertainment, Tokyo, through TOHAN
CORPORATION, Tokyo.

Seven Seas books may be purchased in bulk for promotional,
educational, or business use. Please contact your local
bookseller or the Macmillan Corporate and Premium Sales
Department at 1-800-221-7945, extension 5442, or by
e-mail at MacmillanSpecialMarkets@macmillan.com.

Follow Seven Seas Entertainment online at
sevenseasentertainment.com.

TRANSLATION: Diana Taylor
ADAPTATION: Maggie Cooper
COPY EDITING: Betsy Aoki
COVER DESIGN: Nicky Lim
INTERIOR LAYOUT & DESIGN: Clay Gardner
PROOFREADER: Jade Gardner
ASSISTANT EDITOR: J.P. Sullivan, Nibedita Sen
LIGHT NOVEL EDITOR: Jenn Grunigen
PRODUCTION ASSISTANT: CK Russell
PRODUCTION MANAGER: Lissa Pattillo
EDITOR-IN-CHIEF: Adam Arnold
PUBLISHER: Jason DeAngelis

ISBN: 978-1-626928-69-5
Printed in Canada
First Printing: June 2018
10 9 8 7 6 5 4 3 2 1

God bless me?
CONTENTS

This is dedicated to my friends, both in this world and the other.

— FUNA

CHAPTER 1

Reincarnation

"WHERE...?"

When the young woman awoke, she found herself in an unfamiliar room.

White walls, windows draped in pale pink curtains, an antique desk and armoire, hand-sewn stuffed animals...

The room was undoubtedly for a little girl. Yet sleeping on the bed was Kurihara Misato, an eighteen-year-old—no, that was wrong. She was Adele von Ascham, ten years old.

Wait. What? I'm...Kurihara Misato, ten years old, the eldest daughter of the Ascham family... N-no, wait! That's not right. What's going on? My... my head is killing me...

The girl must have fallen unconscious because the next time she opened her eyes, the pain in her head had vanished, and she remembered everything.

"Ah... So that's what happened."

She had died. Ten years ago.

Kurihara Misato was born to an ordinary family. Her parents were both honest, kind people, and she was the eldest of their two daughters. The younger, her junior by two years, wasn't perfect, but she was a cheerful girl with a lively disposition. Misato herself proved different: a wunderkind with talents beyond those of other children her age.

From the moment she was born, glimpses of her gifts could be seen.

She learned language early, and from the moment she could stand on two feet she was walking, much sooner than the average child.

Studies. Sports. Art. Shogi.

In kindergarten and grade school, she displayed, again and again, signs of this unusual intelligence, and as the years passed, everyone had high hopes for Misato. Much too high.

Grandparents and other relatives flitted about her. "This girl is a genius," they proclaimed. "She's going to be famous one day!"

One side of Misato's family had once been well known in the country, and the other descended from a noble line. By now, however, both had been reduced to common folk, rich only in pride. Soon, a battle began between the two sides, each eager to name Misato as their heir and lay claim to her intellect. As Misato's grandparents vied for her attention, they pitted her against her cousins—and even her own sister—with no thought for how difficult this must be for the girl herself.

Discord spread throughout the family, and Misato's only salvation was that her parents, unconcerned with such things, raised their children as normally as they could. Her younger sister was jealous of the attention Misato commanded but nonetheless grew into a fine, happy child.

Yet while Misato was granted a reprieve at home, predictably, she stood out at school. She was never bullied, but neither was there anyone she could call a close friend. Everyone treated her as though she were special.

Furthermore, this unhappiness was an area in which Misato was by no means a "genius."

When it came to loneliness, Misato's giftedness was no help. Perhaps, if she truly had been a genius—the sort of person for whom ideas and innovations are more valuable than companionship or support—perhaps then, her life would have been a little bit easier. But Misato wasn't like that.

In many ways, Misato was completely average. She was quick-witted and highly logical. Because she loved to read, she was knowledgeable about many things. But beyond that, she was just an ordinary girl with a high IQ and excellent test scores.

For Misato, living with such extravagant expectations—always being thought of as someone extraordinary—was painful. All she really wanted was to be able to gossip after school and swoon over boys, just like her classmates.

She was surrounded by others, but at the same time, she was all alone.

This continued even through high school. Misato, who had no friends to go out with, was left with little to do in her down time besides playing games, reading, and studying. Perhaps because of this, she was eventually admitted to Japan's most prestigious university, just as everyone had hoped.

And then came graduation day. After delivering a flawless valedictorian speech, Misato left high school behind. *At university, I should be able to live more freely*, she thought. *Finally, I'll be surrounded by other people who think just like me.* But just as she finished this thought...

Most of the people walking along the street were other graduates, flooding out from the school. The rest of the students had yet to be dismissed.

These students—no, former students—were giddy with freedom, talking and goofing around as they walked. Among them, one girl was swinging her bag as she chatted to her friends. A little girl around ten years old cycled by them on the edge of the road. The bag hit her as she passed, sending her tumbling off her bike and into the street.

An enormous vehicle came bearing down. Perhaps the driver had taken his eyes off the road or had been unable to react quickly enough—whatever the reason, it looked as if he wouldn't be able to brake in time.

By the time she realized what was happening, Misato's body moved on its own, flying into the roadway toward the little girl.

Why am I doing this...? she thought. *Someone standing closer should've had more than enough time to save her. Why didn't anyone move? I'm not going to make it in time...*

No one else moved to act; they only stood, their eyes on Misato.

"That girl is so brave!"

"She's going to save her, isn't she?"

Just as Misato scooped the girl's body up and flung her onto the sidewalk, there was a resounding screech. The vehicle, which had just begun to brake, struck Misato's body, shoving her to the ground.

"So, you have awakened, Miss Misato Kurihara."

When Misato returned to consciousness, she was lying on the ground. A young man of about twenty stood nearby, looking down at her.

"I-I was struck by a car, wasn't I...?" Misato muttered, coming to.

The young man made a troubled face and spoke. "Yes. And then you perished."

"Wh..."

What on earth are you saying? That was what she wanted to say, but on a certain level, it made sense. There was no way she could have possibly survived the accident. Besides, as she became aware of her surroundings, she could see that everything in the room was white. The floor, the ceiling—even the robes that the young man was wearing. *What's going on?*

While Misato sat, confused, the young man politely explained the situation.

"This place is what is known, in the common parlance of the populace, as 'Heaven.' And I suppose, by that same token, I would be called 'God.' Though I'm not entirely sure that is an accurate description..."

According to the young man, this was the state of things:

The world was governed by the laws of increasing entropy.

Entropy was defined in thermodynamics, statistical mechanics, information theory, and elsewhere, as a quantity of disarray.

Within a closed system, without external interference, entropy would always tend to increase.

If one placed a cup filled with hot water and another filled with cold water next to each other, touching, they would eventually become the same temperature. In contrast, if one placed two cups filled with lukewarm water side by side, they would not turn into hot and cold water. Strictly speaking, that assertion could not be confirmed within the theory—but still, it was usually a safe assumption to make.

For the most part, natural phenomena and the elements of life existed because of an inherent imbalance of matter and energy. If everything were to be mixed equally, it would be a world without any variations in energy. In other words, it would be a world where nothing changed: a world of sleep, or death.

Everything in the world trended toward death.

This was not the work of the Devil. It was wrought by the hand of the absolute god known as the Laws of Physics.

However, there was one thing that opposed all this: life.

By separating that which had been mixed, one could produce items that possessed regularity: cold water, hot water. This was an activity that gave the appearance of reducing entropy. In truth, when viewed through a wider lens, it could be said that the reverse was true. In order to separate matter and create new things, energy had to be consumed—and with that consumption came the increase of entropy.

It came as no surprise, then, that once the activities of life evolved into a civilization, they would—in many cases—eventually fall to ruin. Indeed, the probability of that greatly exceeded the theoretical probability value of the event.

And yet. There was a certain beauty to that frenetic activity, and sometimes it seemed as though the Laws of the World had a will of their own.

When a civilization reached dangerous levels, these Laws interrupted the Laws of Physics—offering only the smallest reprieve, in the most serious cases. The Laws were subtle: they granted only hints, suggestions planted in individual dreams and visions. But there was a twist, for nearly always, the recipients of these hints died at an exceedingly high rate. Even the Laws themselves didn't understand the reason for this. No matter how much it was studied, no explanation could be found.

Which left only a question: would the balance of life crumble in an instant? Or was there, perhaps, a will in the world that would save humankind?

"Huh?" Misato's head was spinning. "You're saying that my suffering—my death—those are all your doing...?"

"That is incorrect."

"What, then?!"

"The one I aided was the little girl whom you saved. You weren't involved in this plan. Your suffering is entirely your own fault."

"My own...?" Misato fell forward, her hands planted on the ground.

So this had been her fate from the beginning.

"To tell you the truth, the reason I summoned you to this place was to offer you my thanks."

"Huh...?"

"Despite my watchfulness, the little girl should have died there. I kept a sufficient lookout for accidents and illnesses, yet somehow that fall occurred—and somehow, there happened to be a car whose driver was distracted by his cell phone. My short-term predictions never accounted for such an event! I still don't understand how it could have happened.

"In the moment, I searched for something to protect the girl, but nothing suitable turned up. The people nearby didn't react in the slightest. Why? It was as if that girl's death was determined from the start, determined as a part of the world's preordained harmony.

"And then, just as I was about to give up, thinking that all the hardships I had faced in preparing this girl had come to nothing... you appeared. You were so far away that I was sure you would never make it in time. There were others far closer—you shouldn't have felt any reason to move. You were completely outside of the scope of both my desperate search and my short-term predictions.

"You are but a normal human being, and yet you flew in the face of that preordained harmony, escaping the view of my predictions, making a martyr of yourself and saving that little girl.

"Did you know? One day, that little girl is going to form the foundations of the theories that will allow humanity to travel to other star systems..."

And so, it became clear. *Even though I never accomplished anything myself,* Misato thought, *I was still able to make a difference. My life, my existence, do still have meaning.* With the knowledge that her life hadn't been for nothing, Misato felt a sense of quiet satisfaction.

"With the deepest gratitude in my heart, I would like the chance to grant you a new life. That is to say: you will be reborn, with your memories intact."

"H-huh?!" Misato was shocked. This was just like those games she used to play when she took breaks from studying. *Although if this is a game,* Misato thought, *there will be more coming...*

"So that you may live unhindered in a world whose society is somewhat behind your own, I would like to grant you some manner of enhanced abilities. I will offer you a choice: what sort of abilities do you desire?"

There it is.

Misato's reply was immediate. "Please, make my abilities average!"

"Excuse me?" At Misato's reply, the young man known as God appeared absolutely dumbfounded. "I don't think you understand me. The world into which you will be reborn is far less societally developed than your own. It is a world of swords and sorcery—lawless and overrun with bandits and monsters. Do you see? Without some sort of enhanced ability, the odds of you living a peaceful life are..."

In spite of God's concerns, Misato's mind was made up.

"I don't care. This rebirth means that I will live as a human, right? When I am reborn, I want my abilities and appearance to be completely average by my new world's standards. Please. I want to achieve happiness through my own efforts. As long as I retain the knowledge that I have right now, I think that should be enough of an advantage for me."

Seeing that Misato's decision could not be swayed, God nodded. "I understand. Now, regarding this world: We have been interfering with this place on something of a large scale, as a test case, which has caused it to become a world where magic is usable. We have disseminated a number of nanomachines, which multiply automatically until they have reached a fixed density. These react to the will of living things, which causes a variety of phenomena to occur. Chemical changes, physical changes, etc... Well, for someone like you, I suppose it could only be regarded as 'magic.'

"In truth, this world has collapsed a number of times, leaving only a scant number of survivors with meager skills. To offer relief measures, and as to conduct an experiment, we decided to interfere on a scale beyond what we would normally attempt. However, the pseudo-magic that arose from these nanomachines proliferated far more than we hoped it might. As a result, the progress of the civilization's renaissance has stagnated.

"For that reason, this world has been judged an enormous failure. Recently, it's been left to its own devices, with no one to look after it. Although there are those among us who feel guilty about all this, the people of the world in question have been content to continue living their lives regardless. You might say it's not such a bad place, after all—however, progress is minimal, security is weak, and dangers abound. Death is both common and swift..."

Wait just a second—this is what he calls "not such a bad place"? That was Misato's first thought, but then as she mused further on the matter, she began to reconsider. Wasn't it likely that the dangers God described could be avoided, particularly if one were born a woman and stayed close to home, avoiding travel?

Because she wouldn't be returning to her previous form, but rather, was going to be born anew as an infant in that world, there was no need for Misato to hear all the details about life on the other side. It would be best, she thought, to take her time and learn as a normal child would. So rather than asking questions, she only listened vaguely as God explained the basics of this new world and how she would come to enter it.

"Let us begin with the process of rebirth: The couple who will be your new mother and father were destined not to conceive, so there's no concern of displacing the soul of a child who should have been born otherwise. A newly fertilized egg has been prepared specially for you. As for me, I'll be praying that you live a happy life. Even if it is a strange to hear a prayer from a so-called 'god' such as myself.

"In the meantime, I thank you truly, from the bottom of my heart. Because of you, I believe that the day will come when the people of your former world will be able to rise up and achieve a higher order of being. Please, have a good life..."

And then, Misato was Adele von Ascham, age ten, the only child of the noble Ascham family—or at least, she *should* have been.

Something, however, was off.

Her memories returned when she was ten years old—that was fine. It seemed rather late for such a thing to happen, but accepting the spirit of an eighteen-year-old would have been a huge burden for a baby. She would've had to feign childish behavior, and it would have been bothersome if she already knew how to speak. It was probably a boon that she did not remember her former life until she had grown older.

However, as Misato ruminated on her memories, she found that she had a great deal to ponder.

It had happened two years ago.

Adele's parents had been scheduled to attend a party at the estate of a neighboring lord, but on the day in question, her father had suddenly fallen ill. The family arranged for Adele's grandfather to attend instead, but on the return trip, brigands attacked the duo, and both Adele's grandfather and mother perished.

The family's lands were relatively secure—bandits had not been seen for some years—but somehow, on this one occasion, they had appeared.

The day after the funeral, a woman was brought into the Viscount's home, bringing along with her a girl the same age as Adele. From then on, Adele's father attended parties with this woman, introducing the girl, whose name was Prissy, as his only daughter. Adele was left behind.

In time, most of the staff members of the residence were also replaced, and before long, those in the kitchen were all who remained of the old guard.

It was a familiar story, but an ironic one, for in her previous life, Misato's parents and sister were the only people whom she truly loved, and in this world, the three people who fulfilled those same roles were her greatest enemies. Her parents, and her new stepsister, who in all honesty was most likely her father's own child, born of an affair... All three had spent the last two years ridiculing Adele, bullying her, or else pretending that she didn't exist at all.

Now, however, only three days of that life remained.

Perhaps to wash their hands of her, the Viscount and his new wife had decided to send Adele away to a boarding school in the capital. She was scheduled to depart in three days, and for Misato—or rather, for Adele—this was an enormous relief.

The three days passed, and without so much as a word of farewell from her family, Adele boarded a carriage bound for the capital.

True to form, the Viscount hadn't even provided one of his own carriages. Thus, Adele carried little luggage: only a few changes of clothes, some toiletries, and a few other scant personal items.

She was on her way to Eckland Academy. It was a school primarily for the children of lesser-ranking nobility and middle-class merchants—though exceptionally talented commoners occasionally attended on scholarship. There was another academy in the capital as well, but this school was attended by only the very upper classes: royals and other aristocrats, the heirs to the wealthiest merchants, and the like.

Of course, her stepsister—or, in truth, her half-sister—was set to attend this more prestigious academy. Prissy would arrive there the following week, no doubt in one of the Viscount's stately carriages, accompanied by both their parents. And even once she began at school, Adele knew, Prissy would return home often.

With nothing else to do, Adele passed the long carriage ride thinking about her situation, how eager her family had been to sweep her under the rug. It seemed now that she was nothing but a bother to them, an awkward reminder of her mother, with no place in her father's new life.

It made sense, after all. With Adele around, people couldn't help but deduce that any daughter of her same age must have been born out of wedlock. But with her gone, they could call Prissy a stepdaughter, with no connection to the Viscount's bloodline. That way, there could be no scandal, and Prissy might be adopted by the Viscount, thus becoming his heir.

For them, Adele thought, *it's simple. They have to send me away so that Prissy can take my place.* Even when enrolling at the academy, Adele's parents forbade her from using the Ascham name.

It was possible, she supposed, that they would have a son at some point, and he might inherit. But either way, Adele would have no part in any of it.

She told herself it could have been worse. At least she wouldn't be killed—she'd just been set aside. Perhaps someday, she would be called back on a rainy day, when her father might marry her off for money or power. *Or perhaps they simply think that killing me would attract too much attention.*

In any event, Adele had her own plans: she would spend the next three years at the academy, learning about the world, and then, on the day of her graduation, she would vanish in the dark of night. It was clear already that she had no future in the Viscount's household, where the best possible outcome would be a political marriage: human trafficking under the guise of society matchmaking.

So she made her decision. Somehow or other, she would gather her wits, amass some funds, and escape. That would be her true goal for the next three years, regardless of her father's wishes.

Why? Adele asked herself. *Why did I have to be born into a noble family? I asked for my abilities and appearance and everything to be average, so why... why this?*

That was the question Adele had kept returning to over the last three days, ever since her memories had returned, and finally, in the carriage, the answer came to her.

Royalty, Duke, Marquis, Count, Viscount.

Slave, Peasant, Knight, Baron, Viscount.

The fifth from the bottom. The fifth from the top. Her family was exactly in the middle.

But something wasn't right, for that didn't account for the numbers—for the fact that there were many more peasants than there were dukes.

Not only was Adele's status not the average, it wasn't even the median. The median, she remembered, was derived by taking the center point of all available items, not simply the center *category*.

And even if that had not been true, it really should have been the mode, or most commonly occurring value, that was used.

By all accounts, whether you looked for the mean, median, *or* mode, Misato should have been a commoner! There was no reason that *this* should have ever been her position.

Eventually, she grew weary of thinking about all of it, and on the second day of her travels, Adele found other ways to occupy herself, such as carving dolls out of twigs. In her previous life, she had been quite dexterous and had thus acquired many such hobbies.

The knife she used was a tiny thing, the sort that a nobleman's daughter might be expected to keep on her person. In other words, it was a knife that might be used to end one's own life, should one come under attack from a robber—or some other man—and face the threat of defilement.

That's ridiculous, she thought to herself as she carved. Rather than killing one's self, would it not be preferable to use the knife to attack one's assailant, even if the blade in question was not truly suited to such things?

It was strange, she observed, that a knife like this cut wood as easily as if it were butter. Was it a particularly good knife? Or a particularly soft wood?

Stranger still, the doll that she was carving had an uncanny quality to it. It was less like a rustic toy and more like a figurine.

The other passengers in the carriage were uneasy, watching the little girl with the knife, worried, with every cut, that she might cut off one of her own fingers.

It was the second night of the journey to the capital.

The carriage ride wasn't exactly a luxurious way to travel. The sort of people who took a shared carriage ride were not the sort who could afford to shell out more money just for a place to sleep, and so, Adele and the others were resting in a meadow by the side of the highway.

As a gentlemanly act, the male passengers had offered the carriage to the women, while they themselves slept out on the grass. They indicated to Adele that she, too, should sleep inside the carriage, but after a long day squished like a sardine inside the tiny interior, she disembarked to join them in the meadow, instead. She knew that, if any of the women were restless sleepers or heavy snorers, such cramped quarters would be unbearable.

Lying there in the meadow, Adele suddenly recalled something that her father had told her. *The exam.*

In order for commoners to enroll in the academy, they had to pass an entrance exam. Nobles were not required to do this; however, as Adele currently was unable to carry her family name, she typically would have needed to take the exam as a commoner. Yet, perhaps to save money or avoid the extra bother of an additional trip to the capital, her father had made alternative arrangements. He'd written to the dean, revealing her nobility to guarantee her position, but demanding the school's discretion:

"The fact that she is a noble, as well as her family name, must be kept a secret. She must be treated the same as the commoners' children." Her father's plan ensured that Adele could not use failing the exam as a reason to return home.

The noble students also took an exam, a placement test to assess students' current abilities. Thus, although the academy had agreed that she was to be treated as a commoner, Adele nonetheless had a test she would have to take upon her arrival at the school.

Adele worried that, if she took this assessment along with the other nobles, her fellow students would be able to determine her status. However, none of the adults seemed particularly worried.

In any event, thinking about it would not do her much good. Adele decided to focus instead on practicing her magic.

Magic.

The word itself was exciting.

For Misato, who'd never had any friends, magic was something that appeared in the cartoons she watched as a child, and in the games that she would play, every now and then, while taking a break from her studies. In the world she was now in, magic was a reality—and she could use it. Just the sound of the word made her heart race! Magic!

But of course, she had known all that.

In this world, there were plenty of people who could use magic, just like the kind she had seen in cartoons so long ago. There were court magicians, magical societies, and casters associated with both the wizards' guild and hunters' guild...

However, she was but a child of ten years old.

According to Adele's memories from the time before knowledge of her past life had returned to her, her own magical abilities were average—or at least, she had an "average" aptitude for a ten-year-old girl, which was to say that her talents were fairly underwhelming.

Currently, she could only make enough of a spark to light a campfire and produce enough water to fill a single basin.

Still, this was actually quite useful. The fact that she would never have to worry about water while traveling meant that she could get away with carrying far less luggage than most. Complaining of her abilities among those who could not use magic at all would have been downright sinful.

Strictly speaking, she could be considered slightly above average in magical ability, but Adele wasn't about to issue a complaint to God in that regard.

Besides, she supposed, *in the average between "people who can use magic" and "people who cannot," someone who can use magic a little bit* would *be right in the middle.*

While the world's magic could generally be divided up into categories such as "water magic" and "fire magic," typically speaking, magicians themselves weren't classified according to such distinctions: one would never hear of a "fire-user" or "water-user."

This made sense, as the different kinds of magic were not derived from a "spirit of fire" or "spirit of water." Instead, all magic found its origins in a singular type of nanomachine. Thus, using it was dependent on whether or not one could assert one's own will onto the nanomachines in order to create a magical phenomenon.

This talent depended on a variety of factors: whether or not one's will could be concentrated into a pulse, whether or not that pulse could be received and interpreted by a nanomachine, and whether or not the contents of that pulse were something that could be made reality. Also, the image of what one hoped to create had to be clear in one's imagination. Whether or not the intended effect was something that would be classified as "forbidden interference" was another factor

As a result, it was impossible to break magic up into separate areas of study by type, though it was entirely possible to have strengths and weaknesses. Problems arose most often around the "image" portion of the magical equation. After all, people living in the desert would be hard-pressed to visualize the image of water or lakes.

Yet, in general, skilled magicians were skilled in every type of magic. Magicians whose abilities were less impressive—well, that remained true no matter what type of magic they used.

As the means to use magic resided solely within Adele's memories, Misato—now Adele—hadn't used magic once since the memories of her past life had returned. In order to avoid any accidents, she'd been forbidden to use magic within the family's mansion. So, she thought, it would be wise to practice at least once before she reached the capital.

With that in mind, Adele decided to try producing water. She settled against using fire at night, as that would draw too much attention and—in the event that something unexpected happened—it could be dangerous, as well. Water, at least, would be safe. Not only that, but it could be used to wash up, so it was quite handy, too. Their route was far from the river, and the small quantity of water the carriage was able to carry was intended for drinking, not bathing.

It would have been kind to offer water to the others, but as she had few attachments to people, as either Adele or Misato, the thought did not so much as occur to her.

Adele took a towel out of her bag, which she'd brought down from the carriage, and moved into the tree line, just a short way away and up a mild incline.

It was the first time she'd used magic since recovering her memories of her life as Misato, so Adele decided to try appealing the nanomachines, which she had heard about from God. She thought back to the times when she had used magic, before her memories returned, and stretched out her palms, reciting an incantation.

"Gather, oh water, and come to me! Aqua Ball Generation!"

Nanomachines, she thought, *don't let me down!*

...UNDERSTOOD.

"Huh? I swear I just heard somethi..."

Splash!

"Gaaaahh!!"

A great flood of water came pouring out of the sky in a single mass, washing Adele down the slope.

"Ugh! Ubb-glugg! Grk ugh blugg... I'm drowniiing!"

Adele flailed, swallowed up by the sudden torrent, fighting for her life as water rushed into her lungs.

It was not until sometime after that she was discovered face down at the bottom of the slope by some of the other passengers, who had rushed over to see what was happening.

I don't understand. Why did all that water...?

Once she had a chance to calm herself, Adele sat pondering this question. The other passengers helped her change and wring out her clothes; one older woman even lent her a baggy garment to wear until her own garments were dry enough to put back on again.

Adele knew that she had said the words correctly. But clearly, something had gone wrong. Was that really a problem, though? After all, she had been able to summon a huge amount of water from a botched spell. Or was what had just happened an indication of a new, powerful magic that she had somehow uncovered?

Have my magical abilities increased? Did regaining my memories impact my magic?

It certainly seemed that this was the case; however, that didn't change the fact that Adele's magical ability was supposed to be "average." Up until her current journey, Adele had rarely left the mansion, but she had read books and studied a great deal. From what she knew, there was no way that a ten-year-old child could possess the magical strength to produce the amount of water she had. Even if it were just another confusion of terminology, between "median" and "mode"...

This is bad, she thought.

Tomorrow she would arrive in the capital, and then, the academy. There was no more time to practice, and even if there had been, it would have been unfair to upset the other passengers again.

Later, she could determine the cause of all this. For now, she would simply have to see what happened.

Didn't I Say
to Make My Abilities
Average in the
—— Next Life?!

CHAPTER 2 |

Eckland Academy

THE FOLLOWING AFTERNOON, when the carriage arrived in the Kingdom of Brandel's royal capital, Adele collected her luggage and headed straight for the academy. She carried only one bag, and it wasn't heavy.

Ardleigh Academy, the school Prissy was to attend, was located near the King's castle in the center of the capital. Eckland Academy, Adele's school, was located on the outskirts near the capital's northern gates. The main gates of the city were to the south, and the difference between the two school locations would have been clear to anyone.

The carriage station was located in the central square, but after a long walk, Adele reached Eckland Academy. She showed her entrance permit at the gate and then followed the gatekeeper's directions to the girls' dormitory.

Would their matron be kind? Or would they be more like

a strict warden? For the next three years, Adele's fate would be determined by this individual. Grimly, she knocked on the caretaker's door.

A bespectacled elderly woman answered, her eyes harsh. A warden.

At Adele's greeting, she simply glared, then handed over the keys to the girl's room.

"Is that your only luggage?"

"Y-yes..."

"What's inside?"

"A change of underclothes, some toiletries, and writing implements."

"That's all?"

"Yes."

"I see..."

After a long pause, the warden continued.

"If you should like to do any work on the weekend, come and speak to me."

Well, Adele thought, *perhaps she's not such a bad person after all.* With this thought, Adele climbed the stairs to the second floor in search of the room assigned to her.

Upon opening the door, she found herself in a private room: her very own little palace for the next three years. The room was about eight feet square. The bed took up roughly half the space, and the rest was filled to capacity with a desk, chair, and armoire.

It was, Adele supposed, a typical school dormitory. She was fortunate enough to have her own room, so she could not say she was dissatisfied. At the very least, it would be far more pleasant than living back at home.

Unpacking her things took her all of forty seconds. She placed her toiletries on top of the armoire, her spare undergarments inside, her stationery on the desk, and was then done unpacking.

If she ever had to flee in an emergency, and was given only forty seconds to gather her belongings, she could more than likely manage it with ease.

The entrance ceremony was in four days. In two, she would take her placement test along with the other nobles, and in three, she would receive her uniform and other supplies and begin to prepare for the entrance ceremony. The next day would be her last day of freedom.

Adele lay flat on her bed and fell deep into thought once again.

What was the source of that water magic?

Where could so much water have come from?

Adele pondered this as she rested.

If she thought about what she knew of how the world worked, if she thought about God's explanations of magic—what conclusions could she draw?

Option one: Her own magical ability had grown, and accordingly, the intensity of the pulse she generated had been greater...

But weren't her magical abilities supposed to be "average"?

Option two: Her powers of visualization were particularly strong, and therefore, their conversion to magic especially efficient.

This was certainly possible, Adele acknowledged—her knowledge of the modern world might, after all, have some kind of impact on things. However, it seemed far-fetched to imagine that visualizations alone could confer the kind of strength she had summoned.

Which brought her to...

Option three: An external force.

What had she done differently? Something besides reciting the spell...

Oh.

Nanomachines, don't let me down!

That's what she had thought.

Could the water have been the nanomachines' reply? *No way,* she thought.

Although these *were* nanomachines, seeded by godlike beings. They couldn't be compared to the sorts of machines that had existed in Misato's old world. Unsurprising, then, to know that each and every one of them possessed their own sort of artificial intelligence. A machine of more singular function would never be capable of receiving and implementing people's thoughts in such a way.

What if these beings were to receive the pulse of a spell one normally would not cast, judge it to be a request, and actualize it? What would happen if someone were to call upon them by name?

It was a possibility.

However, there was no time for Adele to test this theory.

Practicing in her room was out of the question, as there was too great a danger of destroying something. As for a practice room, well—she could hardly borrow one before she was fully enrolled. Even if she could have, people would see her and ask questions.

"If only I could just ask the nanomachines..."

IF YOU HAVE A QUERY, WE SHALL ANSWER IT.

The voice rang in Adele's ears, startling her and causing her to thump her head against the wall.

"Gaaaahh!!"

She groaned and curled forward, clutching her head.

IF YOU HAVE A QUERY, WE SHALL ANSWER IT.

The mysterious voice persisted!

There was no one in the room besides Adele. Who else could the voice be speaking to?

Gingerly, Adele called out.

"Hello? Nanomachines?"

YES. THAT IS THE NAME OUR CREATOR HAS GIVEN US.

On Earth, Adele knew, nanomachine research was already underway. The computer had transformed, within a matter of decades, from something the size of building to a machine that could fit in the palm of your hand.

With that in mind, it was impossible to imagine the capabilities of nanomachines that had come into existence well before humanity, designed by godlike beings rather than scientists and engineers.

Even Adele could see that merely accepting humans' requests and answering them would be a fairly simple matter. What she couldn't predict was whether the nanomachines were merely responding with the words indicated by their programming, or whether they possessed a will and personality of their own.

This was the perfect opportunity to learn the answers to these questions.

"What I'd like to know is this: why is my magical power suddenly so great?"

PLEASE WAIT A MOMENT...

After several seconds' pause, the nanomachines replied.

OUR DATA INDICATE THAT THE INSTRUCTIONS YOU PROVIDED DURING YOUR LAST MAGICAL EXERCISE INCREASED THE EFFICACY OF THE PROCEDURE BEYOND NORMAL LEVELS.

So she had been right about that much. That was a relief. But Adele still had questions.

"By how much did the result increase?"

ROUGHLY 3.27 TIMES.

"Hmmm..."

Clearly, that was too small an increase to explain the phenomenon entirely.

"Why else was my power stronger than an average ten-year-old's?"

THAT IS SIMPLE. YOUR THOUGHT PULSE WAS STRONG, AND THE IMAGE IN YOUR MIND WAS CLEAR AND CONCRETE. TO BE SPECIFIC, YOUR THOUGHT PULSE POSSESSED ROUGHLY HALF THE STRENGTH OF THAT WHICH MAY BE PRODUCED BY AN ELDER DRAGON, THE MOST POWERFUL CREATURE IN THIS WORLD.

Adele couldn't believe her ears.

"Um, sorry. You said half of...what?"

The nanomachines spoke slowly and clearly.

THE. STRENGTH. OF. YOUR. THOUGHT. PULSE. IS. ROUGHLY. HALF. THAT. OF. AN. ELDER. DRAGON'S.

"A-and what about compared to a human?"

IT IS ROUGHLY SIX THOUSAND, EIGHT HUNDRED TIMES STRONGER THAN THAT OF THE AVERAGE MAGIC-WIELDING HUMAN.

"S-six thousand..."

Six thousand, eight hundred times.

Whap!

Adele smacked her head against the wall.

Fwoomf.

She collapsed onto the bed.

"Wh-why...?"

After taking some time to recover, Adele had more questions for the nanomachines.

Thinking that she would have plenty of time to learn later, she had neglected to ask God very much about the details of magic, but now, the stakes were higher. If she made a mistake, she might cause a disaster, so it was critical that she got a firm grasp of the situation as soon as she could.

The nanomachines were full of explanations.

IN EFFECT, WHAT YOU REFER TO AS A HUMAN'S MAGICAL STRENGTH IS A COMBINATION OF THE STRENGTH, ENDURANCE, AND CLARITY OF THE THOUGHT PULSE THE INDIVUDUAL CAN PRODUCE. TO COMPARE IT TO A VOICE, IT IS AKIN TO VOLUME, STAMINA, AND CLARITY OF VOCALIZATION. THE CLARITY OF IMAGE IS NOT A MATTER OF MAGICAL STRENGTH, BUT IS INSTEAD DEPENDENT ON THE LEVEL OF TECHNIQUE. IT IS A SKILL ACQUIRED THROUGH TRAINING, NOT AN INNATE PROPERTY.

"So, you're saying that I'm proficient at all of that? The reason I can attain such a clear image is because of my previous knowledge, but as for the rest... *Oh, no.*"

Suddenly, it was all clear to her.

The nanomachines spoke the words anyway.

THE STRENGTH OF YOUR THOUGHT PULSE IS HALF OF
THAT OF AN ELDER DRAGON, WHICH IS THE STRONGEST
FORCE IN THIS WORLD.

It was exactly as she had calculated. Between those in this
world with the least and most magical strength, she was directly
in the middle.

Bang! Bang! Bang!

Adele slammed her head against the wall again.

"This is wrong! This is all wrong! That isn't how you calculate an average! All… all I wanted was to live life as a NORMAL
GIRL!!!"

Once again, she hadn't even been placed at the median.

Certainly, it would be troublesome to compare the powers of
all creatures in existence, but shouldn't dealing with numbers of
such magnitude be a small feat for a god?

Or, had God done this on purpose? An attempted favor out
of concern for Misato's safety in this world?

After taking some time to calm herself, Adele continued her
interrogation.

"Has anyone ever asked you all these questions before?"

NEVER BEFORE HAS THERE BEEN A HUMAN WHO WAS
AWARE OF OUR EXISTENCE AND ADDRESSED US DIRECTLY.
MOREOVER, WE ARE NOT PERMITTED TO RESPOND TO ANY-
ONE WITH LESS THAN A LEVEL THREE AUTHORIZATION.

"Authorization?"

ONLY THOSE AT LEVEL THREE HAVE THE AUTHORITY TO
CALL UPON OUR POWER. TYPICAL CREATURES, INCLUDING
HUMANS, ARE INITIALIZED AT LEVEL ONE AUTHORIZATION.
ELDER DRAGONS BEGIN AT LEVEL TWO AND OCCASIONALLY

LEVEL THREE. IN THE PAST THERE HAVE BEEN HUMANS WHO HAVE REACHED LEVEL THREE, BUT IT IS AN EXTRAORDINARILY RARE OCCURRENCE.

SUCH HUMANS HAVE BEEN VERY ELDERLY, REACHING LEVEL THREE ONLY SHORTLY BEFORE THEIR DEATHS. FURTHERMORE, THEY CONSIDERED US MERELY TO BE THE SPIRITS WHO CONTROL MAGIC. THOSE WHO HAVE HEARD US APPEAR NEVER TO HAVE CONFERRED THIS INFORMATION TO ANYONE ELSE.

IN ORDER FOR OUR FORMS TO BE CONVEYED DIRECTLY TO THESE HUMANS' BRAINS, WE HAD TO STIMULATE THEIR RETINAS AND FORM OUR VOICES BY CREATING RESONANCE IN THEIR TYMPANIC MEMBRANES...

"Huh? So, what you're saying is..."

TO OTHER PEOPLE WE APPEAR TO BE NOTHING MORE THAN VISUAL AND AUDITORY ILLUSIONS. TO OTHERS, YOU YOURSELF WOULD NOW APPEAR AS A LUNATIC, HAVING A CONVERSATION WITH YOURSELF.

"Eep!"

WORRY NOT. CURRENTLY, THERE IS NO ONE IN EITHER OF THE ADJACENT ROOMS.

The nanomachines continued, while Adele looked frantically at the walls to her left and right. IF YOU DESIRE, WE CAN CREATE VIBRATIONS IN THE AIR SO THAT OTHERS MAY HEAR US AND BEND THE LIGHT WAVES SO THAT OUR FORMS ARE VISIBLE...

"No, no! You can stay as you are."

After all, she was just a normal, average girl. She had no need for magical spirit friends.

Now was the only time she intended to question them. Unless something else pressing came up, she wouldn't be speaking to them again.

Adele thought back. "So, the reason you are able to answer my questions is because I'm level three?"

OUR CREATORS, WHO HAVE THE HIGHEST POSSIBLE AU-THORIZATION LEVEL, ARE LEVEL 10. YOU ARE LEVEL 5.

Of course. The average, dead center between 0 and 10.

"Can you explain what counts as prohibited interference?"

THERE ARE CERTAIN CASES WHERE LIMITS HAVE BEEN IMPOSED ON THE TYPE OF MAGIC THAT CAN BE INVOKED TO PREVENT THE INFINITE PRODUCTION OF BACTERIA AND VIRUSES, NUCLEAR FISSION, NUCLEAR FUSION, RADIATION, AND ANY ACTIONS RELATING TO OUR OWN EXISTENCE.

"I suppose that's to be expected."

As Adele continued asking questions, she hit upon something else that interested her: *loot boxes.*

She asked whether there existed a magic that could access other dimensions, ones where the passage of time and progression of decay didn't exist, and the nanomachines answered that amongst the infinite dimensions, there were in fact worlds where the space-time continuum had ruptured. There, the concept of time ceased to exist; if one were to open a dimensional rift to one of these locations and place an item inside, the result would be a loot box or something similar. Moreover, because this loot box would occupy a pre-existing dimension, no additional energy would be required to maintain it. The nanomachines would be more than capable of storing and retrieving items in this way.

Apparently, some magicians were capable of using so-called

"storage" magic, which was very useful, if hindered by both space constraints and the fact that time continued to pass within the "storage" space. If Adele feigned this sort of magic, then she could use a loot box even in front of others, who would assume that she was simply using "storage" magic rather than calling on the power of the nanomachines.

After another series of questions meant to ascertain how she might lower her magical output to that of a normal human, Adele was through.

"Thank you for everything," she said. "With this information, I think I should be able to proceed as a normal girl."

ARE YOU...A NORMAL GIRL?

It sounded like a loaded question. Adele puffed out her cheeks.

"I am going to be a normal girl, live a normal life, and achieve a normal happiness!"

WE PRAY THAT YOU FARE WELL.

Upon finishing her conversation with the nanomachines, Adele felt a sudden sense of dread. She had never felt particularly strong before now, but in the wake of all that had happened, she began to wonder...

A coin would have been most useful, but at the moment she hadn't a penny.

As she searched for something else to use, her gaze landed on the metal handles of the doors to the wardrobe. Seeing no better option, she gripped one with her fingers and gave just the tiniest squeeze—

Crack.

So, even her physical strength was half of an elder dragon's?
What garbage!

Adele was so absorbed in her thoughts that she ended up
missing dinner.

Already accustomed to skipping meals, this was hardly cause
for concern. What worried her more was what she was going to
do moving forward.

She was currently penniless. Her parents hadn't provided her
with her a single coin.

Her tuition had been paid for, though, including her meals.
At least getting three meals a day wouldn't be a problem. She
could simply eat at the school cafeteria. On the other hand, buy-
ing snacks or eating out would be impossible, and she wouldn't
be able to purchase anything else, either. No clothes, no undergarments, no soap... No journals, no pens, no ink...

What was she supposed to do?

Honestly, what had her father and stepmother been thinking?

As she lay in bed pondering her dilemma, Adele decided to
go the next day and pay a visit to the matron's office. She had no
other choice.

Adele nestled under her covers.

This time, she was going to live as a normal person. She'd had
it with being seen as someone special, with being burdened with
heavy expectations.

She was going to be equal in status to everyone else, have normal conversations, and then—then, maybe she could make friends...

"Please give me a job!"

"What are you doing here at this hour?" the matron said, then sighed. "I suppose I did tell you when you arrived to come see me if you were interested in work..."

"I currently have no funds and only two spare changes of underwear! The assessment is tomorrow, so if I don't begin today, I won't have another chance until the coming weekend, and that will put me in quite a bind!"

The matron rubbed her temples, brows furrowed.

"Have you ever worked before?"

"I'm afraid not."

Even in her previous life, Adele had never held a job.

"Come with me."

Adele followed the matron to a humble-looking bakery.

"Mr. Aaron, I've brought you a new counter girl. What do you think?"

The matron explained the situation frankly to the bakery's owner: Adele was a penniless student with no prior work experience who wished to work only on her days off from school.

"Hmm. Well, I suppose if she's one of yours, then there's no problem." The bakery owner turned to Adele. "Here, we do the important work of putting food on everyone's tables, so we can't take even a single day off. I've been thinking for some time now that it would be nice if, one day a week, I might take a little break once the day's baking is finished.

"With that in mind, we've been looking for someone to come in and sell bread once a week, from morning to evening. What do you think? If that sounds good, why don't you come and try working for us? If it doesn't work out, you're welcome to quit at any point."

It seemed like the perfect job for Adele.

Even a ten-year-old girl could easily remember the prices of bread, and the baked goods there couldn't be all that different from what they sold in Japan... In any case, this was Adele. Even if there were a mountain of loaves, she could surely memorize their prices quickly enough for the baker.

Besides, the job was only once a week—how difficult could it be?

"I'm in, if you'll have me!"

And all at once, it seemed Adele would be able to live the life of a normal student after all.

In this world, each week was six days, with six weeks in each month. Thirty-six days in a month and ten months to a year. So, 360 days. The weeks and months were easily divisible, as well as numerous, so this was convenient in a number of ways.

On top of this, at the end of the year, there were the two "Days on Which We Mourn the Departing Year and Offer Our Thanks," as well as the "Changing of the Year Day," and the "Day on Which We Welcome the New Year and Celebrate." This last was actually two days, which made five extra days altogether, for a total of 365 days a year.

Each week, one of the six days was generally a rest day for everyone, including the academy, so this was the day when Adele would work at the bakery.

Of course, this meant that Adele had no days off, but that couldn't be helped. In any case, Adele thought, a school intended for children aged ten to thirteen couldn't possibly be all that difficult for her, so she didn't imagine there would be any problems arising as far as homework was concerned. Though many students would surely study independently after returning to their dorms, that was unlikely to be necessary for Adele.

Today wasn't a rest day, but in order to give her proper training, the baker decided Adele would work the remainder of the day for practice. And so, the matron left Adele there and returned to the dorm.

Adele's training was a success.

In her previous life, Misato had had few acquaintances, but that hadn't been for lack of desiring them. In truth, it was less that she was awkward or uncomfortable in the company of others, but more that few ever reached out to her.

Armed with her memories of Japanese hospitality, it was simple for Adele to play the role of a young shopkeeper, and immediately, the customers took a liking to her.

And so, that evening, Adele headed back to the academy's dormitory, two silver coins clasped firmly in her hand.

The fruits of my labor! My very own earnings! Money that I can use however I like! Adele was walking on air.

However, a sense of unease quickly overtook her elation.

What happens if I lose my coins? What if they get stolen?

There were few thieves who would stoop so low as to target a ten-year-old, but Adele couldn't convince herself to calm down. After all, there remained a part of her brain that was still eighteen years old, fully aware of the world's dangers.

Suddenly, she remembered—the loot boxes!

If she stored her coins in a loot box, they could never be lost or stolen.

At the thought of this, Adele relaxed and cast a silent

spell with her thoughts alone. At once, the coins in her hand disappeared.

Next, she tried retrieving them. In seconds, the sensation of metal returned to her palm. She stored the coins away again at once.

For a moment, Adele's heart swelled with pride at her success, but suddenly, something else occurred to her, and her face paled.

If the spell had gone wrong, she realized, she could have lost all her hard-earned money. Why hadn't she tested it on a pebble first before experimenting with the coins? She'd been an idiot.

Well, she reflected as she plodded on, *at least, I didn't lose the coins*. Everything was fine. But she would have to be more careful going forward.

To compare the currency of modern-day Japan with that of Adele's world, a single copper coin was worth roughly 10 yen. A half-silver was worth 100, a silver worth 1,000, a half-gold worth 10,000, and a full gold worth 100,000 yen.

Fruits and vegetables were cheap, meat and other luxury items expensive, and tools and jewelry an exorbitant price by Japanese standards, meaning a simple monetary conversion would have been pointless. However, judged in terms of what might be required to maintain the average person's standard of living, Adele's wage was quite reasonable.

Typically speaking, the average craftsman with a family took home a salary of around 3 gold pieces a month. Minus rest days, a person worked 30 days a month, for a converted salary of about 10,000 yen per day.

By contrast, Adele's salary was two silver a day, or roughly 2,000 yen, which worked out to about 250 yen per hour. Though it might not have seemed like much, it was a perfectly adequate wage for a child. A monthly salary of 12 silver pieces, or roughly 12,000 yen, would be more than enough to cover her daily necessities. Most likely, she wouldn't be able to purchase any clothing, but as her school uniform was provided, Adele would get by.

In order to maintain appearances, the school provided mending services and allowed students to exchange outgrown garments free of charge. All things considered, though all that was said to be free, in truth, such things were paid for out of the students' tuition.

She would have to deal with her undergarments herself, but at this point, Adele had no need for anything on her top half. While the eighteen-year-old in her did not exactly consider this to be fortunate, for now, it was one less thing to worry about, and she was grateful for that.

In any case, it seemed as though her money troubles had been solved.

From then on, on the days Adele worked, the baker continued to come in before dawn to begin the breads. The locals dropped by to purchase fresh-baked bread for their breakfasts, and those who worked on rest days would pop in at noon to get something to carry them through the day, just like always. In the afternoon, however, the baker left the shop under the care of his counter girl, taking advantage of the chance to get out and enjoy some rest for the sake of his health, or spend time with his wife and children.

The following day was the examination, when all the noble children came together to take placement tests and be sorted into classes.

Of course, truly noble children like Prissy would be attending the far superior Ardleigh Academy. Those at Eckland were the children of far lesser aristocrats—those who had only the dimmest hopes of inheriting, those who would not even prove useful as pawns in a political marriage—those who were, to put it simply, mediocre. Their prospects were hardly better than those of a merchant's child.

The other students *were* those very children of merchants, including daughters from families without sons, sent to make connections that might help them marry into more influential merchant families.

All this was a great deal for a ten-year-old to comprehend, especially a ten-year-old noble raised in privilege, told since birth that he or she was different from mere commoners. And yet, amidst all of this, Adele breathed a sigh of relief. She didn't stand out from the others present at the examination as much as she had expected. Though her clothing was of a far lower quality than what Prissy was granted, Adele's garments were in fact that of a noble's daughter, and despite being quite rumpled from the carriage ride, she found that her appearance was not too different from that of, say, the youngest child of a low-ranking noble. The fact that her clothes had been soaked and had then wrinkled as they dried further aided in the illusion.

The day began with a written exam.

This test covered basic history, the names of the King and other influential figures, facts about neighboring countries, etiquette, basic logic, and a variety of other topics.

Alienated as she was by her family, Adele found little to do besides study. As a result, Adele's intelligence had already been considerable even before her memories returned, and now, armed with her new perspective, she mastered the exam easily.

The mathematics section was similar. Compared to what she knew from her previous life, these calculations were child's play, and Adele worked the problems with all her might. If she didn't end up in the highest-ranking class, she knew that she would be bored to tears. And besides, the concept of a girl who had an aptitude for studying was a fairly ordinary one. It was natural for *someone* to be at the top when it came to exams.

As it happened, most class placements were made according to the results of the written exam. In order to carry on lectures and the like, it was necessary to group students by level, for if the school were to mix students of vastly differing abilities, it would have been difficult to settle on a curriculum that could be completed by all.

Yet this approach wasn't practical in all cases. It would be incredibly difficult for teachers to manage a class filled with geniuses or the opposite. Everyone would require the same amount of attention, after all.

By mixing students of an advanced and beginner level, teachers could leave the more advanced children to their own devices and focus on the students who were in greater need of their guidance. And, should any students show themselves to be at a higher level than even the instructors, there were various methods of independent study that might be employed.

Specifically, when it came to magic and physical education, it was more convenient *not* to divide the students by ability. While this made things a breeze for the more skilled children, some complained that it meant that they didn't have much chance to improve.

Similarly, even those who couldn't use magic were required to take magic classes. After all, in the future, one might become employed as the assistant or secretary to a magician—or, should one become a soldier, one might have to fight against magic users someday. Thus, even if one couldn't use magic oneself, having a basic knowledge of the magical arts was vital.

A physical assessment came after the written exam.

No one was expected to enter the school as an athlete. They only needed to show that they were relatively healthy and fit enough that they could participate in the school's physical education class.

Adele performed each exercise precisely as directed. She couldn't afford to display any abnormalities in this area. She was, after all, a "completely normal, average girl."

So, accounting for the number of children lined up in front of her, she tried her best to adjust her performance to what appeared to be an average level.

They were divided into teams of five and directed to complete various exercises in succession. Adele had been placed in the number two spot on her team, leaving only the one child ahead of her as reference.

She made calculations in her head. The student ahead of her was a boy, but at this age, Adele estimated it wouldn't be too strange for a girl to perform at the same level. Didn't they say that girls grew faster than boys when they were young, anyway?

In any event, as long as she stayed within the average range, it didn't really matter if she did well or poorly. As long as she didn't stand out.

In every event—sprinting, running, long jump, chin-ups, push-ups, and javelin—Adele strove to receive exactly the same marks as the young man ahead of her.

This way, even if she appeared to be slightly gifted for a girl, she could still be counted as a "normal" child.

Finally, they came to magic.

In this world, about thirty percent of all people had some magical ability. Among those, perhaps another third had a knack for it. This meant that true magic users were around ten percent of the total population. Everyone else was only able to complete simple, practical tasks such as lighting a furnace or summoning enough water to quench a mild thirst.

Before her reawakening, it wasn't clear whether Adele would have been able to scrape her way into that top ten percent, even with training. However, she had at least always been one of the thirty percent. If a carriage traveling through the desert happened upon some trouble, with Adele on board, their chances of survival would have been slightly higher.

But now...

To be safest, it would be better for Adele not to use magic at all. She knew that much.

Unfortunately, this strategy was impractical. Because she *was* able to use magic, it would have been a shame not to allow herself to try, just a little. Pretending not to be able to use magic could make trouble later; if there were ever a time when the circumstances called for it, Adele did not want to be unprepared.

So, just as with the physical exam, she planned to adjust her level to resemble that of the other magically-capable students.

Just like the previous time, Adele carefully studied the others who used magic before her, and when her turn came, she calculated her own efforts accordingly.

The average human had about 1/6,800 of her magical strength, so if she suppressed her powers to about 1/10,000 of their greatest strength, the effects would be equal to that of the child immediately in front of her.

Poof.

A fireball of just the right size came flying out, and Adele breathed a sigh of relief. It wasn't a combat-worthy spell, just a dinky little flame.

But everyone, including the instructors, was staring at Adele, mouths agape.

"Sh-she didn't use an incantation..."

Adele felt her stomach fall. She had forgotten to recite the incantation.

Of course, in reality, an incantation was not required to expel a thought pulse. However, for most humans, unable to instantaneously conjure the necessary image or the molecular movements and chemical reactions involved, it was necessary to facilitate the image and thought pulse formation by using a spell: "O, flames! Swirl and gather to me, and dash my enemies!"

The easiest way to actualize this was to recite it aloud, and although not impossible to do silently, it was more difficult, the sort of technique used mostly when a sneak attack was necessary. If one chose not to articulate a spell aloud, the power of its magic would diminish considerably, even if one took the same amount of time to think the appropriate words.

However, Adele visualized and enacted this phenomenon

without her expression even changing. At the same strength as the child before her. Though this also counted as "silent casting," in terms of power, it was so great that the people of this world could not fully appreciate what she had done.

Fortunately for Adele, even the adults watching didn't totally comprehend the magnitude of her casting—though it was obvious to all that her magical abilities were far beyond what would be expected for a child of her age.

Inwardly panicking, Adele strove to justify her mistake. *There must,* she told herself, *be plenty of people who can cast without incantations. It's just that most people don't choose to do so. I'm just a normal girl who happens to be particularly skilled in fire magic. That's it!*

The new students had yet to introduce themselves to one another. So, while under other circumstances the room might have filled with whispers, silence reigned. Despite their obvious shock, the instructors decided to carry on the test as planned. There would be plenty of time to ask questions later.

The class sorting concluded without other incidents, and when the students were dismissed from the training grounds, Adele headed back to her room.

Only one boy remained on the grounds: Kelvin von Bellium, the fifth son of an impoverished baron.

The Bellium family was poor. Despite this, the charming Baron, after being blessed with three sons and a daughter by his wife, had relations with her lady's maid and acquired two more sons, as well as another daughter.

The Baron wasn't some immoral philanderer. He provided

richly for the maid who had granted him these offspring. He allowed her children to live in the mansion and raised them as his own. His wife and her children were never cruel to them, treasuring them as family would.

And yet, the maid's family still wanted for money.

Originally, the Baron had planned for his wife's sons to attend Ardleigh Academy, but this would have left no tuition money for the sons of the lady's maid.

The eldest son was the Baron's heir, and the second, his spare should something happen to the first son. The third would, God willing, become a knight or a guardsman, or else a high-ranking bureaucrat. If he were lucky, he could marry into the family of a baron or viscount with no male heirs of his own.

Normally, all three girls would have been sent to Eckland Academy, whose tuition was one-tenth that of Ardleigh's. However, with the necessary assets, there was the possibility that they might be able to wed themselves to the heir of an aristocrat or the son of a prominent merchant, thus raising the family's fortunes. In order to give his daughters a better chance of finding eligible spouses, it was necessary for the Baron to send them to Ardleigh, even if it meant overextending the family's meager accounts. Such were the gambles a poor noble's family had to make in the hopes of being freed from their hardships.

As it turned out, the maid's daughter was a beauty. So much so that, even as the illegitimate daughter of a baron, she was sure to marry well. With the maid's daughter set to attend the more prestigious school, it was impossible for the Baron to send his eldest daughter, the Baroness's, to the lesser academy. If he did, people might wonder whether something was wrong with the girl, thus destroying any chance she had of making a good marriage. Therefore, though it was beyond the means of the poor baron's family, both of the daughters were sent to Ardleigh Academy, and the family prayed for the younger's beauty to bring them a fortune at long last.

Thus, it came to be that the Baron's fourth son—his first with the maid—and the fifth son, named Kelvin, were set to attend Eckland Academy. That was how it would be.

Yet, the fourth son had a magical talent. It was just enough that the boy would be able to make a living on the road—or even, depending on the circumstances, become a court magician or enter the wizards' guild.

His parents were elated, and at the last minute, it was decided that he too would be sent to Ardleigh, leaving only Kelvin, the fifth son, to attend the Eckland Academy all on his own.

Out of seven children, he was the only one.

How? Why? Kelvin railed against the injustices of the world, even though, deep in his heart, he knew that it couldn't be helped. Sending one's children to a prestigious academy was no small burden for the family of an impoverished noble.

Even after the high entrance fees, there was three years' worth of tuition, textbooks, food, lodging, uniform fees, and more to account for. Multiply that times seven, and there was simply no way the Baron's family could manage it. The unexpected cost of the fourth son's tuition had already probably put them in quite a bind. They even sold some of the wife's jewelry and took on loans. It was a huge gamble to take on the child of a lady's maid.

Rather than complaining at the cost of educating her maid's children, the Baron's wife apologized profusely. If only there had been money for Kelvin to attend Ardleigh with his siblings—but there was none.

And so Kelvin arrived at Eckland Academy, which was, when all was said and done, one tenth of the cost of an Ardleigh education. He was the fifth son, born to a maid, and although he was physically strong, unlike his brother, he had no magical abilities.

Yet Kelvin was determined to make the best of his situation.

If I'm going to be stuck in this place, he thought, *I may as well shoot for the stars!* He dreamt of becoming Eckland's top student, excelling far beyond the upper-crust sons and daughters at Ardleigh. He would graduate to great fortune, paying back his mother, his father, and the Baroness for all they had done for him.

Thanks to the time Kelvin spent with his older brothers, he knew his body was strong, and he looked forward eagerly to the physical portion of the placement test.

Right away, I'll show them who's boss, Kelvin had thought.

But then, just after he had shown off his very fastest sprint, the girl behind him provided exactly the same display.

He had pushed himself to his limits when it came to chin-ups, but yet again, the girl stared at him, then completed the same number. Worse still, he could tell that she only pretended to grow tired, stopping at precisely the same number as him even though she could have carried on much longer.

It was the same with the javelin. And long jump. And push-ups.

She stopped when she matched his record in every one, even though she still had more in her.

And on top of all of that, she could even use magic.

Dammit! Dammit! Dammit!

She was tormenting him, but next time, Kelvin resolved, he would beat her.

Kelvin von Bellium, the Baron's fifth son. That was the moment his goal for the next three years was decided.

It was the day after the assessment: the long-awaited textbook distribution day.

In truth, Adele was not particularly excited about receiving her course materials. What she really wanted was clothing, which was distributed at the same time.

There were two uniforms, one for summer and one for winter, as well as two gym uniforms for the same, along with a variety of shoes and stockings.

Finally, she would have fresh clothes to wear, and, as long as she was in uniform, no one would notice if she wore the same thing every day. Even better, if she outgrew her uniform or gym clothes, or if either were seriously damaged, she would be able to exchange them. If there were too many exchanges, she might receive used items that other students had outgrown, but that prospect didn't particularly concern her.

Her new possessions were too numerous to carry in one load, so after several trips to the supply room, Adele changed into her uniform. She had been given one that was slightly too large, in anticipation of a growth spurt, but this gave off a very "average" sort of feeling, which she relished. Her single item of personal clothing had grown somewhat tattered from being worn for so many days running, and to keep it safe, Adele decided to store it inside a loot box.

Facing the mirror, she took in her appearance.

I hope I make a hundred friends! Adele, who had yet to make friends in this life or her last one, beamed with hope.

That afternoon, she went down to the announcement board to find that the class rosters had been posted.

Later that afternoon, they would be lining up according to these rosters to practice for the entrance ceremony. Tomorrow would be the entrance ceremony itself, followed by self-introductions. Classes would begin the following week, after the rest day.

As she expected, Adele had been placed into Class A.

In truth, this was not actually the "A" from the alphabet of Misato's world—but as it was typically the first character taught in that country's writing system, "A" made a good substitute.

The entrance ceremony practice, and the actual ceremony the following day, went off without a hitch. Some of the children's families were in attendance, but in many cases, their homes were too far for them to make the journey. In addition, although there were more than a few lower-class noble families who lived in the vicinity, Eckland's entrance ceremony took place at the same time as Ardleigh's. If parents had children at both academies, they invariably attended the festivities at the higher-ranking of the two schools.

Those children from poor families and those who had been sent to Eckland to get them out of their parents' way were also alone, and as one might expect, Adele was amongst them.

Following the ceremony, teachers showed the students to their classrooms.

After having little time to converse with one another, it was finally time for the children to get to know their classmates. Adele's heart was roiling with anticipation and anxiety. Would she be able to make friends easily? Or would she be no good at it, ending up as lonely as she'd been in her past life?

The homeroom teacher for Class A was a man of solid build, around thirty years old.

"I am Abe von Burgess, the homeroom teacher for Class A. I will be responsible for each one of you this year. In fact, I plan to be the second-year Class A teacher also, so I will likely be seeing some of you next year, as well. That being said, at the end of the term, the class sorting may change depending on your grades, so I will be saying farewell to anyone who fails to keep up their performance."

Mr. Burgess sounded less like a teacher and more like a slightly-aged ruffian, the sort who would be a mid-rank hunter in the local guild. Yet the "von" in his name indicated that he was an aristocrat, and it was clear that he meant to warn any particularly thick-skulled noble children that their status would be no substitute for hard work.

"Now then, let's start with introductions. Why don't we go down the line, beginning with you?"

"Y-yessir!" The boy at the front of the far left row began his introductions, as directed. "I'm Marcus, the third son of the Buick family. I'm from the capital. My strengths are..."

The class was made up of twelve boys and eighteen girls—thirty students, all told—and each gave their names, hometowns, strengths, interests, hopes for the future, and the like: a fairly standard introduction.

It was only natural that the girls outnumbered the boys in this class. To start, there was a higher proportion of girls at the academy in total, as the sons of lower class nobles and merchant families were more likely to attend the superior school, while any girls not likely to make an advantageous marriage were sent to the lesser school. Beyond this, many boys put their effort into athletics rather than their studies, meaning that their grades weren't as sharp as the girls' were.

Adele had always struggled to remember faces, but as she was determined to make friends, doing so would be an absolute necessity. As each student gave their introduction, she stared intently, memorizing their features. Those who noticed this strange behavior began to grow flustered, their cheeks burning red, yet Adele hadn't the slightest notion she was doing anything wrong.

"I am Kelvin von Bellium, aspiring knight. My specialty is swordplay. It is also my hobby. My goal while at Eckland is to become as strong as I can!"

Kelvin's declaration, so different from the rote introductions that had come before, couldn't help but pique Adele's interest. Of course, it scarcely occurred to her that this was the same boy she'd shadowed so closely during the physical assessment earlier that week... Nor did she notice the glare that Kelvin flashed her way as she looked toward him.

The introductions continued down the line, until finally it was Adele's turn.

"I am Adele. I have no special abilities. No matter how you look at it, I am a completely normal, average girl."

Everyone in the classroom, other than Adele, all had the same thought at once.

She's lying.

They were in total agreement. This girl, who could casually cast combat spells at the same level as those incanted by those of the greatest magical ability, who precisely matched the physical achievements of a noble son in peak form, when she clearly could have gone farther—she had to be lying. Perhaps she had meant to help the boy save face, but in truth, she had done him a disservice—though she didn't seem to realize that that was the case.

Was that her true nature? Or some kind of act? Since the moment the placement exams had ended, whispers such as these had been circulating amongst the noble children in the common areas and the dining hall.

"This is my first time in the capital," Adele went on. "My interests are reading and eating delicious things. I haven't had many friends before now, so I hope to get along well with all of you." She smiled.

She'd done it, she thought. A perfect introduction by a perfectly normal girl. This was the beginning of her new, "average" life at Eckland Academy.

Adele, however, had no idea that the other children had seen so easily through her act during the physical assessment, nor did she realize that she'd had the bad luck to copy only the children at the top of each field. There was more: despite claiming that she was a commoner, she had taken the assessment along with the children of nobles. Furthermore, she'd made the outlandish statement that her interests were "reading and eating delicious things," despite the unlikelihood of a commoner having access to expensive books or tasty morsels. Stranger still was her declaration that she'd reached the age of ten friendless.

Yet Adele truly believed that she would fit in as a completely average student. She had no idea what her classmates truly thought.

After the introductions came orientation. Mr. Burgess explained the layout of the school, its routines and regulations, and the lessons that would begin at the start of the next week. Then, the students were dismissed. It was only a half-day, and he instructed them to use the afternoon and the following rest day to take care of any necessary shopping to prepare for the week to come.

Adele's situation was different. The next day, the baker would be expecting her, and besides, she still didn't have any money with which to shop. Purchasing her absolute necessities, such as soap, notebooks, and ink, would easily use up the coins she had made on her first day in the bakery. As those were all considered luxury goods, they were expensive. Her existing funds would barely be enough.

It would be best, Adele determined, to set aside tomorrow's pay for something equally important. She would've liked to purchase two more changes of undergarments at the very least, but that would have to wait for another occasion.

As she stood pondering her dilemma, Adele found herself surrounded by a knot of boys.

"Adele, would you like to go shopping with me?"

"No, come with me! I grew up in the capital, so I know all the best shops!"

"No, I do!"

Adele withdrew reflexively. And yet...

Although the boys had surprised her, they didn't seem to have bad intentions. Did this mean she was...popular?

Adele stood for a moment, perplexed. As Misato, she'd been gorgeous. Despite being born to parents who were utterly plain in appearance, Misato was a classic beauty, with sharp features, the kind one might expect to be pursued by talent scouts and modeling agencies. Still, she had never been the slightest bit popular in school. Because everyone assumed she was out of their league, no one had ever dared to ask her to spend time with them.

While Adele had a nice, symmetrical face, her appearance was otherwise unremarkable. She was not glamorous or striking; rather, she had the sort of pleasant appearance that tended to put people at—

Wait.

In that moment, Adele remembered a TV program she'd seen many years before. The presenter had explained that, if one could average the features of hundreds of human faces, the result would be "universal beauty"—not standout looks, but a pleasant appearance, one that made people feel at ease.

If one could average the features. If one could average...

No. When she'd said she wanted an "average" appearance, she had meant average as in normal, generic—just another face in the crowd. Not average as in universally beautiful!

"I-I'm sorry." Adele stuttered. "I've already finished my shopping!"

Seeing Adele flustered and blushing, the boys only pressed harder, the competition turning fierce.

"Boys! Settle down!" A girl with the air of a council chairman scattered them with a roar. Adele offered her thanks and fled the room, her mind swirling.

Until now, whether in her life as Adele or Misato, the boys in her class had never said a word to her beyond "Lemme see your homework!"

Upon returning to the dormitory, she slipped into the washroom and examined herself in the mirror, which was little more than a polished piece of metal.

She was slightly shorter than the norm. She had odd, silver hair, inherited from her mother. She didn't exude beauty in the way that Misato had, but her face was well-arranged, and it did, she suppose, give off a sense of equilibrium.

Am I attractive?

A bubble of laughter rose in her chest.

Walking by the washroom door, the other girls averted their eyes at the sight of Adele's strange expression.

It was all wrong, anyway. She wasn't supposed to be attractive. She was an average girl, and she certainly didn't need a pack of suitors—especially not before she was grown up.

Yet as Adele shook her head at herself in the mirror, another thought occurred to her.

It was strange, wasn't it, that at age ten, she had barely begun to develop? In this world, the more precocious girls began to hit puberty around seven or eight years of age. Misato herself had started to develop as an eight-year-old, and by the time she hit eighteen, her bust size had been slightly above average. Adele, on the other hand, showed no signs of any kind of development. There were already plenty of girls in her class with noticeable breasts, but this was one area in which Adele was nowhere near "average."

Why was that?

It was true that she hadn't eaten much in the two years

after the death of her mother and grandfather. Perhaps that had stunted her growth?

Adele sighed. She looked like an elf, or a dwarf...

Oh my god. Adele was aghast as a horrible thought occurred to her.

Together, humans, elves, and dwarves made up the class called "humanoids." However, if God considered them all to be a single race...

She should have been an average height, but in fact, she was shorter. Her chest was almost entirely flat.

No no no no no no no!

There were far fewer dwarves and elves than humans. Including them in a calculation of the average should scarcely have had any effect...under any normal circumstances.

But in a special circumstance...it would have been a bother to calculate an average based on the entirety of the world's population, so what if one were to simply look at an "average human," an "average dwarf," and an "average elf," for ease of comparison?

And what if a certain idiot assumed that these three individuals could make for an accurate average?

Wait wait wait wait wait wait wait wait!

Adele looked around her room frantically. It shouldn't be. It *couldn't* be.

At least orcs and goblins weren't considered humanoids...

Bang bang bang bang bang!

A few minutes later, Adele's classmates found her smacking her head against the wall of the dorm hallway.

Lying on her bed later that afternoon, Adele attempted to console herself.

And at least dwarf girls are pretty cute...

In fact, female dwarfs weren't all that different from their human counterparts. They were a bit shorter and somewhat rounded in appearance, but they weren't stocky like the males, and of course, they didn't grow beards. They weren't much different, Adele thought, than a petite adolescent girl. That was something.

Besides, if Adele did have dwarf characteristics, then the equivalent aspects of an elf's physique would cancel them out. Both male and female elves were tall and slender, so that rather than having a huge influence on Adele's figure, her dwarflike qualities would be mostly negligible. Or so it would seem.

Yet Adele's height, combined with the matter of her chest...

She shook her head. This was all just speculation.

If she were to ask the nanomachines, then the truth would...

I can't ask them about that! What happens if it all turns out to be true?! It's all too awful.

You rang?

"I DID NOT!!" Adele screamed at the top of her lungs, then looked to her left and right in a panic. Thankfully, it seemed that the occupants of the neighboring rooms were out, so she received no complaints about the disturbance.

CHAPTER 3 |

Friends

ADELE BEGAN THE SCHOOL WEEK in high spirits. On the rest day, she had received another two silver pieces from her job at the bakery, and on top of that, she was allowed to take leftover bread with her, which she could store in the loot box without having it go stale.

The moment she stepped into the classroom, she was bombarded with questions.

"Morning, Adele!"

"What'd you do on your day off?"

"Let's eat lunch together today!"

Attack of the boys!

Adele was a bit of a hot commodity.

She had the smarts to make it into Class A, the physical prowess of a lady knight, impressive magical talent—plus, a personality so demure as to try concealing all of this.

Furthermore, though she was passing herself off as a commoner, she had entered the academy without taking the entrance exam, and it appeared that her family themselves had paid the full tuition. Most importantly, she was beautiful, too.

Though they were only ten years old, in three years Eckland's students would make their first steps into society, and two years after that, they would be considered adults. It was not strange that, in the midst of this gifted class, many were already trying to forge connections for the sake of their futures—romantic or otherwise.

"Do you all never learn?! Look, you're smothering her!"

Once again, the girl with the chairman-like air—perhaps it was easier just to call her the chairwoman?—intervened on Adele's behalf.

"Th-thank you. I'm not really good at talking to boys, so..."

As she spoke, Adele could sense the boys considering her carefully. Half, it seemed, might give her space, not wanting to intimidate such a retiring beauty. But the other half looked ready to press harder in order to take advantage of her inexperience, to test her reaction.

The other girl smiled, and all at once, Adele realized something. What the girl had done—that was something a friend would have done. The girl might be...a friend! And if she were, she would be the first friend Adele had ever made—her previous life included.

The first week of instruction took place in the classroom.

As one might expect, the students didn't launch directly into physical or magical exercises. Instead, they began with general education, as well as safety practices, and the theory behind their martial and magical training. They wouldn't begin practical studies until the following week.

For Adele, these classroom activities were a breeze. With the memories of an eighteen-year-old from a civilization that was centuries ahead of this one, there was no way she could possibly fall behind her classmates.

Besides, Misato's powers of reasoning remained a part of her. Did God assume that she needed intelligence in order to absorb Misato's consciousness? Or had the intellects of humans in this world continued to advance, even though their civilization had failed to do so?

Even when there were errors in the magical theory that their teacher was presenting, Adele didn't point them out, and the week proceeded without incident.

Then came the day preceding the next rest day.

"Miss Adele, we would like to speak to you about something later." It was Marcela, the third daughter of a baron, flanked by two of her friends. At her words, Adele's heart leapt.

"O-of course!" Adele stuttered. "But where...? Oh! My room should be big enough, shouldn't it?!"

"Uh... sure, that's fine..." Marcela replied, bewildered by Adele's eagerness.

A friend! And an invitation! This was the moment she'd been waiting for.

Viewed from afar, the three girls—Marcela, a baron's third daughter; Monika, the second daughter of a middle-class merchant; and Aureana, a commoner who was attending the academy on scholarship—looked like nothing so much as a noblewoman and her attendants.

Marcela was a typical aristocratic type. However, she was also quite the generous spirit, and along with Monika, a friend of Marcela's from before the academy, she had helped to relieve Aureana, the commoner, of a number of worries. It was, she claimed, a noble's duty to alleviate the suffering of the powerless.

This time, though, the three of them were acting together.

"What could she mean by 'my room is big enough'? All the rooms have the same layout, do they not...?"

"Who knows? I guess we'll find that out when we get there."

"Let's go teach that cheeky girl some manners!"

"Yes, ma'am!"

Marcela could not stand her—that girl Adele. She hadn't witnessed it for herself, but she'd heard about the impressive power Adele displayed during the assessment. That much was fine. Every person had her own strengths.

However, what she could not abide was the way that one glance from Adele sent the boys into a tizzy.

Once she returned home after graduation, Marcela would be groomed as a bride, and two years later, if things went well, she would become the second wife of a middle-aged aristocrat, a trophy bride, or—at worst—the mistress to a powerful noble. Until then, she needed to keep her options open.

The fact was that the academy was filled with girls in search of romance, and any individual who threatened to monopolize the attention of the school's male students was breaking an unspoken rule. Marcela, the poor baron's daughter, was determined to make this apparent.

Without the expectations that came with noble blood, Monika and Aureana were not as troubled by all of this. However, for the sake of their friendship with Marcela, both girls offered their support.

At the sound of knocking, Adele jumped up, rushing to open the door.

"W-welcome! Please come in!" Her heart fluttered with joy and nerves. Even in her previous life, she had never had the experience of welcoming a classmate into her own space.

But as her guests entered, Adele realized... *I don't have any chairs but the one!*

Why had she been so careless?

Having a visitor sit on one's bed was surely bad form. Moreover, having *three* friends on the bed while she sat in a chair would create an odd sort of one-versus-three situation.

"I-I'm so sorry! I forgot to prepare any seating! Please wait a moment, while I borrow some chairs from the common room."

She flew from the room without waiting for a reply.

"What a scatterbrain!" Marcela said.

Monika nodded. "She certainly is. But at least I understand now what she meant when she said her room was big."

It was true: the space felt large. But in fact, Adele's room was the same size as everyone else's. The difference was that, in this room, there were no chests, no luggage, and no lamps. There wasn't a single decoration, accessory, or stuffed toy. The room was practically vacant.

Even Aureana, the commoner, had outfitted her room with a cheap, used chest that she had purchased in town and decorated using trinkets gifted to her by her fellow villagers.

Looking around Adele's room, she spoke in a stunned voice. "It's amazingly empty..."

Marcela seized the handle of the built-in armoire.

"Milady! You musn't—"

Ignoring Monika's warning, Marcela flung open the doors. "She has no clothes!"

All that hung inside were the uniforms the school had provided.

Next, Marcela reached out to open the drawers below.

"W-we can't! It's not—" Monika tried to grab Marcela's hands, but the drawers had already slid open.

Once again, there was nothing inside.

"Empty..."

Just then, there was a pained shriek. Marcela and Monika pulled back their hands and turned to see Aureana standing over the desk drawer, an awful expression on her face.

"What is it?!"

Marcela drew closer to peek inside the drawer, and Monika followed suit, looking apprehensive.

They looked inside the drawer and gasped.

Marcela stood, stunned, and Monika had tears in the corners of her eyes. Aureana was already weeping.

In the drawer was one thick bone.

It was on a plate, but there were no scraps of meat. The bone was clean, covered in knife marks, as though it came from a kitchen.

Marcela eyes were wide. "Is this...her snack...?"

By the time Adele returned from the rec room, carrying a pair of small chairs, they had returned the room to its former state and dabbed away their tears.

"Sorry to keep you all waiting."

"I-It was no bother..." Marcela cleared her throat. "Anyway, there is something I would like to ask you."

Adele arranged the two chairs she had brought in a semi-circle next to the one that had already been in the room. She herself sat down on the bed. Even in a room as empty as hers, there was not much space for seating.

"What is it?"

"It seems that you didn't sit for the entrance exam when enrolling at the academy. So we'd like to know—are you, in fact, a noble?"

So, Adele thought, *they've found me out.* However, she couldn't bring herself to lie to her new friends, and so she answered frankly.

"Well, yes... It's true. But if I were to use my family name, it's likely that I would be killed—by my father and my new stepmother, whose child is meant to take my place."

Marcela fought desperately to remain composed and do credit to her noble pedigree.

Aureana was silent, her face white as a sheet.

Finally, Monika gulped, her voice wavering. "I-I see... W-well, are you gifted at sports or magic, then?"

"Hmm?" Adele asked. "No, I'm fairly normal. Even during the assessment, I only performed as well as whoever was in line ahead of me..."

Marcela began to understand the rumors that were circulating. This girl was clueless!

Was it possible that she really had *no* idea that the people ahead of her had been top of the class in each of their respective fields? Could she truly not know that everyone had noticed the way she deliberately held back in order to match the others?

Perhaps her parents had instructed her to conceal her exceptional abilities, so as not to cause trouble for this stepsister.

"I-I see. Normal, yes. Normal..."

"Yes! It's nice to be normal, isn't it?"

".........."

In the long pause that followed, Marcela remembered the reason she'd come to Adele's room in the first place.

"Miss Adele," she began. "You seem to get along awfully well with the boys..."

Adele leapt at the bait. "That's true! Although I can't figure out why... I'm awful at talking to boys in general. The only man I've ever really spoken to before is my father."

Adele continued: "I certainly have no plans of getting a boyfriend right now. I'd be perfectly content just to find one once I'm out on my own, as an adult. I just wish there was some way of getting them to leave me alone..."

"Wha...?"

The three girls were dumbstruck. There was something very wrong with this situation.

The thing that they had originally come to speak to her about no longer seemed important, after all.

To break the silence, Marcela asked the first question that popped into her head.

"Well, do... do you have any plans for tomorrow?"

"Oh, yes. I spend the rest days working. I have no funds and receive no allowance... With the pay I get tomorrow, I should hopefully be able to buy at least one more spare undergarment!"

The way that she said these words—so cheerfully!—was too much for the three girls to bear.

Aureana trembled, her face pale.

Monika was bright red, her teeth clamped down on her lip as tears welled in her eyes.

Marcela, meanwhile, prayed desperately for serenity.

"W-well, we won't trouble you by overstaying our welcome. Perhaps we should get going..."

"Oh, you're welcome to stay..."

Marcela replied, standing, "There will be plenty of time for that later. We still have three years here, after all."

"Of course!"

The girls bade farewell to their classmate and returned to their own rooms, leaving Adele overjoyed.

"I did it! I can finally cross 'having friends over' off my list! Three of them, no less!"

What Adele didn't know was that the three of them had walked home in complete silence.

Meow.

"Oh, you're back!"

A little black cat slipped into Adele's room through the open window.

Adele pulled the plate from the drawer and set it atop the desk, as the cat jumped eagerly for the bone.

"You really like that bone, huh? I'll try to get you a new one next time."

It was the beginning of the second week in the Class A homeroom.

"Miss Adele, do you have a moment?"

"Oh, Miss Marcela!"

Adele bounded happily toward Marcela, who shoved a paper bag in the other girl's direction.

"I accidentally bought the wrong size for myself, but I thought that they might still fit you."

"Huh? For me?"

The bag was rather large.

"Thank you! Can I open it?"

"N-not right now! Please open it when you return to your room!"

Judging by the redness of Marcela's face, Adele was able to form some idea of the bag's contents.

It wasn't something that a girl would normally misjudge the size of.

"Miss Marcela..."

Adele inched closer, then hugged Marcela tightly.

"St-stop that! Miss Adele, let me go this instant!"

Marcela struggled, turning bright red—but there was no escaping Adele's inadvertently forceful embrace.

Their classmates looked on, envious of Adele's attentions.

From the next day on, Adele's classmates began bringing her gifts of sweets and dried meat, girls and boys alike.

Adele found this odd but accepted the presents gratefully. Still, there were no more joyful embraces.

"Why didn't I get a hug from Adele? Hey, tell me!"

"I-I don't know anything about that."

The other girls in the class pressed Marcela for answers, with more and more students joining in.

"Marcela, what exactly did you give Adele that time that she hugged you?"

"I-It was nothing!"

"It wasn't nothing! What on earth did you give her?"

"I-I don't remember!"

"Please, tell me! I want a hug from Adele!"

"Me too! I want Adele to hug me!"

"And I want to hug her!"

"Me too!"

A male voice piped in. "Me too..."

"YOU BOYS STAY OUT OF THIS!"

CHAPTER 4

Training

T HE FOLLOWING DAY marked the start of their practical training.

"All right, you lot! Time to start your training!"

Apparently, their homeroom teacher, Mr. Burgess, was also in charge of their physical education.

All the students wore leather guards over their gym uniforms, and unlike the uniforms themselves, these hadn't been provided beforehand. Instead, they were shared by the various classes, and the stench of leather and other people's sweat filled the air around Adele and her classmates. Although the students at the prestigious Ardleigh Academy no doubt received their own guards, as well as weapons and armor, the Eckland students didn't have the luxury of complaining.

"I *should* start with the fundamentals of strength training and technique, but I get the feeling that that'll bore you all to tears," began Mr. Burgess. "So, we'll start with a practice battle so that you all can grasp the importance of mastering the basics.

"Let's get a good example... Those with prior experience, step forward!"

Several of the boys stepped forward at his command.

"One of you—go ahead and show me what you've got!"

However, no one seemed eager to volunteer.

Just when it seemed that Mr. Burgess would have to give up and pick someone himself...

"I will!" Kelvin, the baron's fifth son, took a step forward.

"O-ho! Kelvin, is it? All right, let's go! I'll allow you to select your opponent."

At the academy, rank was rendered irrelevant, so even the children of nobles were addressed by their first names.

As Kelvin looked over the pool of potential opponents, everyone carefully averted their eyes. Half of the children assembled were nobles who had already witnessed his prowess during the physical assessment.

After taking the time to leisurely assess each student, Kelvin pointed a finger.

"You there! Let's go!"

It was Adele. She stared back, mouth agape. "Huh? Why me? I-I don't really have any experience..."

She looked to Mr. Burgess, hoping for an out.

However...

"It's Adele, right?! Okay—well, this should be an interesting one. Let's do it!" Mr. Burgess grinned. Rumors about Adele had circulated among the teachers as well as the students, and he was pleased with this chance to test her abilities.

"Huh...?"

Adele, for her part, was bewildered. Suddenly both Kelvin and her teacher wanted her to fight?

She had only just learned the face and name of the boy who had called her out—the boy who she always seemed to catch staring at her. At first, she'd wondered if he were in love with her, but his attitude suggested the opposite must be true.

In fact, his sharp gaze seemed to label her as his rival.

But if he had to choose a rival, Adele thought, wouldn't it be better to choose someone of exceptional ability—not an average, ordinary girl like herself?

"Please be gentle with me..." Adele pleaded, as she lifted her wooden sword, but Kelvin only readied his weapon, silent.

Adele steeled herself. Kelvin seemed quite serious. These might only be wooden swords, but if he hit her hard enough it would still hurt, even through the leather armor.

Her strategy was decided.

Fighting in Normal Girl Mode, at the level she'd been at before her reawakening, would mean an instant loss. What's more, she would have to continue to perform at that level in future practice sessions, meaning she would never be able to train seriously. That would be a problem.

Although she might be fast and powerful, Adele had absolutely no knowledge of technique. Therefore, in order to prepare herself for life after graduation, she would need to do some serious training. In order to do that, it made sense to show some strength and battle—at least from time to time—with the strongest of the boys, so that she could benefit from the guidance of the instructor.

Even if getting hit would be painful.

Or maybe she could avoid getting hit?

If she could manage that and let her sword be knocked away at an appropriate point, then perhaps the battle could end before she suffered serious injuries.

With this in mind, Adele prepared for the fight.

"Begin!"

Just as the command left Mr. Burgess's mouth, Kelvin rushed toward Adele.

In this world, there was no suri-ashi or okuri-ashi, the stepping techniques of Japanese kendo. Rather, the aim appeared to be simply to take out as many opponents as possible on the battlefield.

Sensing Adele's hesitation, Kelvin moved quickly, swinging his sword down from above. Of course, it would have been frowned upon to aim directly at a girl's skull, so he moved instead to strike her shoulder, which was covered in the leather armor. In kendo, such a move would have been a kesa-giri strike.

Victory was in sight—or so Kelvin thought. But his sword cut through only air, with an empty *whiff*.

"Huh...?"

As Adele easily evaded his swing, Kelvin's confidence wavered. However, he wasn't foolish enough to allow an opening. He quickly raised his sword again and swung it towards Adele's right side, she herself having dodged to the left.

Thunk!

She blocked his blow with her sword.

He sent a swift attack toward her left side, hoping he might catch her off balance. Yet this blow was easily blocked as well.

Kelvin continued attacking, and Adele continued blocking.

Kelvin swore. How could this be happening? The girl had the stance and technique of an amateur. How could she move so quickly?! How could she block each one of his attacks?!

Kelvin was overwhelmed with confusion—but so was Adele.

Eeek! His attacks were getting stronger. How could she gracefully lose the battle without allowing herself to get hurt?

Finally, Kelvin's reckless side emerged.

If Adele was already blocking each move with her sword, he had no choice but to aim at her blade intentionally. Then, at least, he might have a chance of overwhelming her with his strength.

He bore down, aiming for the spot just above the grip of her sword. Drawing on both his strength and the blade's momentum, he focused his energy on the third of his sword closest to the tip. Adele's sword was stationary, and when he struck, he would hit it at the base.

He's going to hit me!

Without thinking, Adele grew tense.

Cra-aaack!

Her sword made a terrible, grating sound.

Thwap!

Kelvin's wooden sword struck Adele's wooden sword near the handle. One sword flew out of its owner's grip, going tumbling across the ground.

"Huh...?"

The one who was left staring down at his now-empty hands was Kelvin.

Rats, Adele thought. But it was already too late.

Just as with her magic and as she had seen with the door handle, it was clear that God had done something to impact her physical strength. And whether it was due to a mistake, a misunderstanding, or a deliberate choice, that did nothing to change the outcome.

In Adele's life up to this point, she had always been able to hold back, almost subconsciously, carrying on her act as a normal girl with normal abilities. It was because of this that it had taken her until several days after the return of her memories to notice anything was off.

Now, if Adele exerted even a bit of strength, even unconsciously, her power would grow to a whole new level.

It was not unlike the gears shifting in an automatic car, the increase in horsepower creating an excess of torque.

What would happen if that level of strength were poured into a wooden sword?

Normally, when two swords exchanged blows, the force of one sword canceled out that of the other. However, if one sword remained stationary, the entire force of the second's blow was reflected back into the arms of the swordsman.

It was as good as striking a lump of iron, and accordingly, there was an extremely high chance that one's arms would go numb, causing the sword to fall. And this was exactly what had happened to Kelvin.

"That's the match!" Burgess said.

"N-no! My hands slipped!" Kelvin protested as their teacher signaled the end of the match.

Burgess's reply was exasperated. "Is that what you would say if you dropped your sword on the battlefield? Would you say to your opponent, 'Oh, just a moment please! My hand slipped! Would you give me a second to retrieve my sword?'"

"Er..."

This was not going well.

Even Adele, who was ignorant when it came to the subtleties of swordplay, could tell that this was not a favorable situation. She, a rank amateur, had bested a boy who was both confident and incredibly strong. Even though she had claimed it was her first time using a sword...

This was no good. For a "normal girl," this was no good at all.

"U-um! I can keep going..." Adele said.

"Oh?" Burgess seemed intrigued as he turned to address Kelvin, who silently retrieved his sword. "What will you do?"

What will I *do?* Adele wondered. If she simply dropped her sword, it would be obvious she was faking. She would have to take a blow.

Adele readied her sword to fight again.

Kelvin's stance changed, and the clash of blades began anew.

Although he hadn't had enough time to recover from his previous exertions, neither had his opponent. And given that girls had little physical strength, it was only natural that she would be terribly exhausted. With this idea in mind, Kelvin charged again and again. Yet Adele continued to block each blow with precision.

As the fight continued, Adele showed no signs of tiring, and Kelvin began to grow impatient once more. Due to the violence of his assault, he was already reaching his limit. He could feel himself getting tired: his grip on the sword was beginning to weaken, and his breath grew ragged.

Why? he raged. *Why can't I land a single blow?! Against this girl—this amateur?!*

Losing was not permitted—not by Kelvin's standards.

As for Adele, she continued to block each of Kelvin's blows almost reflexively, still lamenting the difficulty of losing the fight in a way that would appear natural and would not involve getting hurt.

She would prefer not to be struck anywhere without protection, or indeed, in any place where the leather was thin or weakened. Given that she had hardly wavered in the face of Kelvin's earlier blows, it would look ridiculous for her to simply drop her sword casually. So distracted was Adele by these worries, that it didn't occur to her that this level of speed, strength, and endurance was completely beyond the capacities of a normal ten-year-old. Nor that Kelvin, who was himself leagues ahead of the other freshmen, would be beginning to tire as well.

The battle continued until...

Now!

Kelvin's form was crumbling, and his swings now were considerably weaker than those that had come before. Seeing that any chance to lose the battle would soon pass by her, Adele purposely slowed her own movements, turning her body in such a way as to allow Kelvin's sword to strike her right on the spot where the leather of her armor was thickest.

All she needed to do now was pretend that she had no time to protect herself.

She tensed her body and squeezed her eyes shut in preparation for the pain of the blow.

...Huh?

The attack never came, and after several moments, Adele opened her eyes.

There was Kelvin, red in the face and trembling with rage, and next to him, Burgess, with an expression that said something along the lines of "Now you've done it."

"Stop messing with me!" Kelvin shouted, then tossed his sword down on the ground and stomped away.

Adele stood, slack-jawed, not understanding.

"You know, kid... You ought to be more considerate of a man's pride," Mr. Burgess said. Behind him, the other students nodded.

What happened? What had Adele done wrong?

"Well, it is what it is," their teacher went on. "I don't blame him for getting mad, so I guess we won't punish him for skipping class... this time. Now, the rest of you pair up and try sparring."

The students split up into pairs and began practicing, but with Kelvin gone there was an odd number, leaving Adele on her own. Even Marcela avoided meeting her eyes.

How did this happen? Adele asked herself.

The handle of the wooden sword that she had gripped for so long was now dented with an impression of her fingers, rendering it unusable.

It was the first day of magic lessons and Adele was determined not to mess up the way she had last time.

Among the class of thirty, about six of them showed a spark of true magical prowess, while maybe nine more would be able to achieve at least an everyday level of proficiency. Overall, the proportion of skilled users was a bit higher than the norm, but this was no real surprise. It was only natural that those who hoped to become career magicians would do whatever they could to get into a decent school.

"To start, why don't we try a few of the tasks that you learned about in your classroom lessons? Remember, this goes for all of you, whether or not you are able to use magic. Understanding magical technique, even if only in theory, will be useful to you going forward."

At the direction of their instructor, Ms. Michella, the students began to recite their spells.

Next to Adele, the Marcela Trio was putting in a good effort.

Marcela's abilities were of the everyday sort, while it appeared that Monika and Aureana had no magical capacity whatsoever.

Typically, the strength of a magic user was determined by the power they could produce with a single spell, how long they could maintain that spell, and how much time they would need to recover before repeating it.

No matter how strong the spell you produced was, if it could only last a few seconds or if it took a long time for you to recharge before you could use that spell again, your abilities were not particularly useful. On the other hand, even if your output was weak, those who were able to cast continuously and recharge quickly often proved handy.

In other words, someone who could summon only five liters of water at once, but could do so three times in a row—or someone who could summon only two liters at once, but recovered in an hour—was in far greater demand than someone who could summon ten liters only once per day.

Battlefield magic was the only place where, depending on the circumstances, raw power might be useful. However, this was an exception, not the rule.

Hmm?

As she watched her three friends cast their spells, something strange occurred to Adele. However, they were in the middle of class, so she banished the thought from her mind—she would deal with it later.

After they practiced their incantations, Ms. Michella, who was the perfect sort of person to be a teacher, allowed all those who could use magic to do so, while those who could not looked on in order to "become familiar with the phenomenon."

Although Adele succeeded in using only the most normal of magic, when class ended, she felt a tad disappointed, as though her aim had been off.

"Um, could I have a bit of your time after class?" she asked Marcela, who could not deny such an earnest request from Adele, and readily agreed.

After school that same day...

"I'm sorry to make you come all the way out here."

Adele had brought the three girls to a grove a short walk out-side of the capital's north gates.

"Wh-what are we doing in a place like this?"

"Sorry. There's something that I wanted to talk to you about... But first—can you promise to keep all of this a secret?"

"O-of course, that's fine."

Following Marcela's lead, Monika and Aureana nodded emphatically.

"Um, well." Adele began. "Don't you think it's odd the way that we all use magic...?"

The three girls looked at her, confused.

"Um, well, when I was watching everyone in class, it seemed like they were concentrating really hard on their spells..."

"Well, yes," replied Marcela. "That's because spells are the most important part of using magic... Aren't they?"

"They aren't," Adele said.

"Huh?"

All three girls were stunned.

"Spells are nothing more than a way to assist you in forming the image of the magic you want to produce. It doesn't really matter what words you use. As long as you can form the image, you can use magic without even speaking. Haven't you noticed that people who use magic don't all use the same spells—and some people can do it silently?"

"Th-that *is* true..."

Slowly, Marcela was beginning to understand what Adele was getting at.

"Honestly," Adele continued, "what's most important is forming a strong image in your head—an image of what kind of magic you want to use and how you want to use it. Then, you make that image radiate outside of you. In terms of spells, all you really need are a few words that suit your image."

The three of them stared blankly. Adele's explanation of magic was nothing like anything they had ever heard before.

"A few words?" Marcela exclaimed. "I've never heard of such a thing! Even in silent casting, we were taught that you must still incant the words of the spell before releasing the magic. What do you mean by 'radiate,' anyway?

Adele explained the concept of radiating a thought pulse. The three looked skeptical.

"And as far as images... When you want to produce water, just imagine squeezing it out of the air, like wringing a wet towel. Go ahead, give it a try."

Among them, the most curious was Monika, the merchant's daughter, who couldn't use magic at all. She was the first to attempt it.

"Umm... Water, water, come on out, water squeezed from the sky!"

Ka-splash!

"Huh...?"

About ten liters of water poured down in front of Monika, muddying the ground. Monika, who was supposed to be completely without magical powers! And now, she was exhibiting not the basic magic of everyday convenience, but the magic of someone with real potential—assuming, of course, that she possessed the casting frequency and recovery time of a capable magician. And if training allowed...

"No way." Monika was flabbergasted.

As it happened, water magic had a great deal of utility for a merchant.

Humans required, at bare minimum, two liters of water a day. When journeying in scorching heat, of course, this need became even greater. On top of all that, a horse required something closer to thirty or forty liters a day.

For example, how much water would a driver of a horse-drawn carriage with three guards need to carry to survive a twenty-day journey, with no water sources along the route?

The answer would be roughly 1,600 liters, or 1.6 tons. Combined with food for the humans and horses, that begins to encroach on the space one has for storing one's wares.

However, if you had access to a magician who could produce ten liters of water every hour? That was a different story.

As a middle-class merchant's daughter, Monika already had a number of advantages. Now, on top of those other assets, she was an attractive girl who could also double as a giant water cask. Her value as a merchant had just risen immensely.

More importantly, though she had older brothers and sisters, the chances of her ending up as the mistress to someone of influence had decreased dramatically. At the very least, she would most likely be able to land a man of some wealth—or, better still, the son of a higher-class merchant...

"This can't... this can't be!" Monika fell to her knees.

At this, Aureana cried out, "W-water! Water squeezed from the air, show yourself before me! Aqua sphere, appear!"

The words sounded as though she were reading them from an unfamiliar book.

Splish!

There was nowhere near as much water as Monika had produced, but still, it was something. Enough that she would never need to carry a water skin, or fetch water from the well for cooking and bathing.

"Ha! Aha ha ha ha!"

"I-It can't..."

Monika had watched the other two in stunned silence, but as her senses returned, she made her own attempt at the spell. She had been able to produce water from the start. And so now...

"O, water! Squeeze from the air and become my spear...! Fly forth, to pierce my enemies!"

Ka-splat!

A jet of water struck a tree ten meters away with a splash.

It was not enough to pierce the trunk, but regardless, it was a fine attack spell, one that would at least be enough to disable an enemy.

"I-I did it! An attack spell!" Marcela's voice trembled.

A mere ten percent of people had the magical skills necessary to put food on the table. Of these, most had civilian jobs, replenishing water supplies and replacing fuel. Only one in several dozen was equipped to use combat magic.

Unlike magic that simply conjured water or fire, combat spells came with a number of additional hurdles. Rather than simply producing the substance in question, one also had to condense it, imbuing your spell with enough kinetic energy to propel it forth with sufficient power and speed.

And for those with an incomplete knowledge of magic's true principles, it required considerable talent to radiate a thought pulse silently, without using an appropriate spell.

The people of this world believed that, whether or not you opened your mouth, you needed "words of power" to work magic, and as a result, a great deal of effort went into putting the right words together rather than forming a concrete image of the spell's desired effect. This meant that it was difficult to produce magic continuously or spontaneously.

Rather than casting spells by radiating the pulse of an image, they believed that the effect was contained within the words themselves, which were heard and granted by mysterious beings. And of course, these spells did work as they were intended, thereby confirming this belief. It was thus that the people devoted themselves to researching incantations, never thinking that the success of their spells might be due to other factors.

As for combat magic, those who could manifest it had one of two strengths: the ability to create a clear image or thought pulse, or the capacity to radiate that pulse with great power. In neither case was this a process in which the user of magic engaged consciously; rather, when they cast spells, their subconscious powers allowed them to succeed where so many failed.

Thus, those who could use the so-called combat magic were fairly few.

And now, Marcela had just managed to employ it—with ease.

How many beautiful girls of noble birth could add *that* to their list of accomplishments?

With Marcela as a wife, you would always have a defender by your side, even as you slept. Furthermore, her talent might be passed down to children or grandchildren.

How much value would someone like that have in the eyes of an aristocrat with enemies?

Marcela would be receiving many favorable proposals. Most certainly.

Her imagined future as the second wife of some old man or the mistress of an influential noble was vanishing swiftly in favor of new paths.

"Sniff. Waaahhh..."

Adele had only planned to help her friends as a small thank you for their kindnesses to her and had never thought of the immense difference this knowledge would make in their lives. As they wept, she looked on in complete bewilderment.

Perhaps this had been a mistake?

"U-um, actually, we need to keep this kind of confidential, so... The next time we have magic practice, maybe you could pretend that all of this is a surprise to you? Like 'Whoa, how did I do that?' And could you try, maybe, to leave the 'from the sky' part out of your spells, if you can? Maybe just think that part in your head rather than saying it..."

Eventually, when the three girls were calmer, they understood exactly what she meant.

It would be disastrous for a secret like this to get out. If it were known that the differences between those who could use magic and those who could not were actually negligible—as well as the fact that those differences could be erased with little effort and that magical ability could be increased with only a few simple techniques—there would have been an enormous uproar. Adele would possibly be imprisoned for telling the truth, pressured for information by royal agents, or worse still, killed by her father and jealous stepmother for thwarting their plans...

"N-naturally!" Marcela stuttered. "There is no noble who would ever betray their benefactor... No, their friend!"

"There's no future for a merchant who breaks her bonds!"

"A-and, and... a peasant always keeps her promises!"

"Ha ha ha ha ha ha ha ha ha ha!" They all laughed together.

Two days later, at magic practice, Ms. Michella was ecstatic to see the three girls' magical talents suddenly bloom, one after the other. It was clearly the product of her good teaching.

In particular, she took an interest in Marcela, who showed a level of ability that would be impressive even for an adult magic user. Before long, her fascination with Adele, who could use only standard apprentice-level magic, dissipated.

It had been one year and two months since they first entered the academy.

During this time, Adele, now a second-year student, had managed to lead a fairly peaceful life without standing out from her peers. The majority of their classmates had remained in Class A after their promotion—just a handful had been transferred to other classes due to falling grades.

Adele, whose birthday fell early in the year, was now twelve years old.

In a little over a year, she had earned 144 silver pieces from her job at the bakery, half of which was banked away in her loot box. Were it not for Marcela's generous gifts, she probably wouldn't have been able to save even this much. Undergarments, after all, could be expensive.

As for her body, Adele's chest was not as prominent as it had been at twelve years old in her previous life, but it was starting to grow a little...

The undergarments that Marcela had gifted her over a year ago included some camisoles and brassieres, but until very recently, these had slumbered away inside the loot box with Adele's old clothing and her silver coins.

The thoughtfulness Marcela had shown in choosing padded garments made Adele's heart ache.

Adele excelled in academics. In sports, her technique was lacking, but her strength and speed made her a strong backup player. In terms of magic, she was a perfectly normal "amateur with potential." The only time she had produced anything the least bit remarkable was the piddling fireball she had silently cast during the initial assessment.

That was the state of things for Adele at school.

Marcela, on the other hand, had become something of a rising star ever since her magic had begun to blossom.

Once her family learned of her new abilities, they began sending frequent letters with advice such as, "Don't be hasty," and, "Take care to surround yourself with only the best." Naturally, they hoped to ensure that she would make the best marriage possible. Marcela herself declared that she would wait until the right man struck her fancy and settle for "nothing less than a wonderful gentleman." As a result, there had yet to be any talk of an engagement.

"This is all thanks to you," she told Adele. "I would never have thought that I'd have the power to choose my fiancé."

"No, no, I should be the one to thank you. You were the only one who could draw the boys' attention away from me."

Marcela and Adele grinned at one another.

As soon as others became aware of her aptitude for water magic, Monika also began receiving proposals from the sons of her father's trading partners and a clerk in the family's business, an ambitious young man who hoped to begin his own enterprise.

Yet she chose to wait, also, declaring, "The life of a merchant is risky! Five years from now, my betrothed could be bankrupt, and then what would I do?!" In this, too, Monika was truly a merchant's daughter.

Meanwhile, Aureana, having received a scholarship, would be required to work as a civil servant or teacher in the future.

Though the magic she could use was still very much of the "everyday" variety, suitable for housework and other small tasks, the fact that she could use magic at all continued to delight her.

She would never have to worry about water again, for even if she were stranded somewhere, she would always be able to summon enough to drink. In addition, Adele secretly taught her how to use magic to make water colder, which was quite useful as well.

Of course, chilling magic had always been around, but the method Adele taught Aureana was far more efficient. Even with her relatively modest abilities, she was able to make drinks colder, as well as preserve meats and fish. All of this was very useful.

"Hey! You already know, right?"

"We know. It's match day."

At Adele's response, Kelvin, who had approached the girls aggressively a moment before, turned back with a flat expression.

"There's no deterring that one, is there?" asked Marcela.

"I guess not..." Adele replied, her smile bitter.

Ever since their practice bout at the start of their first year, once a month, Kelvin had challenged Adele. He even made arrangements with Mr. Burgess to hold a practice match during their physical education lessons, so time was no problem. Still, as far as Adele was concerned, the whole thing was an ordeal.

She knew that he was putting in an enormous amount of effort, and it wasn't as though she didn't understand his feelings, but she hated seeing the way his eyes burned with animosity, or his blank, speechless face when he inevitably lost. They were classmates, so Adele put up with it, accepting his challenges each time, but she certainly didn't enjoy them.

Besides all that, however, Kelvin seemed like a decent sort of boy who got along easily with his classmates. Adele often wondered why he treated her the way he did, and the longer she pondered this, the more her discomfort increased.

She could no longer lose on purpose, not after Burgess's lengthy private lecture on the "fragility of man."

"Come on now, you can't just fake it!" her teacher would tell her. "If you keep doing this, he'll know for sure. Honestly, try to consider the man's pride..."

It was hard to meet Kelvin's eyes each time one of their bouts ended.

However, Burgess's lectures on "the nature of boys" had helped Adele—indeed, had helped her quite a bit.

It was time for combat practice.

As always, the class began with Adele and Kelvin's match, and as always, the victory went to Adele.

In terms of technique, Kelvin was leagues beyond her, but that meant nothing in the face of the overwhelming difference between them in terms of power and speed.

Of course, the strength she showed wasn't truly superhuman, but now that Adele had abandoned her "normal mode"—in other words, the amount of power that might be expected of a girl her age—there was no way a preadolescent boy could best her, no matter how talented he was. Not unless she lost on purpose.

Yet not only had Burgess forbidden her from doing that, but Adele had, by now, become painfully aware of her own lack of acting skills.

Kelvin's expression was unpleasant, and that day, seeing him glare at her the way he always did, Adele began to grow agitated. Why did he have to look at her like that? She had never done anything to deserve it. They had been through this routine at least ten times now, and every time, he had made that face and given her that look. This time, somehow, it angered her—as though the rage had been accumulating inside her and now escaped all at once.

"I'm not going to fight you again," she said. "We're through!"

"Huh...?"

For a moment, Kelvin stared at her blankly, as though he could not comprehend her words. Then, he flew into a red-faced rage.

"Wh-what are you talking about?! Until I beat you, I..."

"Can you not see how selfish that is?! What does that have to do with *me*?"

Kelvin opened his mouth to reply, but Adele cut him off before he could do so. "After all these times, are you really going to be satisfied and think, 'Oh yeah, I'm the strongest!' after winning just once? If you've got one win to twelve losses, are you really just going to stop? Are you stupid?!"

"Wh..."

"What, exactly, is it that you would gain from beating me? From beating someone who's not even aiming to be a knight? What would you say to them? 'Yes, that's right, my three years at the academy were occupied by attempting to defeat a little girl who works at a bakery. And now, that girl is preparing to be a bride.' Is that really what you want to say?!"

"Pfft!"

A number of their classmates burst out laughing. Even Mr. Burgess had to hold back his laughter. A conscientious teacher mustn't be seen laughing at such a thing. Certainly not.

"You're aware that I'm a magic user, aren't you? I'm not great with swords. Are you going to tell them that, too? Just proudly announce, 'Oh yes, I had fourteen sword battles with a mage who sucks at swords, and on the fifteenth try, I finally seized victory?!'"

"Gaha! Bwah ha ha ha ha!" The conscientious Burgess finally caved.

"Wh-what are you...?"

"That's what you're doing, isn't it?! You've never once battled me at magic, which is my specialty; you only come at me when we're practicing something *you're* good at. What's so great about beating a mage at a sword fight?"

"Uh..."

"Uh?"

"Uh-I, I... Waaaaaaaahhh!"

Kelvin went running.

"Adele, my girl..." Burgess looked troubled. "Can we chat a minute? There are some things in this world you shouldn't say to someone, no matter how justified you are..."

The remainder of the class turned into another one of Burgess's lessons for Adele about "being considerate of boys' egos," with the other students piping in now and then.

"So, I was wrong?" she asked.

"I'm not going to bother punishing Kelvin for leaving. I certainly wouldn't have been able to bear that dressing down."

Everyone in the class nodded in agreement with the ruling. Except for Adele.

"After that though, hmm..." Burgess turned to Marcela and company. "Wonder Trio, follow me."

"W-wonder Trio? Do you mean us? What is that...?"

The girls looked perplexed at their new title.

"Aah, sorry. That's the nickname we teachers have for you all. A commoner, a merchant's daughter, and a noble—despite coming from three very different backgrounds, the three of you get along wonderfully. More unbelievably, all three of you have seen your magical abilities blossom. It's like you caught the attention of the spirits who control magic, or the goddess was smiling on your friendship. So yes, Wonder Trio, Miracle Trio, Magic Trio... We have a lot of different names for you three."

"Huh?" The three were stunned and began to blush.

"But that's not the point. There's a certain delicate boy who needs comforting, and I'd like to enlist the help of the Three Popular Beauties of Class A, Plus One."

"What's that supposed to mean?"

The three were surprised, but seeing the state that Kelvin had been in, they couldn't possibly refuse.

"I suppose we must—if there's anything we can do to help..."

Yet as one might expect, these three girls still hoped for something in return, even if their actions were for the sake of a classmate.

"Oh, all right," Burgess conceded. "Next time something comes up, I'll take care of it for you."

"That's a promise then. And by the way..."

"Hm? What is it?"

"What did you mean by 'plus one'?"

"Oh, that." He pointed to Adele. "Though I guess, for now, we had better keep the culprit out of this."

And so, as though the three girls had worked some kind of miracle, Kelvin showed up for afternoon lessons.

After the final class was over and the teacher left the classroom, he approached Adele's seat.

At the sight of this, Adele wrinkled her nose, knowing trouble was brewing.

I wish he'd just leave me alone already!

"I won't lose! I am the fifth son of Baron Bellium, and on my name, I..."

"*Oh?*" Adele's low voice echoed through the quiet classroom. Her anger had begun to build again as soon as Kelvin started speaking.

It was then that her classmates knew: the morning's long talk about being considerate of Kelvin's feelings hadn't exactly sunk in.

"Who are you?"

A series of gasps echoed around the classroom, as everyone else was shocked right alongside Kelvin.

"Wh-what...? Are you...?" Kelvin was flustered but tried to save face.

Adele ignored his babbling.

"The one I've been fighting is a boy named Kelvin, a classmate who, no matter how many times he loses, keeps forcing me into one challenge after another. The one who I put up with time and time again, in spite of his mysterious grudges and creepy glares.

"And now? You aren't the one called Kelvin, my opponent and classmate, the one who keeps fighting and wants to be a knight, you're some creature called the 'baron's fifth son'? What business do I have with a thing like that?"

"Huh...?"

"What is a 'baron's fifth son' anyway? Is that impressive? Is that supposed to mean something? All it means to be a noble is that a long, long time ago, your ancestors did something the king liked. Until then they were just normal peasants like everyone else.

"Sure, maybe that person was amazing, but just being their descendent doesn't make you special. Or does your blood run a different color than a commoner's?"

There was an intake of breath as Adele and Kelvin's classmates reeled at this scathing critique.

"Um, actually, being a noble doesn't mean that you were born a noble," Kelvin said. "It means that you were born to *become* a noble. You're raised with your parents' example, and educated as a noble, and your heart is filled up with a noble's spirit—*noblesse oblige*, a 'noble's obligations.'"

The tables were turning! The classroom breathed a sigh of relief, but Adele continued. "What are you right now? You're studying among commoners, you haven't been trained as a noble, you haven't contributed anything to this country or its people. You haven't done anything but live off our taxes. What right have you to declare yourself anything at all?

"You think you deserve to call yourself a noble, when your only qualification is that special family name? Really? And you're willing to take the chance of sullying that name?"

"Uh..."

This was not going well. Seeing Kelvin backed into a corner, the students began to panic. It was beginning to feel like a repeat of that morning.

"...Is your heart burning?"

"Huh...?" Kelvin stared blankly, unsure of what she meant.

"Was all the passion you've poured into practicing combat

really born of your own desires? Or was it something you were duty-bound to do, to protect your pride as a noble's fifth son?

"Did you even enjoy your training? Were you glad to grow stronger? Or was it difficult and painful—did you have to force your way through?

"And when you did, did your heart grow dark and cold? Or did you burn hotter and brighter, believing in a future when your own strength would shine through, regardless of your family name?"

Kelvin was silent, his face bright red again.

"To me, you aren't just a noble or a 'baron's fifth son.' You're a boy, one who believes in his own power, who keeps training because of his own will, and who keeps on fighting to improve himself, regardless of his upbringing. That was what I believed, and that is why I always answered your challenges.

"Did you know that there's a place where the word 'Kelvin' is used to measure the temperature? It isn't a nice little scale, where water freezes at zero degrees, and boils at 100.

"In Kelvin, it's 273 degrees below zero. That is the temperature at which all matter freezes solid—even the motion of time. It's a terrifying sort of scale that fixes that point as zero degrees—or as they call it, 'absolute zero.'

"As for high temperatures, they'll give you a blazing world where even rock and iron melt and evaporate!"

With a snap, Adele pointed a finger at Kelvin.

"Are you a meaningless child with no merit outside of your position as a 'baron's fifth son'? Or are you a man who lives beyond that family name, who has a heart that blazes fiercely and a soul that shines with brilliant light—'Kelvin, the Inferno'?!"

"Uh—I... I..."

Seeing Kelvin's eyes beginning to well with tears, Adele snapped back to her senses. She looked around her to see her classmates gazing in awe, as though they had just witnessed something unbelievable.

Oh dear. Had she overdone it?

Flustered, Adele looked to Marcela, but Marcela simply shrugged her shoulders and pointed silently toward the door.

Following that admirably succinct advice, Adele hurried out of the room.

The following day, Adele entered the classroom timidly to find an atmosphere of unexpected calm. The other students greeted Adele normally, as they always did.

She was relieved.

However, the strange part came later.

Not that it was a bad thing.

It was just that everyone seemed to be putting forth an exceptional amount of effort.

During their classroom studies, during physical education, during magic practice...

They worked enthusiastically and asked productive questions. The noble students' efforts were particularly noticeable.

This was a good thing, surely. However, their attitudes were completely different from those of the previous day. Adele was greatly confused.

Even Kelvin had an oddly calm demeanor and seemed perfectly normal as they sat for lessons. There wasn't a fragment of the irritation or agitation he had shown every day for the last year.

Mr. Burgess was convinced that this was due to the efforts of the three girls, and news spread amongst the teachers that these three were particularly useful. More and more teachers began to put various requests upon them until it began to be a bit of a bother.

Adele couldn't help but comment on the changes.

"You know, Marcela... You managed to draw all the boys' attention away before, but lately it seems like it's started to turn back toward me, hasn't it?"

Marcela shrugged and replied, "Miss Adele, have you ever heard the expression, 'You reap what you sow'...?"

CHAPTER 5 |

Goddess Incarnate

I T WAS SEVERAL DAYS after the incident in the classroom, and Adele was busy at her job at the bakery.

Due to the nature of the business, the bakery was open even on rest days, but sales on these days were a fair bit less than during the week. This was to be expected. Most people used rest days to relax, and even working mothers stayed home, preparing all three of the day's meals. Naturally, there weren't many people who came in to purchase bread on their lunch breaks. Besides, not everyone needed bread to begin with. Many people baked their own, after all.

Nevertheless, the baker was the ally of the single person and the tired housewife. For the sake of the small segment of the population who needed bread, he opened his shop.

And as it happened, this whole problem of selling less bread on rest days was now a thing of the past.

Ever since Adele had started working, rest day sales began to increase, and now the bakery often sold as much bread on rest days as on weekdays.

Why was that?

"U-um, I'd like these ones please!" An apprentice from a nearby shop, a red-cheeked boy of fourteen or fifteen years, pointed at several pieces of bread.

"That comes to two half-silvers and three copper."

Adele smiled as she loaded the bread into the boy's basket and made change for the three half-silver pieces. As she handed him the coins, the boy's hand jerked, his fingers trembling.

"Thanks very much!" she said.

"U-um, I was wondering... Are you free after the shop closes?" the boy asked.

"Sorry, but when we close, I have to hurry back, or I won't make it in time for dinner. I don't have the money to buy my own food. Besides, the school gates close early, and since the matron was kind enough to allow me to work here, I can't risk breaking curfew..."

"I-I see..." The apprentice boy, who had painstakingly worked up the courage to ask Adele out, let his head hang in disappointment.

"Please come again!" she said.

"Y-yes, I'll be back!"

The boy headed home, his cheeks still burning at the memory of Adele's smile.

Adele was a good-looking girl, with a politeness born of her memories of Japanese hospitality. By this world's standards, she was so incredibly considerate that it was no surprise young boys often mistook her good manners for genuine interest.

Furthermore, Eckland Academy—though inferior compared to Ardleigh—was, from a commoner's perspective, a highly prestigious institution. Seeing Adele standing behind the counter of the bakery in her school uniform, most assumed that she must be an extremely gifted commoner, one who had been admitted to the school on scholarship. And as a commoner, boys assumed she just might be within their reach.

There she was, right in front of them: an intelligent, good-looking girl who would probably be able to make good money in the future. And to top it all off, she always had a smile to spare. There wasn't a boy around whose heart wouldn't leap.

A good many young men began appearing to purchase bread for their rest day meals, as well as the next day's share. Oddly, they never seemed to pay with exact change. In fact, it seemed that they always made sure to purchase items that would leave their total at an odd number and paid with coins that were too large—for if they did, the chance that their fingers might brush Adele's was doubled.

"Hee hee hee. You really are a wicked girl, Miss Adele…" A little old lady from the neighborhood teased her after the apprentice boy left.

"No, Granny! What are you saying?"

In her previous life, Adele had few if any fond memories of her grandparents, but in this life she got along well with the elderly.

The little old lady's husband chimed in. "Now, now, she's right indeed! You keep that up and you'll have your own shop and a man to support you in no time."

"Not you too, Grandpa!" Adele protested.

The elders of the neighborhood had also been dropping by the bakery on rest days.

With their children grown up and away from home, they were drawn to Adele's youth, and she was happy to talk to them. They were a nice change of pace from her many would-be suitors, after all.

When it came to work, there was really only one thing she was unhappy about.

Lately, the shop had been so busy that they were selling out of most of their bread by the end of the day, which meant that there was very little for her to take home in the evening.

On this day, after finishing her duties, Adele headed back toward the dorms, only to suddenly find her path blocked by a flock of people.

"Um, excuse me. Is there something going on?" she asked.

An old lady Adele recognized from the shop explained. "Oh yes! The third princess's carriage is coming through! Everyone's hoping to catch a glimpse of her. They say if we're lucky, she might even stop and open her window to wave."

The third princess almost never left the palace, so there were few who had seen her.

Why not? Adele thought. It wasn't every day you saw a princess. She might as well try to catch a glimpse of her. There should still be plenty of time.

Adele took advantage of her short stature to slip through the gaps in the crowd, until she had made it all the way to the front.

A few moments later, a group appeared on the opposite side of the main road.

At the front were four soldiers with swords at their hips and spears in their hands. Behind them were three soldiers on horseback, carrying lances. Following them was a gorgeous horse-drawn carriage, flanked at the back by more cavalry and foot soldiers.

Due to the narrow city streets, the princess's carriage was unable to move quickly, and the foot soldiers had likely been stationed as a sort of perimeter to deal swiftly with thieves or attackers.

The carriage and its guards approached, and just as the first soldier passed in front of Adele, a young boy of five or six was thrust into the road by the crowd's jostling.

"Impertinent brat!" The guard raised his spear and struck the child away with the blunt stone head.

The blow landed on the boy's gut, and he was struck senseless, tumbling to the ground, unable to speak or move. Yet he had been flung forward into the path of the carriage, and to shove him aside, the soldier struck the boy once more.

He's going to die!

By the time Adele realized what she was doing, her body was already moving, jumping out of the crowd and flying toward the fallen boy.

It felt like déjà vu...

It was just like before, wasn't it? Would she die a second time?

Yet she didn't stop moving, and as she threw herself over the boy's body, a thought rang out in her mind. *Lattice power, barrier!*

A translucent wall appeared in the air, deflecting the soldier's heavy spear just before it struck Adele.

Shing!

This was lattice energy, the cohesive force that bound atoms, molecules, and ions into a grid when a matter changed from a gas to a solid.

As she cast her mind about for something to protect her, Adele remembered the barriers she had seen in anime; however, just watching the shows gave her very little idea as to the principles behind the kind of protection she was trying to manifest. If she could imagine it concretely, then the nanomachines would be able to manifest it for her somehow or other, but even as she tried to conjure an appropriate image, it occurred to Adele that her knowledge of defensive energy was sparse. Instead, another term popped into her head: "lattice energy," something she had read about it in a book once, in her previous life.

Lattices. Cohesive force. It sounded like something that could form a shield.

While she didn't fully comprehend the meaning of these terms, Adele's instincts sensed that they might be able to help her.

Indeed, using this notion of a lattice, Adele formed a dazzling image, a barrier that, when it appeared, was not a smooth, solid hemisphere, but a surface of what appeared to be innumerable connected glass plates.

"Wh...?"

Startled, the soldier raised his spear again and again to strike through the barrier. However, it did not crack.

"Move!"

At some point one of the mounted cavalrymen had descended from his horse. Now, he was approaching.

From his appearance and demeanor, it was clear that he was

of a higher rank than the foot soldiers. He had been on horseback, so he was probably a knight...

He brandished his own spear, swinging it full force, with the point of his blade pointing straight at Adele.

Shing!

"Impossible!"

Oh God oh God oh God!

Adele was panicking.

As if getting into a scuffle with the royal guards wasn't bad enough, now there was the issue of this lattice barrier, which had formed from her instinct to survive.

To the best of Adele's knowledge, magic like this was unheard of in this world.

There was magic that could be used to dissipate other magic in a duel between magic users. There was also magic that could raise the earth to act as a shield against swords or spears or arrows. There was protection magic that drew on wind and water. However, even in books and legends, there was no such thing as magic that could shield one against physical attacks without the use of another one of the elements.

Anyone who could conjure such magic would be invincible in battle. With your enemy unable to strike, you could launch a one-sided assault.

They were definitely going to take her to the palace, where, Adele suddenly realized, she would probably be executed for attempting to assassinate the third princess.

This was very bad. She had performed unthinkable magic in broad daylight and inadvertently threatened the princess's life! This was a double whammy. What could she do?

While still covering the boy, Adele wracked her brain desperately, trying to devise some plan. However, panic began to cloud her brain. She was fresh out of ideas.

"Wh-what are you, fiend?! Are you a monster or a demon?!" the guards shouted, fear on their faces as they edged away from Adele's shield.

...A demon? Like an evil spirit? Wait a minute!

At this flash of brilliance, Adele dispelled the barrier.

With a sound like shattering glass, the lattice exploded into shards, which dissipated into thin air. There was no danger in dropping her shield now. Even if one of the soldiers attempted an attack, Adele was confident that she could grab a spear in time to stop it.

She stood slowly and turned to the soldiers, her expression blank.

"What impudence is this, to visit harm upon an avatar of the divine?!" she said.

"Huh?"

"How dare you attempt to cause injury to my vessel?!"

"Huh?"

Uncertain as to what was unfolding before them, the assembled crowd of soldiers and onlookers appeared taken aback.

The knight was enraged at Adele's sudden hubris.

"Y-you're speaking nonsense! Oi, you lot—seize her!"

At the knight's command, the soldiers approached Adele with some trepidation.

"Lightning! Visit your wrath upon these fools who dare to raise their blades against a god!"

KABOOM!

Four lightning bolts crashed down, striking the tips of the soldier's spears.

"Waaaaaaaaaaaaahh!!"

The soldiers dropped their spears in agony, falling on their behinds.

"Wh-what just..."

It had not been flame magic. It was honest-to-goodness lightning, straight from the heavens.

It was a power unlike magic at all.

"Was that...the power of God...?"

The soldiers huddled in fright. Suddenly, they were no longer soldiers who fought for a living—they were human lightning rods.

What had really happened was that Adele had gathered negative electrical charges below the clouds and positive charges above, inducing a lightning strike by drawing the positive charges to the tips of the soldiers' spears.

She had collected a low, secondary current that ran from the spear handles to the ground, so as to form an insulating membrane around the soldier's hands and not accidentally shock the life out of them.

Next, she began a silent spell.

Refract and diffuse the light! Gather moisture into ice! Neutralize gravity and maintain formation...

Adele solidified the image in her mind and released her creation in a wave.

Shining particles of light began to float and swirl around Adele's body and ice crystals gathered at her back.

"It's... a goddess..." the knight whispered weakly.

Indeed, a young girl now stood before the soldiers, her body bathed in light and platinum wings sprouting from her back.

"What divine punishment shall I visit upon you? Shall I level your palace? Or shall I eradicate the nobles, the royals, and the soldiers as well? Better yet, perhaps the entire Kingdom..."

"Please wait!"

A girl flew out from the ostentatious carriage and ran desperately toward Adele, pushing past the two knights at the door.

She was golden-haired, fourteen or fifteen years of age—undoubtedly, this was the third princess.

When she reached the knight's side, she fell to her knees, her head bowed.

"Oh, Goddess, please forgive them! This carriage before you is mine. So please, level all your punishments at me and spare the others!"

"Y-your highness, what are you doing? As captain of the guard, this is my responsibility. I should be the one to take the fall! Your highness is entirely innocent."

"No! It is only natural that the person in the highest position should take the punishment, is it not?!"

Hmm, Adele thought. Rather than fighting to pin the blame on each other, these two were scrambling to take it. Perhaps they weren't such bad people, after all...

The crowd was beginning to grow restless, and Adele's original purpose had been simply to distract everyone for long enough to save the boy. She needed this over with.

She was already treating the boy's wounds with silent healing magic. She made certain to ensure that any injuries to his bones or internal organs were healed, and there was no damage or internal bleeding around his skull.

"Silence! I detest such blabbering! Very well. Thanks to the generosity of your princess, I shall spare this place. However, I'll show no such kindness next time. Do you understand?!"

"We understand! We offer the utmost gratitude for your forgiveness."

What a humble speech from a princess!

If Adele was found out, she would most certainly be beheaded.

It was time for the finishing touch.

Adele turned and faced the soldier who had struck the boy. The man was still on the ground.

"You there. I understand that you thought merely to fulfill your duties, but you were foolish and rash. The blood you would have spilled would have been on the *Princess's* hands! Would you wish for a rumor to spread throughout the lands that this country's third princess was a cruel tyrant who murdered children standing in the way of her carriage? Could you live with that on your shoulders?"

At these words, the soldier was overwhelmed with the gravity of what he had nearly done.

"And now, I must depart," Adele said, then added, "But just one thing before I do! This vessel I am inhabiting knows not of my presence. You must not speak of it to her. Understood?! You must never speak of this incident to anyone!"

Everyone, the crowd and soldiers alike, gazed intently at Adele.

They nodded emphatically, faces pale.

"M-my Goddess, I have a favor to ask!" the captain of the guards said.

"What is it?"

"At the very least, permit me to speak of this to the king..."

For some time, Adele mulled over this request from the captain of the guards, before finally nodding slowly.

With so many soldiers aware of the incident, it would be unthinkable not to tell their king.

"I suppose I must. You may. However, you may speak only to the king and no one else. This must be kept secret from the other nobles."

"Y-yes. Yes, we will be sure."

Just then, a bright idea popped into Adele's head.

She turned to the captain of the guards, making something of a troubled face.

"Hmm. This girl—my vessel. She is impoverished and somewhat lacking in nutrition. Perhaps you will spare her a bit from your coin purse? Call it a 'commendation for her bravery,' or whatever you will."

"Ah! Yes, of course, your Greatness!"

The captain's reply was immediate. He could not possibly refuse.

Excellent, Adele thought. The captain's money would be some consolation. Now, to end this charade!

Keeping her face stern, Adele fanned her hands over the boy.

"Light of healing, ease his wounds!"

The boy's body was surrounded by particles of light—though this, of course, was just for show, as his wounds had already been mended.

Once the light and brilliant wings vanished, Adele returned to her position on top of the boy, where she had been when the shield had first risen.

"Hmm, yes, I believe it was just here. Now, each and every one of you had better keep your promises!"

Taking one last look over the nodding soldiers and the crowd, Adele closed her eyes, then opened them, blinking to feign shock.

"H-huh? What? I'm not hurt? What happened to the soldier with the spear?"

She looked around as she spoke.

Apparently, her acting skills had improved somewhat over the past year.

"Mmm... Huh? Who are you, miss?"

The boy had finally awoken. Thanks to the magic, he showed not even the slightest sign of pain.

The crowds who witnessed the scene muttered among themselves, but they didn't want to risk saying something careless.

The captain of the guards called out. "U-um... No, uh, you there! Girl!"

"Hmm? Do you mean me?" Adele clasped both hands under her chin conspicuously, her eyes wide.

This time, at least, her surprise was artificial.

"Y-yes. I must commend you for standing up to my subordinate's in order to protect that boy. It was courageous, and so, I would like to offer you this reward."

The guard pulled a coin purse from his breast pocket.

Yes! It was all going perfectly according to her plan.

Adele fought fiercely to hold back her grin as the guard handed her the purse.

She was surprised at the weight of it.

It was then that she realized that everyone was looking—at her and the impoverished boy.

However you looked at it, the boy appeared far poorer than Adele, who was wearing an academy uniform.

How would it look if she took the money and ran?

Another problem.

"Y-you take this!"

"Huh?"

"That knight over there—he said it was an apology, for frightening you!"

"Really? Thank you!"

Adele groaned inwardly. There went her escape funds.

Still, she handed over the coin purse. Her hands trembled softly.

Seeing this, the captain of the guard bristled.

All the color drained from his face, but there was nothing he could do to stop the purse from changing hands. He could not violate the goddess's orders by speaking of what had come before.

Just then, a voice rang out to save the captain, who was by now dripping with sweat.

"Allow me, as deputy captain, to reward this brave young girl in the captain's stead."

Thank goodness! the captain thought and reminded himself to thank his deputy. He had seen his life flashing before his eyes.

Adele was equally relieved. *What luck! Now I should be able to add to my escape fund!*

In order to save a child's life, Adele had reflexively used a barrier, a type of magic unknown to this world. On top of that, she had feigned possession by a goddess, tricked a pack of soldiers, and forced everyone to pretend that nothing had happened.

And thanks to this whole improvised scheme, she had even

ended up with some money in her pocket. Adele was filled with an innocent joy.

But she was naïve, lacking in experience. She knew nothing of the cunning of man.

Those weaknesses left her wide open.

It was the evening following the incident.

Inside the palace, three individuals gathered in the king's office for a discussion.

They were the king, the guard captain, who was called Bergl, and the third princess, Morena.

"Is this all true?"

"I would never dream of telling you such a lie."

"Father, you must believe him!"

"Hmm..."

The king thought for a long time, and then made a decision.

"Very well. Bring that girl to the palace."

"Father!"

"Your Majesty, we mustn't!"

While Bergl and the princess panicked, the king spoke plainly.

"With so many people having seen the incident, there is no way we can stop the news from spreading. We cannot assume that such an important person would be left unmolested. Though some day she may still catch the attention of some other noble or the ruler of another country, for now, would it not be beneficial to ingratiate ourselves to the goddess?

"We can say that we are simply giving thanks to the girl who used her own body to shield a child, who prevented the tarnishing of the princess's image. Is there any fault in that? Is it not a perfectly natural course of action, for a king and a father?"

"Ah..."

"Morena, you must give thanks to the one who shielded you from disgrace. You must befriend her, no matter what."

"O-of course, I will gladly. That is all I could wish for..."

"All right, then. Bergl, as you know the girl's face, I will leave to you the task of tracking her down. Begin your search at once!"

"Yes, sir!"

The search concluded swiftly.

Adele had been wearing her uniform, and the guards were quite familiar with the uniforms of both of the city's academies. On top of that, Adele's splendid silver hair made her stand out even more than she might have otherwise. Finding her was easy.

Straight away, Guard Captain Bergl met with the dean of Eckland and described Adele's appearance.

There was no way that the dean could lie to a royal knight, who had come on the king's imperial decree. Naturally, he ignored the viscount's gag order and told the knight Adele's full name and status.

The dean did this without ill intention, thinking that it would give the girl a better position. He truly believed that he was setting a young girl on the road to prosperity.

And so, the guard captain reported the results of his investigation to the king. Soon after, the honorable young daughter of Viscount Ascham received a message, inviting her to come to the palace straight away.

"...That is to say, the King would like to extend an invitation to the honorable young daughter of Viscount Ascham. Here is the letter."

The messenger, a certain Viscount something-or-other, handed her the envelope. Adele stared down at it, a hand to her head.

How could this have happened?

Even with a goddess's decree, it was impossible to expect that many people to keep a secret—or assume that kings and nobles would be happy to leave a girl who was touched by the goddess alone. Yet this thought had not occurred to Adele, who naively imagined that she would be able to continue living a normal, peaceful life. That all changed the afternoon a teacher called her away during lessons, leaving her to languish alone in the reception room with this messenger.

If I don't do something, they're going to lock me up or restrain me. Or even worse—will they strip me down and dissect me? No goddess is going to come leaping out of my belly!

What do I do what do I do what do I do?

I have to think!

Work, you stupid gray matter!

Suddenly, something occurred to her.

This noble messenger before her hadn't been present at the time of yesterday's incident, and the guards, who would have recognized her, weren't present.

Furthermore, the messenger's discussion with Adele made no mention of the goddess or of yesterday's incident. He had merely offered an invitation to the "third princess's benefactor."

Even though he had said nothing of the goddess to Adele, it was still possible that he knew about it. However, given his fairly natural comportment, it was most likely he did not.

He hadn't asked her anything about the goddess or the particulars of the incident. *He's just an errand boy!* Adele realized. *He must not know anything about it.*

Thanks to that fact, she realized she had an out. It was time to test that newfound confidence in her acting skills!

"Hmm? I am to deliver this to young Miss Ascham?" she asked.

"Huh?"

The messenger gaped at her unexpected reply.

"What I am asking is, do you wish for me to deliver this invitation to the daughter of Viscount Ascham, who attends Ardleigh Academy?"

"What? Huh?"

Adele continued to press the increasingly confused messenger. "The honorable young daughter of the Ascham household attends the upper-class Ardleigh Academy—on the other side of the city. The Ascham family generously donated money so that I might attend this academy, but I do not carry the Ascham family name. If I were to claim otherwise, I would be killed! Someone has made a mistake of some kind."

"Wh-what?!"

"Please do not reveal that you came to me in error. I'll be in a great deal of trouble if I displease the Viscount and lose my financial support."

"I-I understand! Don't worry, I won't tell a soul. I'm so sorry..."

With that, the noble messenger swiftly departed, no doubt heading for Ardleigh.

The invitation had been for tomorrow morning, Adele thought.

I guess this is it...

It was time for her to escape.

When she returned to the classroom, Adele was inundated with questions from her curious classmates. She'd caused a fuss by being called away during class, but she quashed the whispers with a simple explanation. "They had the wrong person."

Marcela and the girls still looked worried, but they calmed down when Adele whispered, "They were looking for my stepsister."

Upon returning to her dorm at the end of class, Adele quickly began her preparations.

First, she had letters to write.

One to her three friends, one to all her classmates, one to the matron, and one to Aaron, the baker. In each, she apologized for her sudden departure, expressed her thanks for their friendship and assistance, and explained that, due to unforeseen circumstances, she was dropping out of school.

Halfway through, she stopped to eat dinner, and by the time she was finished writing, it was already late at night.

And now, the next step... At least I don't have much packing to do.

In the little more than a year at the academy, Adele hadn't managed to accumulate any new luggage. Her spare clothing and the wages she'd saved were all stored away in the loot box. Her room appeared as vacant as ever.

After going back and forth for some time, Adele decided to keep the uniforms and gym clothes she had been lent. They were getting fairly worn, so it was likely that they would be disposed of rather than passed on to another student. She decided it should be fine if she kept them.

After all—if she *didn't* keep them, she would have nothing to wear. As was only natural, Adele had grown in the year since her arrival. The clothing she had brought with her initially was now too small.

She lined up the letters on her desk and borrowed just one blanket from the bed, which she shoved into the loot box. Then, she looked around the room.

It was empty. Perfectly empty.

"Farewell!"

She uttered a soft goodbye, and then, suddenly remembering, took out from her desk drawer the plate with the bone.

Cats weren't fond of humans who fussed over them too much, so Adele, who only scratched behind the cat's ears or on her neck or face when requested, was the perfect companion. The cat visited often, and Adele let her sleep on her bed as she pleased.

However, in terms of food, Adele was only able to provide bones, which left the cat dissatisfied. It hadn't taken Adele long to realize that the cat was wandering to the other girls' rooms for handouts.

For some reason, though, it was only the girls' rooms. She never visited the boys...

"You were a stray to start, so I'm sure you'll be fine," Adele whispered. "Besides, when the other kids mention the name of the cat they're taking care of—Blackie, Goldeneye, Crooktail, Cricket Eater, and so on—I think they're all referring to you!"

Adele nodded to herself, then said, "Now that's enough of that. It's time to escape!"

The next morning, Adele didn't appear in the classroom when the day began, and the worried instructor asked another teacher to go to the girls' dorm and check for her. Upon arrival, the teacher found only the abandoned room and the four letters that had been left there. Soon, a panic arose.

Even though she had always hoped to be completely average, no matter how you look at it, Adele was an outstanding pupil, beloved by students and teachers alike.

Yet upon opening the letters, they found that her disappearance had been of her own free will. Furthermore, because she had expressed her intent to withdraw from the academy, the school had no further recourse. The best they could do was to contact her guardians.

"What's the meaning of this?!" Kelvin demanded when he found out, his expression disturbed.

"Of what?" an unhappy Marcela asked.

"You know what I'm talking about! Adele! Where did she go?! Why did she leave?!"

He was as insufferable as ever, but Marcela could tell that, unlike before, his blood was boiling out of genuine concern for Adele, so she had no choice but to acknowledge him.

The letter addressed to the students contained only an apology for not saying goodbye and a thank you for all their kindness up until that point. Without any other explanation, it was more than natural that he would come to Marcela and the other girls, who had received their own, separate letters.

"Family problems. A conflict of succession. It's not such a rare thing among noble families."

"She was the successor?"

"No, she was in the successor's way. They would've made her disappear, so she vanished herself first."

"Wh..."

Kelvin was lost for words, but Marcela simply sighed.

"What are *you* so worried about? Whether that girl will make it out there? You should be happy that she'll be living freely, without the burden of her meddlesome family. Just what have you seen in her all this time?"

"I just... I never got to apologize, or to thank her..."

"She was always saying that she wanted to 'live normally,' but do you really think that's possible for someone like her?" Marcela said. "Somehow or other she's going to slip and end up center stage. Wouldn't it be best for you to work hard to become a man who can proudly show his face in front of her, when that time comes?"

"........."

As Kelvin silently walked away, Marcela watched with a tender gaze.

Seeing this, the other boys began to whisper among themselves.

"Marcela... She's a nice girl, isn't she?"

All the boys nodded in agreement.

In the palace's audience room, the king, the third princess

Morena, and a number of nobles gathered. Other matters of the day had been dispensed with, leaving only the girl. Morena sat beside the king, prepared for the meeting.

Initially, she had thought they would meet privately, just the two of them, but this girl was to become an important acquaintance of hers. Therefore, it was determined they would wait until the end of the daily audiences, then bring the girl forward, so that everyone could see the princess with her.

"Presenting Viscount Ascham and the honorable young Miss Ascham!"

At the herald's announcement, the Viscount and his daughter Prissy promenaded into the audience room. They proceeded forward, dropping to one knee before the throne, their heads bowed.

They were both utterly delighted.

Yesterday, an agent of the palace had suddenly arrived, telling them, "The third princess most sincerely wishes to welcome the honorable young Miss Ascham to the palace, so that the two of them may become friends, if it so pleases her."

A friend to the princess!

Having a friend in the palace was an extraordinarily valuable connection, and the princess herself would have a direct line to the princes and even His Majesty. There was a strong possibility that Prissy might even catch a prince's eye.

She didn't know what had caused them to seek her out, but perhaps the fourth prince, who had just entered the academy this year, had already come to desire her...

With these possibilities in mind, Prissy's fancies flourished wildly, and the Viscount's were not far behind.

"Show your faces."

At the king's order, the Viscount and Prissy lifted their heads, eyes sparkling.

The king looked to the third princess, Morena.

However, Morena only stared blankly, not speaking.

"Hm? What's wrong?"

"Ah, well, um... Who might these two people be?"

"What? Is this not young Miss Ascham here before you?"

"I don't know this person..."

Overhearing the king and the princess's conversation, the people assembled began to whisper. There had been some sort of mistake. Viscount and daughter, not understanding the situation, were dumbfounded.

"Where is Bergl?" asked the king.

A royal guard answered, looking troubled. "Ah, well, he went to the audience waiting chambers not long ago and then left in something of a hurry."

A voice was raised from amidst the assembly. "Your Majesty, might I be granted permission to speak...?"

"Hm? Oh, Count Bornham. Yes, you may speak." Perhaps this man would know something. The king gestured for him to stand.

"Thank you very much!" Count Bornham said, then turned to Prissy, the young Miss Ascham, and inquired, "Young lady, where might your mother be at this moment?"

"Mother? Why she should be at the Ascham estate here in the capital right now..."

"Hmm... Well then, your beautiful golden hair—I presume it was inherited from her?"

"Y-yes, that's true..." Prissy answered, without understanding precisely why she was being asked such a thing.

Count Bornham now turned and addressed the king.

"My wife was close friends with the Lady Ascham during their time at Ardleigh Academy. Twelve years ago, we received word that she had given birth to a daughter, and my wife and I paid a visit to the Ascham home.

"The infant we saw at that time had gorgeous silver hair, inherited from her mother... However, that mother lost her life three years ago in an accident. Something peculiar is happening here..."

"That child has nothing to do with us!" Prissy suddenly exploded. "She was his first wife's child! We Aschams have no need for her! So we flung her from our home and forbade her to use the family name! She—"

Viscount Ascham frantically clapped a hand over Prissy's mouth, but it was too late.

Count Bornham continued, calmly. "A father has every right to raise his daughter as he pleases, but in this case, there is a bit of a problem with the situation.

"As I just said, my wife was close friends with the *Lady Ascham* during their time at Ardleigh Academy. Ergo, the Viscount only married into the Ascham family. The Ascham family blood runs through neither the Viscount who stands here nor this daughter, but through his previous wife's daughter, who was chased away."

"Usurper!"

"He overthrew the family line! That's the worst a noble can do!"

"A crime worthy of the highest punishment!"

One voice after another cried out from the assembly, now in uproar.

Viscount Ascham was frozen, his face utterly pale.

"What say you, Viscount Ascham?" The king's voice was firm.

Everyone grew silent, awaiting the viscount's confession.

However, Viscount Ascham remained silent, making no move to reply.

After some moments of this looming silence, the door of the assembly hall opened, and a single guard entered.

"Oh, Bergl! Where have you been?" asked the king.

Bergl drew an envelope from his breast pocket.

"Well, when I went to the audience waiting room where the girl was to be, I saw a young woman I didn't recognize standing there. Thinking there must have been a mistake, I rushed to the school attended by the girl we were seeking. However, it seems that she left the school this morning for a destination unknown, leaving only four letters behind...

"As could be expected, three of the letters were addressed to classmates and teachers and the like. Yet there was one more letter, addressed to a trio of girls who she was close to, which contained a few more clues as to the particulars of the situation. The trio allowed me to borrow this letter on the condition that I return it, thinking that it might be able to help their friend."

"Tell us what it says," the king ordered. Bergl looked over the letter in his hands.

"Yes, sir. In summary, she was called, by her family name, to come to the palace, despite having been forbidden previously to bear that name. Were she to do so, the girl explained, she would likely be killed, just like her mother and grandfather. She decided to run but told her friends not to worry. She planned to carry on a happy life somewhere out in the country. That is all."

The king rumbled. "Killed like her mother and grandfather, you say?"

Now, Count Bornham responded.

"The previous Viscount Ascham and his daughter were assailed and killed by bandits. However, theirs was the only case of anyone having been attacked by bandits in that area within a period of quite some years. What, we must ask ourselves, are the chances of this attack falling on the *one* occasion that the carriage carried not husband and wife, but the rare combination of the old viscount and his daughter...?

"My wife always had her suspicions, but I did not wish to slander a household without evidence. I have kept my suspicions silent until this day..."

Viscount Ascham's face had gone beyond pallid and was now pure white.

"Throw those two in the dungeon at once!" the king ordered. "Take the necessary agents to the Viscount's estate and apprehend his current wife. Launch an investigation into all parties who may have been accessory to the murders of the late viscount and his daughter. Consider all those who turned a blind eye or accepted bribes to be an accomplice.

"Until the rightful heir is prepared to take over the Ascham family estate, their lands will be under the Kingdom's control.

"Now, Bergl, you must find her. She is a young girl, so she couldn't have gotten far in half a day's time. It should be simple. Use as many men as you require. You must protect her and treat her well.

"Everyone, move out!"

With the king's decree, all directed parties sprang from the room.

The attending nobles were a tad surprised, as the king was not known for making such hasty judgments. However, they knew that even a gentle king took speedy action when needed, and they graciously accepted their orders.

However, none of them knew of the rage that boiled in the king's heart...

Once the remaining nobles left the audience hall, the third princess spoke.

"Father," said Morena. "That missing girl is..."

"Don't say it."

The king held his head.

Bergl had to find her. And fast.

Didn't I Say
to Make My Abilities
Average in the
——— Next Life?!

CHAPTER 6 |

Fledgling Hunter

I**T WAS TWELVE DAYS LATER.** In a certain regional capital located in a country far from the Kingdom of Brandel—the land of Adele's birth—there stood a hall, which sported a signboard etched with a crossed sword, spear, and staff.

It was not the home of a blacksmith or a weapons shop.

No, this was the hall of the Hunters' Guild.

And in front of it, stood a young girl, alone.

Of all that she had saved, only three silver coins remained. She had used the rest of her money to purchase a tunic, trousers, boots, and a leather breastplate. After that, she had picked up a cheap secondhand sword at a weapons shop. As a normal sword would have shattered if she had swung it at full strength, she had inevitably needed to rework it.

She purchased a relatively short sword to suit her stature, then implored the nanomachines to gather iron sand from the silt of the river bed to incorporate into her blade. Iron sand, she knew, was the same material used in Japanese katana, and the new blade was strong and durable.

In order to emulate the techniques of a craftsman, she gave the nanomachines only simple, direct instructions, to be enacted with earth magic.

What she wanted was an unbreakable sword, one that wouldn't bend or weaken. The sharpness had to be normal and the materials equalized to achieve the optimal carbon content.

I don't care if you turn it into mithril or adamantine or orihalcum or hihi'irokane or any other rare metal, she told the nanomachines. *If you need to rework the molecular structure, then go ahead and do that, too. Just make sure it looks like a normal sword!*

And so, her mysterious blade was completed.

Even the girl herself had no idea what it was truly made of.

She could never have crafted the whole thing alone—it was too difficult to picture a grip or scabbard from the raw materials, so these had a standard appearance. But the blade was the sword's real strength.

She was ready to defeat some monsters—to become a perfectly normal, average hunter. With that aim in mind, the girl opened the door to the hall of the Hunters' Guild and stepped inside

The guildhall was empty.

It was early afternoon, hardly the busiest time of day.

There were no hunters talking, drinking, or trading stories of the day's adventures.

The girl turned to the empty reception window. "Excuse me, I'd like to register as a hunter," she called hesitantly.

"Oh, h-hello!" A flustered girl of seventeen or eighteen years, who appeared to have embarked on this line of work only recently, greeted her. "Um, d-do you know how to write?"

"Yes, I do."

"All right, then. Please fill this out for me."

The girl accepted the blank form from the clerk and moved to a registration desk nearby. She placed the form atop it, gripping the provided pen as she looked the form over. Naturally, the very first blank was for her name.

My name...

The girl thought hard.

Well, I certainly can't use the name Adele. Not unless I run into some old classmate from the academy...

Misato was the name that she had in her previous life, but now, she needed to come up with something new.

Just then, she recalled a conversation she once had with her father when she was young. It was during elementary school, when they had been given an assignment that required them to ask their parents about the origin of their names.

When Misato asked her father about the origin of her own name, he had said this:

"Well, Misato, you know that your father's work is all about airplanes, right? In the world of aviation, we use a measure of distance called a mile.

"There are both sea miles and land miles, but even within the category of land miles, there are international miles, survey miles, statute miles, and a number of others—all of which differ in length by country. It's a huge pain.

"However, when it comes to the land and sea, in the aviation and maritime industries, everyone uses the same nautical mile as the main unit of measurement. The sky and sea are connected throughout the whole world, meaning it would be a problem if every country used measurements of their own.

"Unlike land miles, which follow a number of different standards, nautical miles have only one measure. If you travel once around the world, from north to south, you would go 360 degrees. Each mark of that latitude is 60 miles, and so 1/60th of that will always be one mile.

"The kanji for 'Misato' can also be read 'Kairi.' And that word is the Japanese term for a nautical mile.

"No matter where you go in the world, a nautical mile is always the same. I wanted to find a name that conveyed those universal qualities, and that's why we picked your name.'

The girl let the feather pen glide along the page, inscribing her name.

Mile.

And so, the rookie hunter "Mile" was born.

Mile filled in the rest of the fields on the form.

Gender? *Female.* Age? *Twelve.* Occupation? *Magic user.* Specialization? *None.* Seeking a party? *No.* Past history and commendations as a hunter? *None.*

She returned the completed form to the clerk at the window, who accepted it without protest. "Miss Mile, is it?" she said. "Are you from around here?"

"No, I was born deep in the mountains, but both my parents passed away. Now I have to make it on my own, and there is no other work I can do..."

"I-I'm so sorry. I overstepped... Well, let's get you acquainted with the guild!"

The explanation that Laura, the clerk, proceeded to give her was more or less the same as what she'd heard from the boys in her class.

Hunters had eight ranks, lettered G through S.

G-rank was reserved for what were called "guild hopefuls"— children six to nine years of age who were given odd jobs around the town or tasks such as accompanying those who went out to collect herbs.

At ten years old, these hopefuls were allowed to become proper guild members, but they started out at F, the lowest rank, and could only be tasked with collecting plants and minerals; tracking birds, deer, and wild boars for harvest; and weeding out jackalopes and other lesser monsters.

At E-rank, they could take on goblins and orcs, and at D-rank, restrictions were finally removed from the hunters.

Still, D-ranks had somewhat of a lesser reputation, and though it was not unheard of for them to be offered jobs such as being bodyguards and the like, most employers only sought hunters of C-rank and above.

Indeed, C-rankers were what would normally be thought of as "full-fledged hunters," and their ranks were the largest. Thanks to this, however, their ability levels were greatly varied—from just beyond D-rank to just before B-rank.

B-ranks were first class, and highly esteemed, especially in smaller towns in the country. A-ranks were veritable legends, while anyone who reached S-rank—the highest tier—was heralded as a hero.

However, there were but a few S-ranks, even within the royal capital.

Promotions were decided by committee, based on a hunter's completed jobs, achievements, and contributions to the guild. However, in some rare cases, only a minimum amount of time was required to be registered before a promotion occurred.

Promotion fraud was absolutely forbidden, and anyone caught undermining the system could be permanently expelled from the guild, no matter their position. In the worst cases, hunters had even been known to be executed. Therefore, there wasn't a soul who would let themselves be led astray by anything less than a king's ransom.

Guild members were expected to settle any internal disputes amongst themselves, so long as they remained petty quarrels. In the event that a hunter committed an actual crime, they were tried and punished by both the guild and the local law enforcement. The guild members were still citizens of the town, and a crime was a crime, so violent conduct and extortion and the like were dealt with accordingly.

As the clerk continued her explanation, the hunter's badge, which she'd apparently started making after receiving the girl's paperwork, was completed. It was a small iron tag, worn on a chain around the neck. On it was engraved an "F" (or rather, that world's equivalent of the letter), as well as Mile's name, the name of the guildhall, and a registration number.

Of course, as it was not equipped with any secret functions that automatically logged monster kills, nor received urgent messages from the guild, it was necessary to bring back a trophy as proof every time one killed a monster. If one relocated to another town, it was necessary for a letter of introduction and an assessment record to be forwarded to the new guildhall before the transfer could be finalized.

In order to preserve confidentiality, the specifics of these transfers were never made public, so there was no danger of revealing one's whereabouts.

"Should you encounter the body of a hunter anywhere," Laura said, "please retrieve and return that hunter's mark. We will need to contact the family of the departed and process their removal from the register. Then, once their hunter's badge has been marked as invalid, we return it to the family as a memento. Whoever returns the tag will of course receive a humble sum from the guild as a reward. In some cases, the relatives will also offer the finder a token of their gratitude. And of course, all items found on the body at the time of discovery, including weapons and armor, become the property of the finder."

As the clerk handed Mile her badge, she continued her explanation.

The reward money was only a pittance, rendering it unlikely that a hunter would continually "find" other hunters' bodies without good reason. This discouraged the hunting of other hunters. Indeed, it sounded as though this system had been put in place just for this purpose, to encourage the proper return of tags rather than the theft of deceased hunter's belongings.

Her overview then complete, the clerk turned once more to Mile and said, "Welcome to the Hunters' Guild!"

That evening, Mile lay in a bed at the inn nearest the guildhall, planning for the following day.

There were many jobs for F-rank hunters. However, these were not individual requests, but rather outstanding orders, or calls for material to be gathered in the area surrounding the town.

Such orders meant that new job requests weren't issued daily, but rather, kept perpetually on the guild's records, so hunters could hunt and harvest as they pleased without giving formal notice and then simply bring back their trophies and goods to the delivery point to collect their payment. The listing was always accompanied by the daily reward for goblin slaying or medicinal herbs or jackalope meat—whatever good or service happened to be in demand during that particular season.

Other harvested goods weren't covered by these outstanding orders, but there were certain items for which one could always find a buyer, provided they appraised well. These included birds, boars, and deer, edible tree fruits and mushrooms, wild vegetables, ores and minerals, and many other items. They were assessed by size and quality, with their monetary value changing according to the prices set in the city markets each day.

If Mile were only taking outstanding orders and harvesting, this would save her the trouble of waking up early to pack into the crowded guild for the daily assignment of new tasks. All she had to do was go straight from the inn to the forest.

There were also certain ways that Mile, an F-rank hunter, could hunt higher-ranked monsters than jackalopes in order to earn more money. One of those ways was to join a party, but that was something Mile wasn't considering. Another way was to hunt down monsters from higher-ranked outstanding orders.

The job ranks were largely in place to prevent inexperienced hunters from taking on jobs they weren't prepared for and losing their lives, as well as to minimize the failure rate for jobs that the guild accepted. On outstanding orders, which were not assigned like individual requests, there were no failure rates: if you failed, you could just do it over again. Plus, the value of materials requested via outstanding orders never changed.

Of course, this wasn't especially recommended, but as long as one acknowledged the risks and took responsibility for oneself, the guild would turn a blind eye. However, Mile had no intention of trying her hand at battling higher-ranked monsters unless they happened upon her. She was just a normal, average F-rank hunter, after all.

As for why she chose the path of a hunter, there were several reasons. Firstly, it was something that anyone could become, no matter their age or appearance. With a hunter's badge, she could easily and openly cross territorial and national borders. Thus, in the event that her name and reputation somehow spread to other countries, she could simply move to a faraway land and start over again as a newly registered F-rank hunter under a new name.

Also, as she would only be facing monsters and beasts, it wasn't a big deal if she slipped up in limiting her power. Indeed, if she acted alone, she could use her magic and sword abilities as she pleased without others noticing. And if something unfortunate happened, she could immediately transfer to another country. By keeping her distance from other hunters, she could disappear without a trace and no one would care.

Besides, if she'd had to tend a shop from morning until night every single day, she would've been bored out of her skull. Once a week had been one thing, but she'd prefer to be able to save up enough to live a peaceful life of matrimony some time in the future.

With these reasons in mind, she couldn't think of any other career that she could possibly wish to undertake—especially considering the fact that, above all, a hunter was a completely mundane, average, normal career, one that any old dunce could do.

The following day, Mile woke up bright and early to hurry out on her first job.

As she could use storage magic, she didn't need any bags. However, if she were to go around empty-handed, people might realize that she was doing something unusual, so she slung a bag over her back. This was only to carry her spoils. The bread for her lunch and her water skin were stored away in the loot box space, so as to keep them from being damaged. The only equipment she wore was her leather breast plate and boots, along with the mystery sword at her waist. She looked very much like a novice hunter.

She was in a remote city, so it was but a short distance from the inn to the forests where the prey lived. It would take an adult about one hour by foot, but Mile arrived in fifteen minutes. Of course, it only took her that long because she slowed down when she saw other people—and because she avoided running at full speed so as to avoid trampling the plant life along her way.

"So, this is the Hunters' Woods..." she mused. She had received a map and directions from the clerk, and now there was no mistaking that she had arrived.

It was a dense forest, and there were no traces of other humans, so Mile let herself think aloud. Walking around in silence got a bit lonesome.

"The more experienced people go deeper into the woods or to a different forest entirely," she muttered as she stepped deeper into the forest. "This is an area intended for novices, so of course there shouldn't be any big, high-reward monsters around here..."

After a brief walk, she spotted a bird sitting on a tree branch. Though these woods were dim, she could somehow see it quite clearly.

However, though she could see it, there was no way her sword could reach a bird up in the top of a tree. Even so, it *was* a fairly large bird—if she could catch it, she would certainly be able to sell it for a nice sum. And if she didn't, well, she might find herself going without food (her lodging, thankfully, had already been arranged).

Mile looked down at the ground, spotted a fist-sized rock, and picked it up. She wound up and pitched it at the bird as hard as she could.

Bwam!

A great roaring reverberated throughout the woods.

The bird vanished from sight. The upper part of the tree, where the bird had been sitting, vanished as well.

Somehow, she didn't get the impression that the bird had fled.

Her vision still somewhat sharper than normal, Mile could clearly see bits of meat and feathers, and a few bloodstains, spattered against the remaining tree.

"Noooooooo..."

Several minutes later, she began walking once more, the pockets of her tunic stuffed with a number of small pebbles, each about the size of the tip of her pinky.

Something that size should only pierce them, she thought, deciding that she would aim for their heads. Mile was, after all, an intelligent girl.

However, perhaps because of the terrible roaring sound, there wasn't another animal in sight. Without any other options, Mile resorted to picking herbs.

However, she had heard that they were exceptionally difficult to find, so she had to employ a bit of cunning. *That's right*, she thought. *It's time for some location magic.*

Mile was the sort of person who figured there was no point in doing a lot of hard work if you had access to a tool that might help you.

"Location magic! Show me the way to medicinal herbs!"

Proceed seventeen steps before turning left, then proceed six steps.

"What are you, a GPS??! Those are just directions! That isn't magic!!"

Well, remember—the thing that everyone calls magic is all our doing, anyway…

"Good point."

Mile fell to her knees, a bit disappointed. Truthfully, she had been hoping for something a bit more magical—like a radar screen with red and blue dots, or a pillar of light that would radiate from the spots where the herbs were growing.

If that is what you wish for, we can create it.

"Can you?!" Mile didn't want to rely too much on the nano-machines, so she tried not to speak to them except when she was working magic. However, this time, she responded immediately.

If anyone were to see her, they'd probably have mistaken her for some kind of weirdo performing a one-woman show.

Before her eyes, the location magic shifted forms to a radar system—sans voice navigation. The signals seemed to be beamed directly to her retinas, and using these coordinates, Mile gathered the herbs. After accumulating a certain amount of one herb, she switched to a different variety, storing the first away in her loot box, figuring that it wasn't smart to collect too many of the same thing.

A little while after she began gathering, the last echoes of the great boom she had instigated had finally faded, and the animals that had hidden away in their burrows and dens started to reappear.

Facing a jackalope that had appeared a short distance away, Mile drew one of the tiny pebbles from her pocket and flicked it with her fingers.

On Earth, there was a special finger technique whereby one could flick a metal ball or coin with one's fingers in order to distract or startle an enemy. Mile's version, of course, was different.

Whoosh!

The pebble struck the animal perfectly in the skull, piercing it right through, leaving the meat, pelt, and—most importantly— the horns undamaged. The jackalope's sale value would be undiminished. Pleased with the outcome, Mile gave up on collecting herbs and switched to hunting beasts.

Jackalopes, birds, fox-like creatures—one by one, they fell prey to her pebbles. After a while, she stopped to replenish her stock of ammo, but was soon back at it with a vengeance.

With a spear or sword, the animals would have run before she could get too close, and the chance of actually hitting a creature with a bow and arrow wasn't very high. As a result, normal hunters tended not to go for birds and other small animals. Then again, they would never have been able to spot them as easily as she was in the first place. Even without using location magic, Mile had an uncanny sense that allowed her to spot prey easily, one animal after another. And thanks to that, even when she missed and startled a creature away, she could still manage to fell it before it escaped her.

She continued her hunting until suddenly a giant boar appeared.

Bwoosh!

It was a huge catch.

Mile started on her path home, utterly giddy. But then, she realized something.

"I'm a mage, but I didn't use magic even once..."

Apparently, she didn't count the search magic she used while gathering herbs as "using magic." Unlike combat magic, the things she had been executing weren't exactly what one imagined a hunter mage doing—however, she couldn't help but think of those things as a kind of roadmap.

Ultimately, at the end of the day, Mile had used neither her attack magic nor her sword.

Mile made her way back to the guildhall to exchange her spoils for money. Her bag, which carried but a portion of what she had gathered, was slung over her right shoulder. Thinking of future situations, Mile decided it was best not to hide that she could use storage magic. Instead, she would make the appeal that it was possible for her to hunt properly while still using it. Otherwise, she would never be able to carry all her prey.

But today, she was only going to be turning in her herbs and jackalopes, as per the standing order, as well as selling off the other meat and materials she had gathered. She headed straight for the reception window but was stopped along the way by a man's voice.

"You have a moment?"

Does he mean to flirt with me? Mile wondered.

When she turned to look, the man—or rather, a boy of about fifteen—continued to speak, looking a bit flustered.

"Oh, n-no! Please don't get the wrong idea! I just wanted to invite you to join our party! We're five now, but we still don't have enough attack power. We were hoping to gather one more person. This is all of us so far."

Behind the boy, some boys and girls of around fourteen or fifteen years of age stood in pairs.

"I've never seen you around here before," the boy said. "Did you come from some other town? Judging by that catch, you must be pretty skilled, but it's easy to end up in a tight spot when you're hunting solo."

"We aren't much older than you, and we already have girls with us, so you don't have to worry about being the only one. How about it? Will you think it over?"

Mile had absolutely no interest in joining a party. If she hunted with others, they would discover very quickly that she was an anomaly. Soon, the other members of the group would start leaning on her—or worse, selling information about her to a noble somewhere.

At the same time, it was pretty peculiar of her to continue standing around talking with her bag on her shoulder. She didn't want to start a quarrel with this young man.

"Um, well... Can I go finish turning in my goods first?"

"Oh, sorry." The boy took her request literally and said, "I'll wait right here."

Mile proceeded to the exchange station and handed over her captured prey, along with her name and registration number.

With this information, a hunter's deeds—even if they were only everyday tasks such as gathering meat or herbs—could be recorded on their achievement log, to be referenced in their promotions.

"Well now, little lady." The old man at the exchange station sounded highly impressed.

"You're young, but you've got a lot of skill. You got a lotta these guys, and their pelts're in perfect condition. I'll put a special mark down fer this."

"Really?! Thank you so much! Oh—that's right—I have a few more..."

She pulled the rest of her prey out of her storage space and piled everything up on the desk. The old man's eyes went wide with shock.

"St-storage magic... And there's so much here..."

"Oh, I—is this unusual?"

"No, er, nothin' unusual..."

When Mile finally pulled the boar from her bag, the old man's jaw dropped.

Yet as unsettled as he obviously was by this turn of events, the man was still a professional. When he picked his jaw back up off the floor, he began sorting out the goods.

The birds and jackalopes were each worth 2 silver coins a piece, the vulpine creature was worth 8 silver, thanks to its pelt, and the boar was worth a whole 8 half-gold! She had brought in five each of the birds and jackalopes, so altogether, her payment totaled to 1 gold, 8 silver. In terms of modern-day Japanese currency, that was roughly equal to 108,000 yen.

Of course, it was thanks to the boar that the sum was so large this time. However, even without it, Mile would have brought in about 28,000 yen. If she worked thirty days out of a thirty-six day month, she would bring in 840,000 yen. That was a considerable salary.

Becoming a hunter was the best decision ever!!! Mile thought.

Overjoyed, Mile left the exchange station before suddenly, she realized something.

Oh wait! I forgot to turn in my herbs...

Having stashed the herbs in her loot box rather than using storage magic, Mile had completely forgotten about them. However, as long as they were in the loot box, they wouldn't go bad. She could just turn them in next time.

Factoring in the herbs, Mile's monthly salary would be ten gold pieces—over one million yen.

When she returned to the boy and his party, something about them seemed a little bit odd. Some were staring blankly. Others were completely agog. It was just like the old man at the exchange station before...

"So, about earlier—" she began to say.

"Hey, you!" A man in his thirties rushed in, interrupting Mile's words. "You can use storage magic? How much can you hold?"

Mile was utterly appalled at the man's arrogant manner. She completely ignored him, turning instead to the boy before her. "Please allow me to ask something."

"Hey, brat!" the man snarled.

Mile continued to ignore him. "First of all, out of all of these hunters here, why would you choose me?"

"Are you listening?!"

"To be frank," she went on, "I am much smaller than everyone else here, aren't I? Did you not think that might hold you back?"

"Quit messing around!" The man was indignant. The boy was flustered.

In the evenings, the guildhall was packed with hunters, so a little quarrel like this was nothing out of the ordinary. Still, everyone looked on out of idle interest to see how the newcomer would handle herself.

"You are much too loud! Please, be quiet. Can't you see I'm trying to have a conversation?"

"Wh-what...? W-well, you were ignoring me, so..."

"Oh! Were you talking to me? I do apologize. I couldn't believe that you would possibly be so mannerless as to butt into someone else's conversation without even a greeting, so I merely assumed that you were speaking to someone who I couldn't see."

"Y-you damn brat! You think you can mess with me... W-well, fine. You're gonna join our party. Then you can do some proper work carrying our bags!"

"Anyway," Mile turned back to the boy. "What is it that you four normally hunt for?"

"Can you even hear me?!?!"

"You, sir, are a nuisance. If you have something to discuss with me, please wait your turn. However, if you've come to petition me for either a loan or a date, I must preemptively refuse. I too have the freedom to choose—"

"You little twit!!!" The indignant man drew his sword, swinging it down at Mile. The other hunters leapt to stop him, but they could never have made it in time.

Shing!

Ka-thump.

Everyone froze. Several hunters stopped in place, as though they had seized up mid-run.

The man stood still and silent, gripping the hilt of a bladeless sword. Mile held the stance of someone who had just swung a weapon. And there, clattering to the floor, was the sword's blade— but it wasn't a broken edge that it had. The massive blade had been cut clean off.

"Wh-wha...?"

Schwip!

With a flick, Mile returned her sword to its sheath.

A beat later, the man's iron cross guard snapped in two.

"Ee..." He stumbled back slowly, then turned on his heel and ran.

Two other hunters, most likely members of his party, followed in a panic.

It was probable that the man hadn't actually intended to cut Mile down; there was a strong chance that he had instead intended to stop short, just to give her a fright. However, Mile was not the sort of optimistic idiot who would assume such was the case and simply do nothing. If she hadn't acted and he hadn't stopped short, then she would've been killed.

"Now, as I was saying..." Mile attempted to return to her previous conversation, but the boy only stared at her with his mouth agape, unable to respond.

As Mile stood there, baffled, another hunter in his thirties began to speak.

"Little miss, that sword of yours... It's amazing... Where did you get your hands on it?"

Oh dear.

It was likely that the hunter had no ulterior motive beyond simply an interest in swords, but if people thought her sword was amazing, then they would covet it.

"Uh, I just bought it at a shop, like most people, you know? It was just a used sword from the bargain bin."

"You're joking me! With an edge like that?!"

What do I do? Ah, wait!

"Um, could I borrow your sword a minute?"

"Hm? Oh, well, sure…"

The man detached the sheath from his waist and handed it to Mile, who fastened it on her left side, beside her own blade.

"Now, could I kindly ask someone to toss a copper piece into the air?"

"I'll toss it!"

A curious crowd began to gather around Mile, and one of the hunters spoke up, pulling his coin purse from his breast pocket to produce a single copper coin.

"Here we go! And…hup!"

Shing! Snap!

Mile swung the man's blade quicker than the eye could see, then thrust her left hand into the air.

"Here you are."

Mile stretched her palm out to the man who had lent her the sword, revealing two clean-cut halves of a copper coin.

"N-no way…" He stared at it, dumbfounded. "W-with *my* sword…?!" The man plucked the coin halves from Mile's hand, staring at them in a daze, his disbelief clear.

"You see? It has nothing to do with the sword. It just takes a knack."

Was this girl serious? Everyone present in the hall, hunters and clerks alike, was confounded by Mile's pronouncement.

However, as members of the guild, they were forbidden to launch an inquiry into another's past or abilities. Invasive questions were frowned upon, so they merely watched and listened intently.

Mile returned the man's sword, glad to finally get back to her conversation with the boy. "So. You were saying something about having insufficient attack power..."

"Y-yes! Right now, we have a sword-wielder, a spear-wielder, and a bow-wielder, as well as two mages, one of whom can use attack magic. The other's more skilled at utility and healing magic... Anyway, things can get a little dicey in close-quarters combat, so we were thinking it would be nice to have one more decent swordsman to act as a rear guard..." This boy, presumably the leader, stumbled over his words as he attempted to explain the situation politely. Nevertheless, Mile understood his meaning.

"But, um, I'm a magic user, so..."

"Whaaaaaaaat?!"

This time the surprised shout came from the hunters behind them as well.

"B-but that sword—? And that thing you did earlier..."

"Oh, well, even as a rear-guard magician, sometimes enemies slip past the front lines and end up in front of you, right? And sometimes you get attacked from behind. So at the very least, I figured I should be able to use a sword well enough to protect myself, should that happen. I'm really a pretty half-baked swordsman."

Bang bang bang bang bang!

Mile heard a strange sound behind her and turned to look, only to see the swordsman-like fellow she had been speaking to earlier banging his head against a wall. Had he eaten something bad? What was all that about?

Yet unlike the flabbergasted advance-guard swordsmen, the rear-guard magic users appeared somewhat relieved. If there were really a swordsman who was also able to use such a rare, high-level skill as storage magic, then there would be no point at all in having magic users of their level around. On the other hand, having an excellent mage who could also cross swords with the best swordsmen... That was thrilling.

"S-sorry... We figured you were a D-rank hunter, just like us, so..."

"Oh, um, D-rank? Wouldn't having a two-rank difference make things difficult?" Mile had been trying to come up with a good reason to refuse, and now, the rank gap would provide her with an out. She had assumed that the boy and his party were also E or F-rank, so, really, this was a fortuitous surprise.

"Two? Ah, you're a B, huh? That makes sense, what with the storage magic and your sword skills. You look rather young, but I assume you must be an elf or a dwarf? Please, forgive my rudeness..."

"Oh no, I'm just a plain, average, ordinary human. I only be-came a hunter yesterday. I'm an F-rank."

Ka-thak!

Thwump!

Smack!

Bang bang bang bang bang bang bang bang!

A variety of noises resounded behind her.

"ARE YOU SERIOUS?!?!?!"

Mile was startled at the sudden ferocity of the voices behind her.

"Come on, even so..."

"There's no such thing as an F-rank like you! Why didn't you put in a skip application when you registered?!"

"Huh? A skip application? What's that?"

At Mile's blithe response, the hunters looked still more horrified, and at the front of the hall, the officials' faces went pale.

"Someone call the guild master!"

At the command of a man who appeared to be a veteran hunter, one of the guild officials ran frantically up the stairs.

"Little miss, who registered you?"

"Umm, she was a lady with blonde hair, about seventeen or eighteen years old. I think her name was Leira? Or Lorrie...?"

"Laura! Damn that girl! This is ridiculous."

Mile shrank back. This seemed to be becoming quite a to-do.

"Is there a problem...?"

"Don't you worry, little miss. You're not in the wrong here. The guild master's coming to sort this out."

After several minutes, the official who had run up the stairs returned with the guild master in tow. It had probably taken some time to fully explain the situation. After all, it would have been unthinkable for the master to meet with someone he had no prior knowledge of—especially now that a problem had arisen.

The guild master who descended wasn't the tall, beefy sort that Mile had imagined, but rather the kind of man you might reasonably mistake for a regional bank manager. Perhaps, she thought, he had been selected for his managing ability rather than his combat skills.

"Is this the young lady in question? Where is Laura, anyway?"

"Yes, sir. This is her. And Laura is off today, but I'll go fetch her straight away," replied a nearby clerk.

The guild master nodded, then turned to Mile. "My apologies. It appears that one of my staff has slipped up, but I'd like to try and get this sorted. Would you mind coming with me for a moment?"

"Yes, of course," said Mile.

The veteran hunter who had spoken up before chimed in. "Mind if the rest of us sit in on this too? We wouldn't want anybody pulling the wool over the eyes of this innocent little lady. Gotta make sure she knows that this was a guild slip-up and not a reflection on all us hunters."

The guild master nodded, and the veteran called over two other older hunters. Together, they all moved into the meeting room.

As they sipped tea, Laura, the receptionist from yesterday, arrived breathless, her face very pale.

"First off, let's confirm Laura's side. You were the one who registered this girl, Miss Mile, yesterday. Is that correct?"

"Y-yes..." Laura nodded, her face still ashen.

"And at that time, did you tell her about the skip applications?"

"N-no..."

"Why not?"

"W-well, she was newly registering at twelve years old, so I assumed she was just a beginner..."

"And what do the guidelines say?"

"Th-that we should explain everything to everyone..."

With this misstep confirmed, the guild master held his head.

"She listed her occupation as magic user, didn't she? Why didn't you confirm her skill level?!"

"Well, she was carrying a sword, so I figured that even if she said she was a mage, the sword was her main means of combat and her magic was fairly weak..."

"You idiot! She bested Matthew with her sword in one blow, and she can use storage magic! That's the skill of a B-ranker at the very least! You would've made a person like this sit around for years collecting herbs and hunting jackalopes! What the hell were you thinking?!"

"I-I wasn't..." Laura, now in shock at the magnitude of her mistake, was on the verge of tears.

Truly, it was all quite understandable. The difference in earnings and reputation between an F-rank and a C or B-rank was as considerable as the difference between straw and gold. Her mistake would have sentenced a promising new recruit to sacrifice valuable years of their life, an irreparable act, and one that wouldn't have occurred had Laura not decided to follow her own judgment instead of the guild regulations.

"Um..." Mile interjected timidly, still not grasping the gravity of the situation. "I'm okay staying like this..."

"Do you really think that's possible?!?!"

The attending hunters stirred in anger.

"Do you know what kind of precedent it would set if the guild just let a mistake like this go?! Think about the other hunters! Since when have there been any F-rank hunters who could use storage magic?!"

As Mile stared blankly, one of the hunters elaborated. Storage magic was a fairly high-level magic, so the people who could use it were few. With such magic, you could carry large quantities of spare armor and weapons, food and water, and of course, collect materials and prey, so your rate of earnings increased several-fold. If you were able to use said magic, others would defend you with their lives, even if you were weak in combat. It wasn't unreasonable that you would be able to join C through A-rank parties.

Thus, if you could use storage magic, no matter how poor your other abilities were, you would be authorized as a C-rank at minimum. And so, given that Mile could use other magic fairly well also, as well as being particularly handy with a sword, it was only reasonable that she would be invited to join parties of B-rank or higher.

"So then, could I just re-register?"

"If that were possible, this wouldn't be such a problem."

This time, the guild master explained. Apparently, in the past, there had been many nobles and dependents of such who tried to forcibly have their ranks raised, whether by bribery or influence. In order to prevent this, the rank promotion rules were firmly set, so that once a person registered, they could not re-register at a higher rank. Generally speaking, anyone who unregistered only to re-register again was placed at the same or a lower rank than before, as in the case of a retiree getting back into the business of hunting.

Early promotion was an option, but there were still obstacles. A minimum number of years participating in the guild were required, and exceptions were incredibly rare unless one was a hero acting in a time of national crisis.

Even if the guild was able to arrange such a thing quietly, thinking they wouldn't get caught, the risks were too high and the punishments too severe: no one would ever dare put themselves in such danger. If one official, or even one hunter, slipped up, and word got around to the wrong people, it would all be over for the guild.

This was part of the reason why new recruits were to have their skills and abilities confirmed at time of registration. If it were found that their background or abilities qualified them for a rank skip, then it would be reported to the guild master, and that recruit would be tested before the guild officials and several high-ranking hunters, who collectively would decide the individual's rank.

It was not uncommon for soldiers and knights to become hunters after retiring, as well as former court magicians driven out of their homes by civil war and other conflicts. Obviously, not everyone started at F-rank.

Even Mile, as things stood, *should* have started out as a C-ranker—even though that was the last thing that the girl herself wanted.

"What the hell do we do?"

"I'm really fine like this..." Mile insisted.

"YOU SHUT THE HELL UP!" The veterans all roared, ignoring the troubled guild master's attempts to quiet them. Mile shrank back.

If she could net ten gold pieces a month, there would be no complaints on Mile's part; however, the veteran hunters could not stomach the thought of someone like her wasting all her time on fetch quests and other menial tasks, day in and day out. Plus, an F-ranker would be excluded from the roster of important folks who were called upon to respond when a great monster appeared, when the guild was asked to escort someone important, or when hunters were needed to participate in a disaster relief effort.

All in all, the guild wasn't prepared to let someone who would be useful in these tasks sit around for years, frittering her time away. In particular, it was hard to overlook Mile's storage magic, which could be used to bolster logistical support in transporting goods and help guildhalls in other cities during emergency situations when they might be lacking in personnel. True, the hunters couldn't overrule the word of the guild master, but it was nonetheless a matter of grave importance, one which would have an effect on their very lives in times of emergency.

"What about the prep school in the capital...?" Laura offered softly, her face still pale and her head hanging.

"THAT'S IT!!!" The guild master and one of the hunters leapt from their seats.

The other two hunters seemed to have no idea what they were talking about. Naturally, neither did Mile.

The Hunters' Prep School.

It had begun operating in the country's capital only six years before. The school was an experimental institute, designed to impart the knowledge and technique required of a novice hunter in just half a year, allowing one to attain a D or even C-rank upon graduation. It had initially been proposed by a nobleman from a hunter's background, who was concerned by the fact that, due to the years of participation before one could become a full-fledged hunter, even the most talented candidates were limited in how much they could achieve before reaching an age for retirement.

"Whether they're noble or commoner—or in certain cases, even slaves—anyone can enroll there without obstacle. Because no one is accepted without a guild master's recommendation, the program has a high success rate; it's part of every guild master's duties to scout for new recruits. They stake their own reputations on these referrals. However..."

"However?"

"If the person a guild master refers is ever judged unfit to attend the academy, the student will be expelled at once. And the guild master who recommended the student in question will be looked at very critically by the higher-ups and should abandon any hope of promotion..."

As one of the hunters explained, Mile glanced in the direction of the guild master, who seemed quietly pleased, his eyes sparkling.

"I believe in you, Miss Mile..."

His eyes were no doubt those of an optimist.

And so, Mile consented to relocate to the country's capital for enrollment in the Hunters' Prep School. She got the impression that if she didn't, Laura, the clerk, would probably be fired, and that the guild master—though his position was secure—would still face some kind of penalty.

Still influenced by her Japanese sense of propriety, Mile felt quite guilty. It seemed that this guildhall had carried on its day-to-day operations just fine until she came along: the anomaly, as always.

Laura learned from the incident, as well. Had she continued in the same manner, it was possible that she could have made the same mistake again in the future, but after this lesson, it was unlikely that she would ever again follow her own judgment over the guild's regulations.

Frankly, it worked out for Mile either way.

She was going to end up a C-rank sooner or later, so it wasn't a big deal when, exactly, it happened. The only reason she would have been a C-ranker in the first place was because she could use a bit of storage magic, and even if that were rare, at least it would still have put her in the category of an "ordinary" C-rank hunter. It wasn't much different from being found out to have storage magic as an F-rank, anyway.

Plus, if she went far away and re-registered with a different guildhall, she would end up a C-rank, assuming she followed proper procedures. If she lied and registered as an F-rank, she would have to keep in line with other F-rank hunters, pretending she could not use storage magic at all—which would have been more than Mile thought she could bear. She had no interest in remaining poor by her own hand.

In the end, it was really only a difference of spending half a year as a student or not. And oh, how she wanted to. She wanted to *so* badly!

Her life as a student at Eckland Academy had ended abruptly, but she had relished it. She had conversed with everyone—like normal. She had made friends, and they had spent time together.

How she had longed to stay! She had wanted to be with everyone until graduation. How she regretted leaving. How her heart yearned.

With that in mind, her response was without hesitation.

"I'll go! I'll enroll!"

During the three weeks after it was decided that Mile would be going to the capital, she worked—worked hard.

According to a fellow hunter, tuition, lodging, and meals at the prep school were all free of charge. Plus, the students were allowed to continue working as hunters while enrolled, so really, the work she did during those three weeks was just to ensure that she had a bit of money to fall back on.

The next enrollment period was roughly a month from when she had decided to attend the school, which left her three weeks to work, followed by an eight-day carriage ride; the remaining ten days, she would spend preparing. If all went well, she would even be able to do a bit of sightseeing and take her time getting used to the lay of the land in the capital.

As has already been mentioned, Adele's world had six days and months that were six weeks, so there were a lot of convenient ways in which the number of days could be broken down.

Now, as Mile did her hunting and gathering in the forest, she fought with magic and her sword rather than pebbles. This work did double duty, for as she hunted, she could also practice limiting her power, a skill she would need once she returned to school.

She had, of course, kept a cap on her strength while attending Eckland Academy; however, limiting one's strength to match that of a typical preteen's was not the same as trying to match the power of those who would also be graduating as C-rank hunters in half a year's time. To do all this while embroiled in sword fights and combat magic would be another challenge altogether.

It is possible, Mile thought, *that they might even conduct practice battles with real, bladed swords—not wooden ones.* There might be magical duels. There might even be students there who were older than her, with more experience.

She caught birds with magic.

She bested jackalopes and vulpine creatures with a finely hewn wooden spear.

And boars and deer, she defeated with her sword.

Though she tried to keep her catches no more impressive than those of any other novice, she was constantly turning in prey that left the old man at the exchange station dumbfounded, and by the time she left she had stashed seven gold coins away neatly in her loot box. Combined with her previous earnings, she now had ten gold pieces in total—about 1,000,000 yen, in Japanese money.

This was more than enough to cover her travel expenses and interim lodging, as well as any other immediate necessities.

Finally, she would be able to purchase some clothes of her own, ones that weren't hunting equipment or school uniforms.

And then, three weeks had passed since the discussion in the guild meeting room.

With the guild master, guild officials, and a few other hunters there to see her off, Mile's carriage departed the city.

They would arrive at the capital in eight days.

Mile would have been able to travel much more quickly on her own, but as there was no need to, she refrained from drawing on that ability.

She was just an average, unremarkable F-rank hunter, after all.

As was only natural, the guild master and Laura shared the cost of her travel and meal expenses for the journey.

"There she goes..." the guild master murmured.

"Yes, indeed." Laura replied.

"In six months, hopefully, she'll come back to us as a C-rank hunter, and then it won't be long—maybe a few years—before she reaches B-rank. She's still quite young. I doubt that even A-rank would be out of her reach. It wouldn't be a bad thing for the guild to have such a one among us."

"Do you really think she'll come back here? She won't simply settle down in the capital?"

"Well, I'm sure she's got family. She'll have to come back for them, won't she?"

"No, Miss Mile was born up in the mountains. She said that she only came down here to earn a living because both of her parents passed away. She isn't from here, and she has no family."

"Hm?"

"Huh?"

"Whaaaaat?!?!"

The guild master fell to his knees.

"P-please, at least let her graduate with honors so that my endorsement means something."

He was nearly in tears.

Behind him, the several hunters who had overheard this conversation fell to their knees in disappointment.

The journey to the capital was a smooth one.

Mile's new clothes were plain and cheaply made, giving her the appearance of a "typical, average" country girl.

Soon enough, the other passengers in the carriage became greatly indebted to her, as she was able to provide an endless supply of warm water whenever they stopped to make camp. Even so long after her time in the bakery, she still remembered a thing or two about customer service.

However, thanks to this skill, and the fact that she could store and produce food with storage magic, it was clear to everyone that she was someone special, plain clothes or no.

"So, you're off to the capital, dear? Is it for work?"

"Um, actually I'm going to a prep school..."

"Ahh, you're going to be a maid there, are you? It's an elite school for hunters, so if you can snag yourself a good man with some potential, you'll be set for life! A girl like you should have no trouble. In a few years, you won't be able to keep the boys away from you!"

The woman who spoke was a bit of a flibbertigibbet, one of the passengers for whom Mile had produced warm water and venison. Mile smiled wryly at her assumption. The other passengers who overheard this exchange chuckled internally.

The idea of someone of such a young age who could use storage magic and summon that much water, working as a servant... The young woman was no doubt attending the school as a student in her own right.

Nine days after departure, the carriage arrived in the capital, a day later than expected.

It rained along the way, muddying the roads, and one of the carriage wheels had broken from the strain, delaying them. However, they had still arrived more quickly than one might expect in the face of an obstacle of this kind.

Except for those who were only stopping in the capital en route to other destinations, everyone disembarked at the central station, which was located directly in the middle of the city's main square, and began to disperse.

"Thanks for the showers, dear!"

"Let's ride together again sometime!"

The female passengers in particular offered their thanks for daily hot showers—a luxury not even enjoyed by most nobles—while all the passengers showered Mile with gratitude in the form of leftover food or trinkets from their hometowns.

"When you become a full-fledged hunter, I'll definitely request you by name!"

At least someone had figured out that she wasn't just going to work as a servant...

Naturally.

"So, this is the capital..."

The city, the capital of the Kingdom of Tils, had a much quainter feel than the capital of her former home, where she attended Eckland Academy. Indeed, in terms of national power—based on a calculation involving land area, population, and economic strength—the country possessed roughly one-seventh the power of the Kingdom of Brandel.

Here too, there was an academy attended by the children of nobles and other wealthy families. If Mile were to attend this academy, she might even make more friends like Marcela. Although the place was really none of her concern, it did prickle Mile, just a little, to think about it.

In any case, she would be residing in the city for at least half a year. She wouldn't be able to move into the school's dormitory until three days before the first of the term, or six days from now, which meant she needed to find an inn before taking a look around the capital. In the event that anything happened, knowing her surroundings could mean the difference between life and death.

But first she needed to secure a room. The sun was still high in the sky, so Mile set out, intending to ask some upstanding-seeming citizen where to find the best lodgings before making her own investigations.

She scolded herself for not simply asking the other passengers, many of whom had been native to the city.

As always, Mile had been quite careless.

That evening, just before sundown...

Mile stood in front of a humble inn.

On the advice of a kindly elderly couple, Mile had narrowed her decision down to three options, based on the conditions that they had to be safe for a young girl to stay at alone, relatively cheap, and provide good meals. From there, she visited each one to inspect the surrounding area, the quality of the other clientele, and the level of cleanliness around the entrances, before making her choice. Since this would determine her comfort, or lack thereof, for the next six days, she was fastidious in this process. If she failed in this regard, she could only chalk it up to her own lack of insight and perhaps a touch of bad luck.

Mile opened the door. "Excuse me, do you have any rooms available?"

"Why yes, we do!" said a cheerful girl in response as Mile stepped inside. The girl looked to be around ten years old and sat humbly behind the counter beyond the front door. She was probably the owner's daughter, helping out while her parents were busy with dinner preparations.

"Well then, I'd like a room for six nights..."

"All right," the girl nodded. "Lodging alone is four silver a night. If you want breakfast, it's three half-silver, lunch is five half-silver, and dinner is eight half-silver. Hot water is five copper for one wash basin or two half-silver for a whole tub."

"Hm, well I'd like to try eating at lots of different places while I'm here, so I'll just have dinner for tonight and breakfast each morning, please. I'll take care of the water myself."

"Ohh, can you use magic?! That's amazing..." The girl looked a tad envious.

Mile was aware of how blessed she was in this regard. Being able to summon water would be a very useful skill for an inn-keeper's daughter.

"The food should be ready any moment, but we only serve until the second evening bell."

Mile had learned that the second evening bell rang around nine o'clock in the evening, while the first morning bell rang at six, and the second at nine. The first midday bell rang at twelve o'clock noon, the second midday bell at three, the first evening bell at six, and the second evening bell rang at nine.

"Ah, well, then I better go ahead and eat now."

Once she had settled in, it would be a bother to come back downstairs, so Mile decided to eat while she was yet on the ground floor.

There were a variety of meal choices, but when Mile took a look at the menu posted on the wall, she found...

> *Orc Steak.*
> *Orc Meat Stir Fry.*
> *Orc Meat Stew.*
> *Orc Kabobs.*
> *Fried Orc Meat.*

It seemed that the owners had a vested interest in getting people to eat orc meat.

Mile stared at the girl.

"Ha ha. They accidentally ordered way too much meat," said the girl, smiling wryly.

It seemed that Mile hadn't much choice. In truth, she had never eaten monster meat before. As was the case with most nobles, the Ascham family had never once served monster meat at their own table. Even at the academy, monster meat had never been served, out of consideration for the many nobles in attendance.

Yet it wasn't as though the meat was poisonous, so Mile was not especially bothered by the thought of consuming it. In fact, she expected that she would be eating like this quite frequently from now on. It was simply a new experience. That was all. And soon, it wouldn't be a new experience at all, as hunting would provide her with many more opportunities to eat such things. Perhaps she would even try cooking some herself at some point in the future. With this in mind, she placed her order.

"One orc steak, please."

And soon, there it was before her. An orc steak, with orc meat soup, and bread and salad on the side. The amount of meat was almost intimidating. They were probably trying to use up as much of it as they could. In appearance, it looked a lot like pork. When she sniffed it, it smelled like pork. And when she tasted it, it tasted like pork.

In conclusion, it may as well be pork, Mile thought. *I was worried about nothing!*

For the next six days, Mile wandered the city with the inn as her base, memorizing the layout of the shops and streets as well as she could. She looked down some rather suspicious lanes and back alleys too, but her clothing, which was plain by provincial standards, was downright shabby compared to the fashions of the capital, and as a result, she was never robbed or assailed. It would seem that the denizens of the slums considered her one of their own.

When Mile realized this, she bought some new clothes in a hurry. Something that would count as garb a normal city girl would wear—plain, but not too cheap, by the capital's standards.

When she debuted her new outfit for little Lenny, the innkeeper's daughter, she was met with an ambiguous expression.

"I mean, the materials are nice, but..."

Clad thus, six days after her arrival in the capital, Mile stepped through the gates of the Hunters' Prep School.

Didn't I Say
to Make My Abilities
Average in the
Next Life?!

CHAPTER 7 |

Hunters' Prep School

THE SCHOOL WAS SMALL. The building she took to be the schoolhouse was a tiny, one-story shack. The building that served as the dormitory was a similarly humble affair, housing both boys and girls. The only other building appeared to house an indoor training ground. Such was the sort of school that catered to only about forty students, all in the same class.

Mile had no interest in standing out, but at the same time, she didn't want the guild master to lose face. Her goal was to stay somewhere near fifth from the top of her class.

After Mile finished registering, she proceeded to her assigned room to find a four-person dorm with two bunk beds. Since the school was funded by the country's tax money, they didn't have the luxury of providing individual rooms.

Still, for now, the room was empty, for it seemed that Mile was the first to arrive. She pondered which bed she ought to claim for herself. With her past education in Japanese courtesy, she could not escape the inclination ingrained in her to hold back and let others have the best ones.

I'll probably be the youngest and the smallest, so maybe I should pick a top bunk...

Thus, though there were a lot of advantages to sleeping on the bottom of a bunk bed, Mile selected one of the two top bunks.

The room had one cabinet, divided into four sections. Apparently, this was meant for them all to share. Other than that, there was only one small lockbox, but since Mile could keep her valuables in the loot box, it wasn't of much interest to her. So again, she selected the most inconvenient spot.

In these lands, ceding an advantage one could grab for oneself was something only an idiot would do, but to Mile, this was no real concern.

"I guess I don't need to spend much time unpacking."

Here, she had no intention of hiding the fact that she had storage skills. In fact, the guild master had written this very information in the referral section of her entry application form, so it would be pointless to try to conceal it. Therefore, it was fine if her standard luggage appeared to be hidden away with storage magic. Even if some of it were actually secured in her loot box instead.

Thus, as she didn't really need the cabinet, she figured that the other three could share the space amongst themselves.

Besides the beds, the cabinet, and the lockbox, the room was completely empty. There was nothing else—not even desks or chairs. At this school, there was no spare money to devote to housing. Any time that students had to loiter around in their rooms was time best spent on the practice grounds. The rooms were really just a place for changing clothes and sleeping. That was the sum of things.

Mile was sitting around staring into space and killing time until lunch, when there was a knock on the door.

"Come in!" Mile replied.

The girl who opened the door was tall, about 170 centimeters, with golden hair and a stern, imposing face. She was probably around seventeen or eighteen years old and looked almost boyish. Immediately, Mile could tell that she was also the sort of person who would be popular with the other girls.

"Oh, a roommate! Let's have a great six months together!" The girl grinned and held out her right hand. Mile smiled and returned the gesture. She got the feeling she would get along with this girl.

"Pleased to meet you. The name's Mavis. I'm a knight. I'll spare you the details until the rest arrive. Which bed are you in?"

"Oh—this one, up here."

"Hmm..."

Mile worried Mavis might think she was an idiot, but instead the girl just patted her gently on the head.

"You're a good kid..."

They would definitely get along! Mile was certain of it.

"I'm kinda big," Mavis said, "so I hope you don't mind if I take the bottom here."

Mavis hoisted her luggage onto the bed beneath Mile, and the two of them chatted until there came another knock.

"Come on in!" Mile replied.

This time, when the door opened, two girls stood outside in the hallway.

The first was a kind, absent-minded looking girl around thirteen or fourteen, with brown hair. The second was a tough-looking redhead of around twelve.

"More roommates, yeah? Hey there, I'm Mavis!"

"And I'm Mile. Pleased to meet you all!"

"Reina. Nice to meet you." The red-headed girl strutted into the room. She glanced at both the beds and then tossed her bags onto the bottom bunk of the vacant one—surely a more typical way of doing things, Mile thought. The early bird gets the worm and all that.

"I'm Pauline. It's good to meet you." The meeker of the two girls gently placed her bags on the top bunk, without a hint of disdain for the girl who had beaten her to the punch.

There was no real need for the students to arrive until the day before the entrance ceremony, but it was no coincidence that all four occupants of this room had arrived early in the morning, three whole days before the start of the term. That night would be the first night that they could sleep there at the school, and it was also the first day that their free meals would be provided, starting with lunch. In short, none of them had money to spare.

Of course, this was not true of Mile, who now had funds of her own. Even so, she had wanted to arrive early merely to familiarize herself with the school and the surrounding area. However, wanting to fit in with the other girls, she didn't mention this. At the very least, she had learned to read the room a little better since her days at Eckland Academy.

Soon, lunchtime rolled around, and they all headed to the dining hall with plans to do proper introductions after the meal.

Although it was only the first day of registration, a great number of other students had arrived early as well; nearly half of this year's class of forty crowded the dining hall. At this point, all of the previous term's students had graduated and gone, so everyone present was a new recruit.

The boys were gobbling food as though they hadn't eaten in days, and though the girls were nowhere near so crude, it was clear they had good appetites. As no one had grown close enough for friendly chatter, everyone ate in silence.

After lunch, Mile and company returned to their room to make introductions.

"How about we introduce ourselves in the order we arrived?"

Mavis's suggestion put Mile first.

"I'm Mile. I'm twelve years old. I'm a magic user and an F-rank hunter."

"Is that all?" asked Reina, the redhead. "Anything else you want to say? Like your magical specialty, or your hometown, or your family, or...?"

At her prompting, Mile had no choice but to continue. "Um, let's see. I can use storage magic—I don't have any use for my spot in the cabinet, so the rest of you can go ahead and use it. I dabble in swordplay just a little bit, for self-protection. And as for my family, even speaking about them is a sort of unpleasant matter, so please forgive me for refraining..."

"........."

There was a long silence.

"Wait a minute—" Reina suddenly interjected.

"Something is weird about this. If you can use storage magic, you should be a C-rank already! What are you doing here?!"

Besides, it takes energy to maintain, doesn't it? How can you be using that in place of a cabinet?!"

"Huh...?"

"Don't you 'huh' me!"

As Reina continued to shout, Mile just tilted her head.

"Um, well, the rank thing was a guild mistake," Mile said. "The guild master sent me here in order to correct it. And I don't know—is that really true about storage magic needing to be maintained?"

"Y-you..." Reina trailed off.

"Well, I guess I'm next up!" Mavis offered, only a little nervously.

Being able to read the room truly was an amazing skill.

"Now that Mile's spilled the beans for us, let me be frank as well. We'll be together a good while, so you're going to get to know me sooner or later.

"I'm Mavis von Austien, seventeen years old. I'm a knight, no magic.

"My family has all been knights for generations, and my three older brothers all became knights too. I wanted to be a knight, just like them, but my brothers and parents were super opposed to it, so I ran away from home. So, now, I just go by Mavis, no surname. Hope we can get along!"

Whoa...

As Mavis spoke, the nickname "Rascal" popped into Mile's head—but that was a name for a raccoon, wasn't it? Perhaps she was thinking of something else.

"N-next up's me, then! Reina, fifteen years old! They call me 'Crimson Reina,' and my specialty's attack magic. Let me just be

clear now that the 'Crimson' part has nothing to do with my hair! I have no family..."

At these last words, Reina looked down, despondent, but unlike Mile, it seemed as though she wouldn't necessarily mind talking about her family.

The other girls all asked the same question. "Fifteen?"

"What?! You got something to say about it?!"

Reina was very short for a fifteen-year-old, no taller than 156 centimeters. If she were Japanese, she would be just around the right height for her age, but for the people of this country, who were similar to Caucasians on Earth, she was about 5 centimeters shy of the average height for a girl of fifteen—closer to the height of a twelve-year-old.

Mile was also short for her age, so she was thankful when the conversation moved on.

"I guess that leaves me, then... I'm Pauline, I'm fourteen. I'm the daughter of the lover of the head of the Beckett Company, a mid-sized mercantile operation."

Whaaaaaaaat?! The other girls exchanged surprised looks.

"My existence is a nuisance to my father, but I'm a genius at healing magic, so he sent me here to try and polish my skills so that I'd be a useful gift to a noble or important merchant."

Stop iiiit!!!

"After I graduate from here, I'll probably end up with some middle-aged man—"

"AND THAT CONCLUDES OUR INTRODUCTIONS," the other three cut in.

Truly, these were roommates who would get along well.

For the next three days, the four girls passed their time chatting in their room and strolling about the capital together. Since none of them had very much money, they only did things that were free.

When they did go shopping, however, there was a problem beyond just money: because their room was very small, they couldn't buy much of anything besides a few changes of clothing and small, consumable goods.

Each of them had very different personalities, but somehow, they all seemed to complement each other. It was clear that they would be very good roommates.

For some reason, Reina seemed to take quite a shine to Mile, who began to realize that the older girl was often standing by her side. When Mile brought it up, Mavis was kind enough to offer an explanation.

"Well, it's probably because, you know, the way your figure— no, never mind, it's nothing."

"Wait, what?!"

Mile demanded that Mavis continue. As polite as she normally was, she had grown comfortable enough now to speak to her new roommates without reservations.

The truth was that when Reina stood next to Mile, she looked much older. She was noticeably taller than twelve-year-old Mile and more developed in other ways, too.

Since Reina always seemed concerned about her youthful appearance, it was only natural that she'd want to accentuate the contrast between them—which meant staying close to Mile's side. For Mile, at twelve, being only a little bit smaller than a fifteen-year-old wasn't so bad either.

Mavis was seventeen, so she wasn't even part of the equation. It was Pauline who gave Reina reason to worry. She was a hair taller than the average girl of fourteen, which meant she was taller than Reina. Worst of all though, was the fact that her breasts were much more developed than average, surpassing even Mavis's.

"Grngh..." Pauline fidgeted uncomfortably as Mile cast a glare at her bust. Just then, Reina returned from the washroom.

"Well, let's get going!"

The waiting was over. It was the day of the Hunters' Prep School entrance ceremony.

The ceremony was drab.

Since the vast majority of the students came from poverty, their families couldn't possibly attend.

While the entrance ceremony at Eckland Academy had been nothing special in comparison to that of the much more prestigious Ardleigh, the school still catered to the offspring of nobles and successful merchants, meaning that they had to keep up appearances. Here, the entrance ceremony felt like not much more than an introductory assembly for the students and teachers alone.

Suffice it to say, while a proper three-year boarding school and an accelerated six-month hunters' prep school were both "schools," it was like comparing a four-year university to a driving school; in other words, it was not a worthwhile comparison. Even the difference in the size of the student body was noticeable to Mile.

And, of course, the school had no uniforms. Everyone wore their own clothes. Still, as they *were* attending an entrance ceremony, the students had all worn their hunting equipment rather than standard garb, which gave them the appearance of rookie hunters.

The student body for this term consisted of forty people, the same as always, and there was only one class. In fact, the school was still in something of a trial run, so its scope was very small, much more like a mission school than a true academy.

"Welcome! I am Principal Elbert!" A man of around fifty greeted them from the platform. He didn't look like a principal so much as a retired hunter.

"I've lived as a hunter since I was six years old, up until about six years ago, when I retired and took charge of this place."

No wonder, then, that he looked like a retired hunter. He was one!

And at any rate, a school of only forty students couldn't have much need for a principal.

They might as well call it a "Hunter Training Center" or a "Hunter Boot Camp," Mile thought.

"The aim of this place is to cram you full of all the knowledge you'd normally gain from the successes and failures of many years in the span of just six months. That way, you can be promoted to a D or C-rank immediately after you graduate! You understand what that means, right?"

Elbert looked out at the students' faces.

"That's right! This place is tough! And anyone who can't keep up gets the boot! Having someone happily graduate and then kick the bucket a few days later—or worse, drag all their party members down in the mud? That's not what we want. So, we don't let it happen! If you don't think you can stick with it, then you can turn in your resignation now!"

To enter the school, everyone present had overcome fierce

competition. They carried their families' hopes on their shoulders. No one was prepared to give up so easily. At least at that moment, there were no quitters present.

Following Elbert's address, the other instructors were introduced, and then the students were dismissed. The small details would be covered later, in the classroom.

As they waited for their instructor to arrive, the students chattered in small groups. Roommates, who had already grown close, talked amongst one another.

"I mean, it's pretty obvious," said Reina.

The other three nodded.

She was referring to the principal's remarks. Everyone there had been perfectly aware of the school's reputation when they enrolled. There was no point in blabbering on about it.

After a short while, the door at the front of the room opened, and their instructor entered. It was Elbert, the principal himself.

"I'm your chief instructor. We don't have a particularly large budget, so you can think of me as your principal-cum-chief instructor-cum-weaponry trainer. Besides me, there're the three others I introduced. And other than that, it's just the cooks who make your meals and the school maintenance staff.

"Our curriculum here is focused on practical education, but there's a classroom portion of your studies, too. If you don't know how to identify medicinal herbs or tell different monsters apart, you're dead meat. And if you don't know how to properly address a noble you're escorting, you're going to end up starting a fight that will end either with you getting cut down or put on a list of criminals. You have to study up."

His words were curt, but no one could argue with the truth of them.

Elbert began writing on the board as he continued speaking.

Total Students: 40	*Boys: 27*	*Girls: 13*
Sword Users	*Boys: 13*	*Girls: 3*
Spear Users	*Boys: 4*	
Archers	*Boys: 4*	*Girls: 2*
Magic Users	*Boys: 6*	*Girls: 8*

Girls' Team A	*5 Members*	*2 Magic, 1 Sword, 2 Bow*
Girls' Team B	*4 Members*	*3 Magic, 1 Sword*
Girls' Team C	*4 Members*	*3 Magic, 1 Sword*

Boys' Team 1	*5 Members*	*1 Magic, 3 Sword, 1 Bow*
Boys' Team 2	*5 Members*	*1 Magic, 2 Sword, 1 Bow, 1 Spear*
Boys' Team 3	*5 Members*	*1 Magic, 2 Sword, 1 Bow, 1 Spear*
Boys' Team 4	*4 Members*	*1 Magic, 2 Sword, 1 Spear*
Boys' Team 5	*4 Members*	*1 Magic, 2 Sword, 1 Spear*
Boys' Team 6	*4 Members*	*1 Magic, 2 Sword, 1 Bow*

"This class is divided into parties by gender and grouped based on your professions. Teams A through C are the girls' teams, and Teams 1 through 6 are the boys'. I'm sure some of you may have noticed already, but these party divisions are the same as your room assignments. So you're bound together until graduation, like it or not.

"If there's someone you don't get on with, it's your responsibility to tough it out. That's part of your training. After all, you're not always going to end up liking your party members after graduation, either.

"Now, there aren't many all-girl parties out there in the real world, but here at school, we don't have the time to be breaking up any lovers' spats or dealing with unexpected babies. It's easier to teach you all separately.

"But that's just for while you're here. After you graduate, you can form your own mixed-gender parties if you want to. That's how it usually works, after all."

At that point, Mile felt that Elbert had been a bit too frank, but he simply continued his explanation.

Seating in the classroom was divided up by profession, so it was easy for the instructors to know at a glance which groups would most benefit from what information. Still, when hunters were out in the field, there was the possibility that they would have to take up the arms of a fallen comrade or a bested enemy, so it was crucial that every hunter trained with equipment that was outside of his or her wheelhouse. In the future, this would help them work better with other members of their party. Of course, it was critical to know the strengths and weaknesses of one's enemies, so joint sessions with students of other professions were also part of their training course.

Finally, it was time for the students to introduce themselves to one another.

"I don't expect you all to memorize everybody the first time around," Elbert said. "This is just to get a feel for the sort of folks who are in your class. We'll start from the right side. Give us your name, age, occupation, specialization, and rank, at the very least. You don't have to stop there, though. Feel free to let your peers know what kind of person you are."

In spite of his encouragement, almost no one gave more than the bare minimum.

Few students were interested in filling a bunch of strangers in on their private affairs, their strengths, or their weaknesses. Even Mavis, Reina, and Pauline gave introductions much briefer than those they had offered back in the dormitory.

Finally, it came time for Mile to introduce herself. "I'm Mile. I'm twelve years old and a magic user. There's no type of magic that I'm especially bad at. I can use storage magic, and I dabble just a little in swords. I'm an F-rank."

Unlike Reina, no one here expressed puzzlement at Mile's knowledge of storage magic. No matter how impressive the skill was, it was not particularly difficult to imagine why someone would have judged it too dangerous to send an inexperienced twelve-year-old out into the field. Instead, they would have sent her here to learn a few things, first. That was also, one could assume, why she was still an F-rank.

Indeed, in the wake of Mile's introduction, the students were whispering amongst themselves for an entirely different reason: recruitment, whether they could get to know her before graduation and cajole her into one of their parties.

She was a good-looking, reliable-seeming girl who could use storage—as well as other—magic, and she was even handy with a sword.

If a girl like that wasn't someone you wanted on your side, then who else would be?

For Mile, another difficult time was about to begin.

"All right! Time for our first-ever party meeting," Reina announced that evening after dinner, when they returned to their room.

The three others stared blankly.

"Don't you guys get it? Something terrible's happened! We need to talk about this!"

"What's so terrible?" Mile asked, unconcerned.

"You! Did you not see it?!" Reina shouted back. "How they were all staring at you?!"

"Huh? Am *I* really all that fascinating?"

"No!!! Weeell, it's not that you aren't interesting, but everyone's after that storage magic of yours! Before you know what's what, they're going to start coming after you to join their parties! And if we don't do something, it's going to be a disaster. Besides, you're already my..."

"Hmm?"

"N-never mind! Anyway, listen: You're going to start getting swarmed by men who aren't interested in you yourself, but in your storage magic! We need to do something about this!"

"What are you talking about?"

At Mile's amazement, Mavis and Pauline sighed deeply.

"Listen, most everyone who goes to this school is fifteen and older. People who join a guild as proper hunters at the age of ten can become a D-rank hunter in just a few years, even if they start at F-rank. And once they're a D-rank, they can start taking on real jobs, so there's no need to come to a place like this. No one's going to be sending any young people out on a mission to fight a high-ranking monster.

"However, none of the people here were able to join the guild at age ten. And even if they did join the guild later, the students here were also deemed to have potential. The higher-ups sent them to school so they could move more quickly through the ranks.

"Obviously, Mile, you fall outside that rule, because you're so young. There's no mistaking that you're here because of your storage magic."

Reina continued. "Most of the people here are already adults. Sure, some of them are only looking for future party members, but some of them are also looking for love. Someone like you, whose storage magic gives her great earning potential, who seems easy to control, and who is, dare I say, pretty cute... You're just too delectable of a prize. Do you see what I'm saying?"

"Um." Mile hung her head, crestfallen.

"Basically, if you get any party invitations from here on out, just tell them, 'I already promised I'd be with my roommates.' And, if anyone tries to ask you on a date, tell them, 'I'm not interested right now. I want to focus on my training.' Got it?!"

"Y-yes, ma'am!"

Seeing Mile's startled, immediate reply and Reina's obvious satisfaction, Mavis and Pauline understood.

So, it's like that.

Yes, it was most definitely "like that."

"Oh, that's right," said Mavis. "We need to pick a leader."

Immediately, the three girls all pointed...

At Mavis.

She was the oldest and the tallest, imposing, but also appealing and sincere.

The others were—of course—made up of the short-tempered Reina, mild-mannered Pauline, and Mile, who always seemed a step behind the rest of them.

In other words, Mavis was the obvious choice.

The following day, the morning was occupied by classroom studies.

Practical training would take place on the grounds in the afternoon.

"All right, the gang's all here. Before we start our normal training, we need to confirm all of your current ability levels. Let's go ahead and see each of your combat abilities, one at a time. Break out of your parties, and sort yourselves by occupation."

As directed by Elbert, the students rearranged themselves into groups by combat class.

The other three instructors were also present. The first was Huey, in charge of short swords, throwing knives, and archery. The second was Neville, a magic instructor, with a particular specialty in combat magic. And the third was Jilda, another magic instructor, in charge of utility and healing spells. Each of them was a former hunter.

Though they all had their own specialties to take charge of, they were by no means unskilled in the other disciplines, and when one had their hands full, the others could pitch in.

As things stood, the sword users and archers were mostly boys, and the number of female spear users was exactly zero. On the other hand, the magic users were mostly girls.

Considering physical ability, it was unsurprising that most of the students in the former professions were male. Even boys who could use some measure of combat magic were likely to choose the sword as their main skill. Moreover, a majority of applicants to the school were boys, anyway.

Still, though there were far fewer girls than boys in the student body, there *were* many more female magic users, likely for the same reasons discussed above.

All the students were wearing their own armor, but as weapons would be provided, no one had brought their own.

Even in a mock battle, if one used a real sword, there was risk of injury, and so, the students dressed accordingly. This was a blessing for Mile, who in spite of always looking rather like a swordsman, didn't look out of place with the other magic users.

They could be called sorcerers, yes, but there was not a robe in sight. Rather, everyone wore the same light leather armor, or if they couldn't afford that, thick, plain clothes, meaning that Mile did not stand out in her boots and leather breast plate.

It was only in her choice of equipment that Mile was exceptional. Other magic users carried staves, rods, or other blunt weaponry, but Mile stuck with her trusty sword. A magic user's life depended on their spell-casting and magic. Therefore, they were usually loathe to carry weapons that required extra attention or special skills. The same went for anything that might get stuck in an opponent's armor, making escape difficult.

As a result, they were inclined to the aforementioned forms of weaponry: light and well-balanced bludgeoning tools that required little thought to use, not meant for felling an enemy but merely for swinging about to protect oneself, should someone draw too near.

However, such things were of no concern to Mile. Additionally, it was much easier to fell an enemy with a sword or spear than with a staff or rod—and that was what counted.

For the same purpose, Mile also considered keeping a

slingshot on hand. Of course, a simple slingshot wouldn't make full use of Mile's abilities, but in fact, that might be a good thing. Even if she were excited or panicked, the string could only be pulled so far, so there was no risk of making an error that would allow her power to get out of hand and cause a mishap. Besides, if something did happen, it would be easy to play it off.

Bows were a bother, since one had to walk around with one's arrows prepared, and that just wasn't an option. Slingshot pellets were much less cumbersome, and one could always substitute them with pebbles in a pinch—and pebbles could easily be refined into proper spheres. If she were on sandy soil, she would be able to gather iron sand as raw material. Besides, as far as accuracy, she could rely on her nanobuddies to provide some course correction, so that wouldn't be too much of an issue.

No matter how one looked at it, slingshots beat bows, hands down.

"Begin!"

While Mile sat pondering these considerations, the duels between the sword users had begun.

Naturally, the students were using wooden swords. The school wasn't horrible enough to let a bunch of beginners use metal swords for training. Nevertheless, the duels were completely different from those at Eckland Academy, though Mile wasn't too surprised by this. These students were elite hunter candidates, most of them fifteen and up. Their technique and power were in a whole different class compared to her former schoolmates.

After a splendid volley between the first pair, one of the two swung his sword to finally catch the other in the side, and the match concluded.

The other matches that followed were close, as well. Indeed, all the students were all close in age, each of them a first-class candidate chosen from his or her district, meaning there were only subtle differences in their abilities.

Mile watched their bouts closely, analyzing everyone's levels. She was a studious girl, after all, and could do anything she put her mind to especially when she combined her diligence with practical experience...

There was an uneven number of male sword users, so the final boy was paired with a girl. That girl was Mavis.

Typically, men were thought to be stronger, but Mavis, the oldest and tallest of the girls, closed the gap easily and secured a splendid victory. The boy, having lost, looked momentarily disappointed, but then congratulated Mavis with a smile.

For a moment, his gaze looked distant in a way that reminded Mile of a certain eleven-year-old brat, but he soon collected himself, and offered Mavis a firm handshake.

They really are adults, Mile thought.

The duels between the female sword users followed, after which, Mile assumed, would come the spear users, but just then...

"Oi, Mile. You said you could use a sword, yeah? Let's see what you've got."

"Huh?!" Mile started at Elbert's unexpected command.

Unbeknownst to the other students, Mile had enrolled in the school without being tested, thanks to the recommendation of the regional guild master. As the principal and chief instructor, Elbert, of course, was aware of this. Since Mile did have storage magic, it was clear that the guild master's referral had been legitimate. However, his recommendation had also stated that Mile's swordsmanship was "on par with a C-rank hunter," and Elbert was curious to test her skills.

I...can't really refuse, can I? Mile thought. *I have to do this.* She had, after all, been analyzing everyone's levels as they fought, in case of such an event. *It will be fine. It will be fine...*

As Mile steeled herself, Elbert selected her opponent. When he asked for volunteers, nearly all of them raised their hands, so he selected one of the weaker-seeming boys who had fought earlier.

Why, Mile wondered, *does everyone want to fight me?!* Was it some kind of conspiracy? Were they picking on her because she was young?

In truth, however, they'd all raised their hands with the intent of sidling up to her later to ask how she was doing, saying something like, "Sorry about earlier. Why don't we get together later and talk about the practice match? I'll even bring some tea and cookies."

"Begin!"

The match kicked off with Elbert's signal, and as Mile blocked the young man's flurry of attacks, he blocked hers in return, their exchange proceeding nicely. Finally, one of the young man's blows caught Mile on the side, and the match was over.

She was an intelligent girl, after all.

"……"

Though the match had ended, Elbert continued to stare

silently, deep in thought. After a short while, he called to the boy who Mavis had fought earlier, and the two of them stepped aside to talk.

As they spoke, the male student flared up suddenly, as though he were angry at Elbert. After that, their mysterious conversation continued, the young man nodding reluctantly as though there was something he didn't quite understand, and finally, the two returned to the rest of the students.

"All right, Mile. Round two!"

"Huhhhhh?!?!"

This time, Mile wasn't the only one to shout her surprise.

"Begin!"

And a second match began.

The young man appeared as unhappy about this as Mile. He was being forced to fight a tiny girl who had just lost to a boy who was not even close to his ability level. To make matters worse, she was a mage—and on top of that, though he had lost to a young woman before, Mavis was at least a sword user, and she was strong. That defeat would linger with him, no doubt, but at least for now, he could accept it.

However, the fight he'd just been flung into was unacceptable. Even if he were to win, it would be an unsatisfying victory, without honor, pride, or prestige. It left a bad taste in his mouth. Still, this was part of their lessons, a practice mandated by their instructor. He had no choice but to do as he was told.

The match began and quickly grew fierce, leaving Mile flustered.

Why is he only aiming for the places where I don't have armor?!?!

Every attack was directed at her arms, neck, or the joints in her armor, all places where it would definitely hurt to take a blow at full strength. She'd be lucky to make it out of this with only bruises. She kept on blocking as though her life depended on it, and after things continued like this for a while, finally, she got her chance.

That one's headed straight for my armor.

Just as with the first match, the bout was concluded with a blow to the side.

Thwap!

Mile was relieved. But when she looked up, she saw that the boy before her was staring agog—but at Elbert, not her.

Mile followed his gaze and saw that Elbert was grinning like a madman.

Huh? Wha...?

It had been a set-up.

However, it was not until later that Mile would realize this.

After the spear and bow users finished their matches, it was at last the magic users' turn to compete. Unlike with the sword and spear users, the archers and mages were not to fight one another directly. Naturally, firing at one another would have been incredibly dangerous. So instead, they compared their rate and speed of fire, their accuracy, and their power when attacking a distant target.

One by one in order, they released their attack spells.

Fireballs, water spheres, fire arrows, ice arrows, rock arrows, infernos, explosions...

They varied in size, speed, and power, but once again, were leagues above anything Mile had seen at Eckland. There were few students there who had even been capable of combat magic to begin with.

The most shocking performance, however, was Reina's.

"Blaze, O flames of Hell! Reduce them to ash and bone!"

A surging, wild crimson flame swirled and hit its mark, incinerating the target.

"Amazing!" Mile whispered.

Reina turned to her triumphantly.

So that's why she's called "Crimson Reina," Mile thought. *Still, it doesn't seem like her magical strength is all that high, and I didn't think she conjured anything particularly special...*

For some reason, that was as far as Mile was able to understand Reina's magic, and she didn't try to analyze it further. She got the sense that doing so would just wear her out. It was a wise assumption on her part.

IT IS BECAUSE SHE IS PASSIONATE.

"Eep!"

Mile shrieked at the sudden whisper in her ear, causing several of her classmates to look her way, perplexed. She attempted to play it off as though nothing had happened, continuing to watch as the other students performed their magic.

D-don't scare me like that!

OUR APOLOGIES. IT SEEMED THAT YOU WERE SEEKING INFORMATION.

I was just thinking!! But, well, since I've got you here, I guess I may as well ask. What do you mean by "passionate"?

WE WILL EXPLAIN. AS YOU KNOW, WE NANOMACHINES HAVE RANDOMIZED RECEPTION AND SELECTION SETTINGS. BECAUSE OF THIS, THE NUMBER OF NANOMACHINES

IN RANGE THAT WILL REACT TO THE ARTICULATION OF A THOUGHT PULSE VARIES. OTHER VARIATIONS ARISE FROM THE CLARITY OF THE IMAGE, WHICH IMPACTS OPERATIVE EFFICIENCY. ALL THIS LEADS TO DIFFERENCES IN MAGICAL RESULTS.

HOWEVER, FROM TIME TO TIME, A PERSON APPEARS WHO CAN USE MAGIC WITH FAR GREATER POWER THAN OTHERS, DESPITE HAVING NO EXCEPTIONAL SKILL IN STRENGTH, CLARITY, OR IMAGE. THIS IS WHAT WE REFER TO AS "PASSION." THAT IS TO SAY—HOW TO PUT IT?—THEIR THOUGHT PULSE IS SO POWERFUL THAT EVEN NANOMACHINES WITH LOW SENSITIVITY WILL REACT TO IT.

Hmm...

With that brief acknowledgement, Mile put an end to the conversation, not really knowing whether she understood the nanomachines' explanation or not. It was her turn to perform magic.

Things are going okay so far, Mile thought, *so it should be acceptable to use fairly strong magic.* She wanted to try to stay at around fifth place in the class ranking. Thus, considering the number of students, being the second-best magician wasn't unreasonable. *I should just perform something a little bit weaker than what Reina did...*

With that in mind, Mile decided to try using the same spell as her roommate but with just about eighty percent of the output.

"Blaze, O flames of Hell! Reduce them to ash and bone!"

Just as when Reina performed it, a swirling crimson blaze arose, surrounding the target and reducing it to ash.

"Wh...?"

The others were a little bit surprised to see Mile using a spell as powerful as Reina's, and so soon after her. However, as Mile could use storage magic, it wasn't particularly shocking that she would be skilled in other areas of magic as well.

There was one person who simply could not accept this, however.

"Mile, I need to speak with you later." Reina glared at her harshly, and the hairs on the back of Mile's neck stood on end.

"Wh-why...?"

After Mile, several more students showed off their attack magic, followed by those with utility magic. Healing magic would be covered at some other time, as there was no one there who was injured, meaning that there would have been no way to perform any demonstrations.

Luckily, this was not a problem. There was no one whose only ability was healing magic, so all the students were able to show their skills off using some type of magic or other.

After the practical training was over, the students were dismissed from the grounds for the day. Reina still seemed agitated, so Mile kept her distance, shuffling behind the other students on the way to the dining hall in the hopes of keeping a low profile.

"Miss Mile!"

"Eek!" Mile shrieked and tensed as someone approached from behind and clapped her suddenly on the shoulder.

"Oh, I'm sorry..."

Mile turned around to find the male student she had faced in the second-round practice bout standing behind her.

"Sorry to frighten you—and sorry about the fight earlier. To be honest, it was all on the teacher's orders... Even if he told me to, though, it was still wrong of me to try and hit the parts of you that were unprotected. I'm really sorry!"

"Huh? Oh, no, it's all right! In a battle, it makes the most sense to aim for an enemy's weak points—and if the teacher said so, then you didn't really have much choice, did you?"

"Thank you so much for saying so."

With that, he departed. Mile was impressed. "Man, adults really are different..."

The moment she turned to keep moving toward the dining hall, she was halted by another male voice.

"Sorry about earlier, Miley!"

This time, she turned to find the student she had faced in the first-round battle.

"Were you hurt? Why don't we get together after dinner and talk about the practice match? I have a bunch of pointers I can give you!"

His nostrils flared on his smarmy, grinning face.

Mile, who could smell his ulterior motive a mile away, was unamused. "Sorry, I have a party meeting after dinner. In any case, I am a magic user, not a swordsman, so it's only natural that I would have a lot of flaws in my sword technique. If I have the time to be polishing my sword skills beyond last-ditch self-defense, I think it would be better spent honing my magic—since that's my main discipline..."

"O-oh, uh, but..."

"Excuse me." Before the boy could come up with a snappy comeback, Mile walked away as briskly as she could.

It seemed that among mature adult men, there were still plenty of bad apples.

As always, dinner was eaten with her four roommates, i.e., her party, in the dining hall. Mile peeked timidly at Reina now and then, but she appeared not to notice and ate her meal normally. Mile was glad to be granted a momentary respite.

However, as soon as the four returned to their room...

"Commencing party meeting number two!" Mavis said.

"Mile! What was that about?!" Reina shouted.

"Huh? What? Was what about?"

"Don't play dumb! That spell that you used! What was the meaning of that?!"

Mile recoiled in the face of Reina's ire.

Mavis and Pauline just sat quietly, watching the events unfold.

"Um, well, I just used a normal fire spell, the same as you..."

"I see... The same as me, hmm? You simply plagiarized 'Crimson Hellfire,' the Crimson Reina's signature, original spell, as a little 'normal fire spell,' did you?!"

"Wha...?!"

After some extended and persistent questioning by Reina, Mile finally buckled. She told Reina everything.

Well, not exactly everything. But she devised a cover story that was close enough to the truth.

"So, you're saying that the minister who was after your power shook hands with the demon king, and the prince helped guide you to safety...?"

"Yes! I really thought I was going to die!"

"YOU EXPECT ME TO BELIEVE THAT?! YOU COMPLETE IDIOT!!"

"Wh... How did you know...?"

"I've read that novel, too!!!"

"Waah!!"

Reina grabbed Mile's hands.

This time, she confessed for real.

"So what you're saying is that you hate to get special treatment, and you didn't want everyone to heap it on you just because of your magical powers and storage skill? And that you ran away from home because you would have been killed, due to issues with your family's line of succession?"

"Yes..." Though Mile had adjusted some of the details, each element of this story was true, so it was far more convincing—at least, more so than the romantic epic she had spun before.

"Well, that I can understand. Most people here have had others try to use them or sell them off for their exceptional abilities, in some way or other. This school doubles as a place to protect those people."

With a pained look, Reina finally released Mile's hands.

"Anyway, Mile, what was the deal with that guy who stopped you on the way to the dining hall?" Mavis asked.

"What?!" Reina, who had just let Mile go, grabbed her by the collar now, pulling hard.

"Wait! Stop! Y-you're choking meee..."

After she told them the whole story of the conversations with both of the men, she was finally released again.

"No surprises there. We better monitor that first one, though— he was probably hiding something. Mavis, if that man ever gets near Mile again, block him!"

"I'll see to it..."

Mavis smiled wryly. Suddenly, another question popped into her head. She turned to Mile.

"But why would the teacher set you up like that? You're an aspiring magic user..."

"Who knows?"

As Mile hung her head, Mavis asked, nonchalantly, "By the way, Mile, why did you stop guarding on the last blow, in that second match? Especially in that bout, you had no trouble blocking all his quickest attacks, but then you let the last one, which was pretty slow, hit you straight on. Why was that? Did you fall for a feint or something?"

"...Huh?"

"Well, I mean, his last attack was a pretty weak one, wasn't it?"

At Mavis's prompting, Mile suddenly remembered what the young man said.

The teacher's orders.

...the parts of you that were unprotected...

And then, Mavis's words.

His last attack was a pretty weak one...

It had happened again.

The instructor was testing her mettle and confirming that she lost on purpose.

"Wh-what's this all of a sudden?!" Mavis asked in the wake of Mile's pensive silence.

Faced with Reina's hounding, Mile, now quite depressed over her latest realization, decided to spill the beans about her ability with swords, too. After all, now that the teacher knew, it was only a matter of time until everyone else did, as well.

At least this way, her friends would hear about it from her first. Thinking about things that way, Mile realized she had no regrets about being found out.

"Friends," huh? she thought to herself. And indeed, sitting there beside her, utterly puzzled by the grin suddenly crossing Mile's face, were her three new friends.

The following days were filled with practical training, during both the mornings and afternoons. This was comprised of everything from improving basic fitness levels to studying techniques, methods for attacking different types of monsters, and everything in between. There was individual training as well as practice battles, sometimes even against the teachers themselves. In addition, they had training sessions organized both by discipline and as a full group. Without an awareness of the work performed by those in other professions, they would be unable to forge a strong relationship with their party members. Besides, when participating in real combat as a guard or fighter, comprehending an enemy's abilities and being able to counter their technique could mean the difference between victory and defeat.

The female-only parties had a larger proportion of magic users, and therefore lacked power on the front lines. Thus, when it came time for the inter-party practice bouts, they came together with the male parties to swap members temporarily. Still, owing to Mile's skill as a swordsman and each of the girls' own individual strengths, Mile's party could more or less fight on their own...

Since doing nothing but practical training would have caused the students to burn out, classroom lessons were held occasionally. During these lessons, they learned how to identify medicinal, herbal, and poisonous plants, exploit the weaknesses of different monster types, and take various safety precautions. They also received a general education on such topics as the histories of nearby countries, the makeup of the guild, and in-depth etiquette relating to interactions with nobles.

Typically, a hunter would learn these sorts of things on the job, taking pointers from more experienced party members or simply copying their techniques. From each, they thus learned to improve themselves through simple trial and error.

However, learning this way took time, and the potential for slip-ups due to lack of knowledge was great. Because of this, it often took years to grow into a full-fledged hunter, using one's many failures, repeated year after year, to fill in the gaps in one's knowledge and experience... Worse than that, however, was the fact that there were many hunters who lost their lives from such failures.

And so Mile, studious as ever, took these lessons quite seriously, writing everything down in a notebook she carried to class. Though there were many others taking notes just like her, some students, while they did seem to be listening to the lesson, never wrote a word.

One day back in their dorm room, when a perplexed Mile asked about this very fact, Reina told her, in a somewhat exasperated manner, "It's because they're illiterate, dummy."

"Huh? But then, how will they read the posted job requests?"

"They'll rely on the guild staff to point them to the right ones—or sometimes, you'll see children hanging around who'll read things aloud to earn a bit of pocket money."

"…"

In her previous life, Mile had loved reading—without any friends, it was, along with TV and games, one of her only pleasures. She could scarcely imagine being unable to read and write and could only think what an incredible tragedy their inability to read was.

"Commencing party meeting number three!"

This time, when Reina made her announcement, a question slipped out before Mile even had time to think about it. "Um, if Mavis is our leader, how come you're always the one leading these?"

"………"

"Um, sorry! Forget I said anything!"

"This meeting's topic is… our next rest day!" Reina continued speaking as though nothing had happened. "As you know, this party is lacking in power, skill, speed, and most importantly, money!" She was speaking in a shout now, her voice painfully loud. "Once we start the monster-hunting portion of our practical training, we'll be able to start earning money by exchanging monster parts. However, we can't afford to wait for that!"

Indeed, Reina had already run out of money—the only times she could eat were during the three daily meals served in the dining hall. Not only that, but she was starting to hit the bottom of her inkwell.

It was the sort of circumstance one might refer to as being at "the end of one's rope" or "hitting rock bottom."

"Mavis, you and Pauline have no experience as hunters and only just registered as F-ranks after coming here," Reina went on.

"Mile, you have a little bit of experience, but unfortunately you're still an F-rank. I, however, am an E-rank, which means that I can accept jobs fighting monsters of any rank up to goblins and orcs.

"If there are extermination requests, we'll take them. If not, we'll collect jackalopes and hunt smaller animals. If all goes well, we should be able to get three or four silver each."

"Hmm..." Mile said.

"What? Do you have an objection?"

"N-no, it's nothing..." Mile was merely surprised at Reina's enthusiasm at the prospect of earning such a small amount. That was all.

That night, Mile lay in bed, thinking about whether or not she should teach her roommates what she knew about magic.

Even if she were to teach them, she knew she couldn't do so in the way that she taught Marcela and the others. Her three friends at Eckland had had little magic ability to start with and would never lead a life where they their own mortality would be staked on their magical skill. In other words, even if she taught them a few special tricks, those three would never become wielders who might influence the destinies of many, nor would they do something careless if they ever faced mortal peril. They, she knew, would be able to keep her secret.

For the students at this school, things were different. Their lives were inextricably linked to their magical skill, and their collective fates rested on the abilities of their party members, not only themselves. If people like that learned how to grow their magical power by an immense degree, they would most certainly share this knowledge with their party members. And when their party dissolved, and they joined another, they would tell *those* people as well.

In turn, *those* people would tell their children—and those children would tell their friends, some of whom would surely be money-grubbers who might open magic schools, or work as tutors for the children of nobles, or sell their expertise to other countries...

In other words, there was no way that Mile's special knowledge would remain a secret.

The other factor to consider was the fact that the people at this school already had significant magical abilities. Their powers of strength, clarity, and image were already far greater than those of other people, meaning that they could use fairly powerful magic. If she were to teach people like *that* her tricks...

When she thought about it that way, Mile realized, she simply wouldn't feel right teaching her roommates the same things she had taught the Wonder Trio. However, she also couldn't bear the thought of any of them perishing shortly after graduation. And as they were all aiming to be promoted to C-rank when they finished, not D-rank, extra magical abilities would be a great help.

What to do...?

Mile fretted over the question until daybreak.

"All right girls, let's get going!"

It was the following rest day.

After waking early and rushing through breakfast—all at Reina's urging—the four girls set out through the capital city to the Hunters' Guild.

Naturally, there was a hall even in the capital.

Because of its location, this hall was a kind of capital of its own, serving as a central place to consolidate the needs of all the individual halls within the country. However, as the Hunters' Guild was spread across many countries, there was still no single place that could be called the true headquarters, which was advantageous. With no "head" in any particular place, there was thus no head that could be easily crushed—nor could the organization at large be taken over.

However, in exchange for this security and stability, the guild was slow to mobilize, and once a decision had been fixed in place, it was no small task to alter it. Whenever a big decision needed to be made, it was decided in an inter-country conference.

It was early in the morning, but the guildhall was already packed.

Or rather, the hall was packed *because* it was early in the morning.

One of the reasons for this was...

"Hey! They're from the school!"

Indeed, it seemed that all the other students, just as short on money as Mile and her friends, had exactly the same idea.

The F and E-rank boards, in particular, had been ravaged. All the decent jobs that could be finished within a day were long gone.

"We're too late..."

Reina slumped, devastated.

"W-well, there's still standing orders and gathering tasks. Right?!" Mile said.

She perked up a little at her encouragement and went to confirm the prices on the request and materials board. Upon finding that the turn-in rewards for birds and jackalopes were fairly good, her vigor was restored.

"Well, that's the capital for you! There are tons of buyers, so at least the price of meat is high. Let's get a move on!"

And so, Team C of the twelfth class of the Hunters' Prep School embarked on their first mission.

"This isn't working..."

Reina collapsed in a heap, both hands planted on the ground beside her.

In order to earn four silver apiece, they would, collectively, need to catch at least eight birds or jackalopes—or two foxes.

If they caught something larger, like a deer, they would only need one, but thus far, no such fortune had visited them.

It had been three hours now since they had begun hunting and was nearly noon. They had caught only a single jackalope and a single bird. At this rate, they would go home with only one silver each.

Even if they worked their hardest in the four hours following their lunch break and things continued as they were, at best, they would only net another three catches. For Reina, who was in the most dire straits of all of them, this was a serious problem.

It seemed she had overlooked something critical. True, the population of the capital was large, but so was the amount of meat all its people consumed—and too the number of fledgling hunters. As a result, the hunting grounds near the city had already been picked clean.

I had better say something soon, Mile thought, as they sat down for a midday break, taking out their food and unwrapping it.

Just then, Reina's gaze landed on Mile's meal. "Hang on, what is that?!"

"Huh? It's just my lunch..."

The other three were eating stale bread they had collected from the cafeteria and rehydrated with some water, but Mile was eating a roast meat sandwich and drinking black tea, which she had pretended to pull from storage space—though in actuality, it had come from her loot box.

"How is it still warm?!" Reina asked. In the end, she stole the lion's share of the sandwich.

"Um, there is something I would like to suggest to everyone..." Mile finally said, as the girls rested after their meal.

Everyone turned to look and Mile continued. "The reason that we haven't been able to catch anything is partly due to the fact that the prey is simply hard to find, but I also think a part of it is that our magic isn't accurate enough. We don't have an archer, so we're relying on long-range spells..."

"Hey! Are you saying that I suck?!" Reina sputtered.

Mile kept speaking in an attempt to pacify the other girl. "Um, I believe I mentioned before that I was skilled in many types of magic, so, well, if you like, I was thinking we could perhaps take a brief break from hunting to study some technique."

"Are you saying you're going to teach us something?"

"Y-yes, well..." She trailed off, well aware that the idea of being taught by someone younger than her wouldn't be good for Reina's ego. Already, Mile regretted bringing it up.

However...

"Come to think of it, you've been letting me take all the shots," Mile said. "You haven't fired off any magic. And sitting around getting frustrated isn't going to get us anywhere. Maybe we should just have a bit of practice—you know, for a change of pace."

In an unexpected turn, Reina agreed with Mile.

Mile was surprised, but she grinned.

It was time for their journey to begin.

CHAPTER 8 |

Power Leveling

"ALL RIGHT—and then, squeeze it. Your opponent is a small animal, so it doesn't have to be very hard. The trade-in value will decrease if you damage it. Try to keep the image of small pellets with high-speed propulsion in mind."

Following Mile's advice, Reina cast her spell, gaze steeled. "Come, O water, to my aid! Sphere of water, form! Now freeze! Change form, into a sharp icicle. Turning, turning, spinning! Now, fly!"

The water gathered and froze, condensed into cylinders of ice, then flew away, rotating quickly.

The icicles shot perfectly, right into the targeted tree branch.

It wasn't a hole-in-one shot like Mile's were, but she could tell that Reina would have no trouble hitting a distant target.

"I-I did it!" Reina grinned widely at her success.

It would be unwise to use fire magic in the forest, and the ground of the location they were practicing in was covered in leaves rather than gravel. However, thanks to Mile's advice, which helped her improve the accuracy of her ice attacks by increasing the compression and speed of the icicles, Reina felt her skills improve immediately. She would never have imagined that she would be able to work with ice magic—which wasn't even her specialty—to hunt more effectively, and yet, there she was.

Mile had devised a series of lessons to get them to this point. At first, she hadn't realized that Reina wouldn't understand that a large ice bullet would be affected by gravity and thus need course correction, unlike the specialized fire magic that Reina usually used at combat practice. Additionally, Mile noticed, the effect of the spell's added guidance in helping conjure the necessary image was immense. Making the icicle bullets spin was another helpful addition.

Now Reina would be able to use powerful magic even in battles and on hunting expeditions, where fire couldn't be used.

Nearby, Pauline was practicing, as well. She already possessed reasonable magical skills, but—whether because of her personality or the fact that she was a bit clumsy—she was no good at attack magic, which required continuous production. In the near future, Mile figured, it would be good to teach her at least one attack spell for self-defense, but the present moment was still a little too soon for that.

Instead, Mile taught Pauline something that she thought her friend might find even more useful.

"Come, O water, to my aid! Sphere of water, form! Droplets dance, like a burning soul!"

Thanks to the spell, a gradually heating ball of warm water appeared.

"Yes! That's perfect. With this, baths and cooking will be a breeze. It expends a lot less magical energy than putting a fireball into water, and it can even be used indoors to make smaller quantities—pretty handy for making tea, you know?"

"Th-thank you, Miley!"

"No worries. I'd like to teach you even more soon!"

Rather than trying to impart to them the fundamental knowledge of how to utilize thought pulses and nanomachine efficiency rates, Mile simply gave them the instructions they would need to grow in terms of general magic efficiency, helping them craft slightly more precise spells to invoke the necessary physical and chemical reactions. At the same time, she took careful precautions in order to ensure that they wouldn't inadvertently stumble onto more power than they knew what to do with.

Even so, the two girls' progress was remarkable, and Reina and Pauline practiced with zeal.

"Um..."

A voice came from behind her. Mile turned to see Mavis, looking sullen.

"There isn't anything you can show me, is there? Like a special technique, or something...?"

"Ah..." For Mavis's sake, Mile thought hard, but nothing came to mind.

She really didn't know much about Western sword techniques, and all the special moves she had seen in anime and games were impossible. If Mavis had been able to use magic, Mile would surely have been able to come up with something, but the older girl had no magical skill...

"Maybe we could do some practice swings?"

"..." Mavis let herself fall to the ground. Mile's suggestion wasn't something that would grant her a particular skill.

"U-um, I'll be your practice partner! I don't have much training, so I have no idea about sword techniques or anything, but I have confidence in my power and skill! If you get used to my speed, I'm sure you'll be able to see through other opponents' attacks more easily!"

"Really?" Mavis sounded doubtful. She was pouting.

"Really! It's true! Probably..." Mile spoke the last word under her breath, so upon hearing her reply, Mavis finally brightened.

When the sun at last began to set, it was time for them to return to the capital.

"We didn't catch very much today, but this was still a productive outing! Thank you, Mile!"

"Thanks so much, Miley!"

"Don't thank me! We're friends, aren't we?"

"I'm your friend too, aren't I? Are you forgetting me?" Mavis was still a bit sulky.

"Of course! That's right!" Mile said. After, there was moment of silence, then she piped up, as though she had suddenly remembered something. "It's going to be super annoying if we go back to the guild like this. The boys will all make fun of us for coming back with so little! I'm going to try hunting by myself for a bit."

She pulled some of the pebbles from her pocket.

"Umm, if you could keep your voices down..."

Fwip!

She walked away briskly and returned with a jackalope in hand.

Zip!

A large bird tumbled out of a tree.

Bwoosh!

Vwip!

Ka-shunk!

"M-Mile..."

Reina's mouth hung open.

"What? I use compressed air to make the pebbles fly. It's really just normal wind magic..." In actuality, Mile was doing it with her finger strength alone—there was no magic required.

"W-well, even if that's the case... how are you finding the prey so easily?!"

"Um... Intuition?"

Mavis and Pauline looked at each other and shrugged, trading looks that said, "There's no point trying to understand this one."

When Mile and company returned to the guild, they turned in their birds and jackalopes and were paid twenty-four silver pieces in total. The male students stared, wide-eyed.

"Thanks, but...are you sure you want to share this?" her friends wanted to know.

"Yep! We all went hunting together, after all!"

"Mile, you—well, that's fine. I will gratefully accept. And I will definitely return the favor someday!"

"I'm looking forward to it!"

The girls split their earnings for six silver each and happily made their way out of the guild, with the young men's gazes still fixed on them, a bit jealous of their productivity.

And so, Mile continued giving Reina and Pauline magic lessons. In order to keep things from getting out, she forbade them from telling others what she was teaching them. They worked in private, going over spells, magical effects, and information about physics and chemistry in their dorm room, saving any actual practice for the hunting trips they took on their days off.

In time, Reina's fire magic became much stronger, and even Pauline began to learn some combat spells. Mile also taught the latter about the structure of the human body—bones, internal organs, blood vessels, nerves, cells, and the like—so that she would be able to use her healing and recovery magic more effectively.

The two of them made steady improvements, and as they practiced hunting, even their aim began to improve, so that they could earn more on their own, without Mile's help.

And they all lived happily ever after...

Except for Mavis, whom Mile had forgotten about entirely.

"Miiiiiiile!" Whenever she spoke Mile's name, dissatisfaction could be heard clearly in her voice.

As it wasn't a huge problem to be seen practicing with Mavis, they used the indoor training grounds during their free time, including their lunch and dinner breaks.

"All right! First, let's try it at about 1.2 times the speed of our fastest classmate."

Clack clack clack clack clack clack clack clack clack!

"All right! Next, 1.3 times."

Clack clack clack clack clack clack clack clack clack!

"All right! Next, 1.4 times."

Clack clack clack clack clack clack clack clack clack!

"All right! Next..."

"W-wait! Wait just a minuuuuuute!!"

"Hm? If we speed up just a little bit at a time, you should be able to acclimate yourself to the quicker speed, right? That's what the ninjas did: they planted a hemp seed, and every day they practiced jumping over it..."

"I have no idea what a ninja is, but this is impossible! Impossible, I tell you! Anyway, I'm assuming what you're saying is that they improved a little bit every day. They didn't get faster every two minutes!"

Mile didn't understand what Mavis was so unhappy about, but since her friend looked as though she was about to cry, Mile tried a new approach.

"Okay. Wrap this long sash around your waist and try running fast enough that the sash never touches the ground."

"Um... Okay."

Mavis agreed, put the sash on her waist, and started running. She didn't come back.

There was no way she could turn around without letting the sash touch the ground. After some time, she finally came back, her feet dragging. She was exhausted, and there was a bruise on her forehead, as though she had run into something.

"Let's... let's try a different method..." she said, still short of breath.

"Well," Mile mused, "there were once people who would hang upside down and move water from a barrel on the ground to one higher up, using a tiny cup..."

"I'll do it. I'll do anything if it will make me stronger!"

Unfortunately for Mavis, every special training method Mile knew came from manga, anime, or movies.

And so, the long days of "Mavis's Speed Improvement Plan" began. The goal was to get Mavis to measure up to Mile. In looking forward to that day, Mavis prepared a name for the special technique that she would surely invent in the future.

That technique was called "Godspeed Blade."

It would be an invincible sword technique, one that could slice down enemies with divine speed—or so she hoped.

In spite of their hunting, Mile and her roommates still didn't have much money to spare.

Because they were responsible for providing their own lighting, their lack of funds meant that they couldn't burn their candles very long at night. However, as they also couldn't possibly fall asleep immediately, they spent every night after crawling into bed talking with one another before they drifted off.

They talked about practice, and their classmates, and rumors they'd heard—but because they spent much of their time together, and always saw and heard the same things, they often ran out of things to talk about.

Even when they talked about themselves, Mavis was the only one who would speak freely of her family and upbringing. As the first daughter, she always had stories to share about how her parents spoiled her, or the way that her three older brothers were just a little *too* doting. Mavis herself was the only one who seemed unaware of how these stories sounded.

Blegh...

Apart from the members of Mavis's family, the three girls probably knew more about Mavis's childhood than anyone in the world—despite the fact that they had never wished for such knowledge. Since hearing only Mavis's stories had begun to feel a little grim, Mile also began joining in with the evening chats.

Her talks were on the fundamentals of magic, but—in order to include Mavis—she spoke of other things, too. She told them folktales and legends from Earth, or stories from action dramas, anime, and games, readapted to fit their world.

Her roommates were hooked. Reina loved the stories of powerful sorcerers and magical girls. Pauline loved the rags-to-riches tales, and of course, Mavis loved the heroic legends and epic adventures.

They pestered Mile into continuing every night, none of them realizing that they had contracted a serious illness—one said to afflict all children around the age of thirteen: the obsessiveness of adolescence known as chuunibyou.

One day, on the way back to the dorm after dinner, Mile realized that she had left a letter behind in the classroom. One of her male classmates had handed it to her earlier, saying, "Please read this later."

As she always did with such letters, Mile planned to take it back to the room to look over with the other girls, then come up with a reply. Forming a reply was always a collaborative project—Reina was always the author and Pauline the editor, while Mile took on production. As for the theme, well, it was always heartbreak.

When Mile returned to the classroom to retrieve the letter

she had left behind, she heard a strange tapping sound from the direction of the lectern. Upon looking up, she saw a boy who appeared to be practicing writing characters on the board.

"Writing practice?"

"Y-yeah. It's embarrassing to do it in my room in front of the other guys, and if I use the chalkboard I don't have to waste my paper or ink. I don't even need a quill for it."

"Oh, I see! That's smart!"

Mile was moved by the boy's pleasant, straightforward explanation. She felt a sense of fondness and kinship welling up, as she remembered how she had been unable to purchase paper, pens, or ink when she had first arrived at Eckland Academy so long ago.

"Um. If I remember correctly, you're a swordsman, right?" she said.

"Yeah. I can also use magic, a little bit beyond basic utility even, but not well enough to actually become a magic user. So, I fight with my sword and just use my magic for the extra things, like drawing water and recovery. It really is a big help, though. It's hard going solo..."

"Solo?" Mile asked, perplexed.

Except for special cases like herself, solo jobs were too dangerous and inconvenient for anyone but a true veteran to undertake. Unless you were an oddball or the circumstances demanded it, solo work was not something one undertook willingly.

"Yeah, I'm an orphan from the slums. Er, well, I guess I haven't left yet, so I'm still a slum dweller... Anyway, I have a lot of little guys to look after, so I can't go off adventuring with a party.

"At the moment, I go check on them after dinner, and on rest days I hunt food for them to eat. If I join a party when I become a real hunter, that means I'll be traveling far away for days at a time, you know? But if I do that, there'll be no way for me to look after those little squirts."

"But wait—once they turn fifteen, they'll be able to live on their own, won't they?" Mile asked. "And the next generation will be able to look after the little ones for you..."

At Mile's words, the boy looked a bit surprised. "That's wise of you. And, well, I guess most of them *are* about that age. I've already paid back the favors that were done for me, so really, I suppose my role has ended. Still, I don't mind keeping an eye on them.

"The thing that really bothers me is that no matter how much time passes, life in that place is never going to change. But if I become a C-rank, I'll be able to take the little ones out on expeditions to gather herbs and things whenever, you know? It's rare for the guild to sponsor guarded gathering expeditions, and even when they do, you still have to pay for the guard's participation. With me, it would be free, and under my supervision, they could even try a bit of hunting. I'll be able to train them, and if they can become D-ranks, forming a party of just us orphans someday wouldn't be out of the question."

He shook his head. "But maybe that's just one man's foolish dream."

Watching the boy smile to himself, Mile thought, *A swordsman who can use magic.*

He was a generous soul who, despite having a chance to escape the slums, remained for the sake of the other orphans. Not only that, but he was obviously a hard worker, studying writing as he did, all on his own.

Since they had begun their power leveling, Mile and her

party had more or less risen to the top of their class. Even if she had placed herself at the bottom of that pack, that meant she was ranked fourth in the class. In other words, she needed one more person ahead of her to put her in fifth.

The term "sacrificial lamb" suddenly popped into her head.

"S-say, just hunting with a sword isn't very effective, is it? What if I told you there was a magic you could learn that's perfect for hunting birds and jackalopes?"

"Huh...?"

"It sure took you a long time just to go and get that letter."

"Oh, well, there was a guy in the classroom, and we were just talking for a while..."

"What? A guy?!"

"It was just a chat! A short chat!"

Reina was smoldering, but Mile simply waved her hands as if it were nothing.

"Anyway, here's the letter in question."

"Let's deal with it like we usually do."

"O-okay!" Mile and Pauline agreed, powerless.

Veil was an orphan.

He had never known his parents' faces. By the time he was old enough to be aware of his surroundings, he was already living in the slums, in the shelter of a crumbling, abandoned house along with the other girls and boys. The eldest was a boy of twelve or thirteen, whom they all called Andy.

It was only a few years after Veil's first memories that Andy disappeared.

Perhaps he had died from illness or an accident. Maybe he'd gone off somewhere to become a hunter.

No one ever told them, and Veil never asked.

After Andy, there had been "Big Sis."

He remembered the day when Big Sis went away.

Instead of the rags she always wore, Big Sis showed up in a pretty new outfit and brought the orphans lots of food and clothing. Then she went away with some adults they had never seen before. She never came back again. That was the last time he ever saw her.

The next leader was Brother Jon. After him was Brother Dahl.

Each of them vanished when they were around fourteen or fifteen years old.

Perhaps they died, or perhaps they simply became adults who could finally live on their own and left the slums for a happier life elsewhere.

Before he knew it, Veil was the second eldest, with only Brother Dahl ahead of him in age.

He thought to himself: *It's my turn now—my turn to protect everyone, to take care of them. To pay back all the help the ones before me gave.*

But this time, I won't disappear. I'm always going to look after them.

Because this is my home, and these people are my family.

The capital was a difficult place for an orphan, and yet in some ways, it was also kind.

If one were caught stealing or picking pockets, one would swiftly be caught and indentured. Several bands of orphans had been captured in this way, and their homes demolished. However, if one did honest work, people tended to overlook the house-squatting, and now and then some charitable adult might even donate a scrap or two of food.

Particularly egregious abuses were rare. The authorities were relatively just and made little distinction between rich and poor. More importantly, many of the local thugs and hunters had come from the slums themselves and were thus kind to their juniors—at least in the cases where they themselves had nothing to lose.

At the age of six, Veil registered as an associate hunter, so that he could do odd jobs around the city and help pay for everyone's food. The moment he turned ten, he registered as an official hunter.

At that time, another hunter, himself from the slums, gifted Veil a cheap sword that was destined for the scrap heap, as he had recently acquired a new one.

Veil was so happy he wept. He had never felt so lucky in his life. Previously, he'd planned to fight with a wooden staff until he could afford to buy a sword of his own.

And then, when that precious sword of his finally broke, he saved up a bit of money to purchase a slightly older, used sword.

Someday, he would give his sword to one of his juniors. He swore it to himself.

So that the little ones could eat.

So that they could purchase medicine when they got sick.

So that, now and then, they could buy new clothes from the secondhand store.

The smaller kids earned a little from odd jobs and guild-chaperoned gathering expeditions, but it didn't amount to much. Even though Veil became an official hunter at age ten, he was still an F-rank, and his earnings weren't enough to fully support a number of orphans.

He had to earn more. He had to get more money.

However, there weren't many parties who would take a boy from the slums with no special skills, and even if he found one, he couldn't join a party that would travel far away and leave him unable to look after the little ones.

There were solo jobs that wouldn't take him far and required no special skills, but they didn't grant him much experience, nor did they let him challenge himself. He spent his days gathering herbs and hunting jackalopes and other small beasts, with no hope of promotion. Furthermore, his skills as an amateur swordsman were his only means of hunting, so his efficiency was low.

There was no point in buddying up with others from the slums, either. They were F-rank amateurs, just the same as him, so the jobs they could accept would be no different, and they had no unique skills that he could learn from them. If he formed a party with hunters the same age as he, he would have no way to progress. The only thing that could change with this method would be if he could become more efficient at locating prey.

And then the day came when Brother Dahl disappeared.

One night, he simply didn't come home.

And that was that.

Maybe he had perished, or perhaps he fled.

If he had left the slums behind and joined a hunting party somewhere, he would be fine. Perhaps he joined a party that had gone off to another town, or perhaps he'd gone off to another town, and then joined a party.

Either way, the orphans were left without their top earner.

Veil, now suddenly the eldest, was caught, anxious, between the weight of his new sense of responsibility and the dark and hazy future ahead of him.

It was then that a man's voice had called out to him.

"You there! You're still rough, but I can tell yer pretty handy with a sword. Whaddya think? You gonna take the entrance exam for the Hunters' Prep School?"

The man, who was associated with the guildhall in the capital, told Veil that while he was in school, he would himself check in on the orphans now and then. And at any rate, even while Veil was at the school, he would be able to go look in on them during the evenings and on days off, too. More importantly, the training the school offered was completely free. Veil would be able to work on his days off, and if he and the other orphans worked hard, in just half a year, the quality of their lives would improve immensely.

If Veil could become a C-rank, everything would be just as the man said.

"As long as you can do well on the exam, anyway," the man explained. "Even if you can't read and write, there's no reason why you shouldn't be able to pass. Still, the chances of getting in are slim—incredibly so…"

Despite the man's warning, Veil replied, "I'll do it!"

And so he had.

Even after he became a C-rank hunter, being able to read and write would make choosing jobs much easier for him. In addition, not being able to read and sign his own contracts and the like could be disastrous. With that in mind, every night after dinner, he returned to the classroom to practice his letters.

With the others in his dorm room, it was hard to find space to practice there, and besides, if he used the board in the classroom, he could save money he might have spent on paper and ink. It wasn't unusual for the other students to return to the training grounds or the indoor practice area after their lessons, but no one came back to the classroom.

That was what he thought, anyway, until someone *did* come.

"Writing practice?"

It was an earnest, friendly girl of twelve, three years Veil's junior, who was said to be able to use storage magic. A lucky girl who was not only smart and good-looking, but would also never want for anything. A flower on a mountaintop, blooming miles out of his league.

And yet there she was, standing before him and talking with him, perhaps due to some passing fancy of her own.

We're classmates, he thought. They'd simply happened to meet alone in the classroom—it wasn't so terrible for them to make small talk, was it? She was probably a nice girl who would never judge someone based on differences in status or wealth.

With that in mind, Veil turned to speak to the girl, but then...

"S-say, just hunting with a sword isn't very effective, is it? What if I told you there was a magic you could learn that's perfect for hunting birds and jackalopes?"

"Huh...?"

What was she saying?

Over the following weeks, the girls' efforts at power leveling progressed swimmingly, with Reina, Pauline—and, to some extent, Mavis—increasing their strength by the day.

Mile didn't bother teaching Reina and Pauline any basics, nor did she instruct them as to how to naturally convert an image into a solid thought for specific magical purposes. Nevertheless, their skills improved.

She took care to stop them both at a level that would rank them only as "advanced," in terms of the school's training, so that no one would be aware of their immense progress. At least, this was her intention. She had no idea whether their classmates and instructors were actually fooled.

As for Mavis's sword training, there was no need to be secretive, so Mile poured all her efforts into the task. No matter what, Mavis was a still a completely normal person and the results fairly standard for the kind of intensive training Mile was giving her. It wouldn't exactly be a huge matter of note if she turned out somewhat more impressive than most. Because her practice partner was so fast, her reactions grew quicker, and her own movements did as well. Still, she remained very much in the category of what one might call "a passionate student with exceptional potential."

That progress, and in particular her improved reaction time, startled Elbert, but as he didn't attribute that success to Mile, she didn't mind him taking note.

Contrary to her fears, he paid very little attention to Mile herself beyond that first day. There were other students to attend to, and even if Mile were pressured into sword training, she would never be able to practice it seriously. Furthermore, it was out of line for a teacher to try and tamper with a student's future profession on a whim, so it was probably just as well that Elbert found other things to attend to.

Besides, it was only in terms of power and speed that Mile's swordsmanship was exceptional. She didn't possess any particular talents in the realm of basic technique—not in terms of handling, footwork, or even reading her opponent's movements. She was probably worthless and uninteresting to a sword instructor. After all, just having exceptional physical abilities did not mean that one had the makings of a true swordsman.

Furthermore, Mile *did* have exceptional magical ability, so it was clear to all that that would be how she made her fortune. It was easy to imagine that the two magic teachers had staked their claim, worried that interference might crush a student with great magical potential.

Even though Elbert was the principal and main instructor, he was still under employ himself. And if something went wrong, the higher-ups would catch wind of it.

"Spill it, Mile," Reina pressed Mile one afternoon as they sat in the classroom.

"Huh? Spill what?"

"Don't play dumb! I've been keeping an eye on you. What are you doing in the classroom with that guy every night after dinner?!"

"Er..." Mile mumbled, which only put fuel to the fire.

"Don't tell me you're *dating*, or that you've made some kind of arrangement..."

"We're not, we're not! I'm just using him as a sacrif... Er, no..."

"What do you mean? Explain yourself immediately!"

Mile explained herself.

Reina was horrified. "What are you thinking? You're making him take a bullet for you just so you don't stand out? I can't believe you..."

I bet that boy has a crush on Mile... Mavis and Pauline thought, sending up a prayer for his happiness.

"Well, it's true that you might be in danger if your family ever caught up with you, so I can't say that I don't understand. And since you've taught us so much, it would be wrong of me to complain. But still. Just keep it casual with this guy, okay?"

"Yes, ma'am..."

Veil, the orphan boy, was making vast strides in his magical skill, thanks to Mile's teaching.

She had quickly realized that Veil had neither immense magical power, nor a talent for spells that were particularly complicated. Anything that required extended concentration was similarly difficult for him. So, she decided to teach him two simple spells that he could easily reproduce.

The first was air bullets.

She figured that this would allow him to hunt small animals with ease.

By avoiding complicated productions, such as summoning, freezing, and shaping water, and by eliminating the need to do something labor-intensive like making or gathering rocks to shoot, he could hunt with something that would always be on hand, no matter where he was.

It was just compressing and propelling air, but it would be enough to kill—or at least render unconscious—any bird or small animal.

Furthermore, when facing larger opponents, it would be enough to break a monster's guard or drive them off, ensuring that the incident wouldn't end fatally. Above all else, the spell was short, fast, and easy to use.

In their world, wind-summoning magic was common, but there were limits to this power, due to the general ignorance of barometric gradients, thermal expansion, updrafts, and rotational power due to the Coriolis force. Certainly, they had yet to stumble upon the notion of compressing and firing air, so Mile's lesson was quite useful.

The second spell was a fatal technique: a magic blade that could cut down large prey and human enemies alike. For the sake of secrecy, and to maintain the element of surprise, the sword's blade was covered in a magical coating only just before launching an attack, a tactic that also helped to conserve magical energy.

By coating the sword in magic, its strength was increased exponentially, and the cutting edge became exceptionally thin. It was strong, durable, and sharp: the three components of a swordsman's dreams, made reality. Even a cheap, scrap metal sword could transform into a divine blade with this sort of magic!

As both were single-step processes, the procedures were easy to use, if a bit clumsy. Furthermore, the time it took to actualize both spells was quite short, so the consumption of magical energy and amount of brain fatigue caused by exerting the thought pulse were both fairly minimal.

Most importantly in the context of battle, the incantations

were short. They would still be reasonable to use, even during a sword fight.

With a magically enhanced blade in hand, Veil had become, without a doubt, a "magic knight."

Time and again, Mile warned him that he was absolutely forbidden to tell anyone else about their trainings. He was to keep these techniques to himself, Mile said, threatening that if he were ever to share this magic, then both he and the people he taught would disappear. However, she didn't bother to say who, exactly, would be responsible for the disappearances. Such details were troublesome to think of.

In truth, the air bullets were pretty easy to understand and imitate once one saw them. The magical blade, though, wasn't something that could be figured out with a glance.

Even so, she told him to keep it a secret. If she became known for inventing all sorts of magic, there would be a big to-do. Moreover, she would hate for her techniques to be used to kill hundreds of people or somehow alter the balance of the world. Still, as long as her name wasn't attached to the magic, maybe it wouldn't be all that bad if a spell did spread—especially if the spell in question was something like healing magic or a technique such as the air bullets, which had non-lethal applications.

Even if Mile's actions had some influence on the world, it wasn't as though God was looking to stop her. In fact, the gods appeared to have abandoned all management of her world, so any influence she might have most likely wouldn't be a problem.

Veil took the lessons he received from Mile every night and tried them out while hunting on his rest days. Then, the week after, he returned to discuss the results with Mile and receive new lessons based on his experience out in the field. Thus, while his skills didn't grow at the same rate as her party members', he nonetheless continued to improve steadily.

After Mile spilled the beans about Veil, he also began practicing swordplay with Mavis during school hours. Mavis was thrilled—not only because she had made a new friend, but because she finally had someone other than Mile to practice with. She sulked much less thereafter, so this was a positive development for Mile and the others, too.

"You know, I just realized something," Reina said one day. "'Veil' and 'Mile' are pretty similar names, aren't they? Is there any connection?"

"Huh? Ah, I guess you're right... No, it's just a coincidence. They both just happen to be short names that end in 'L' sounds! I mean, it would be weird to think that there is some connection between you and our classmate Nina just because both your names end in 'na,' wouldn't it?"

"I guess you're right..."

Despite Reina's pondering, the similarity between their names really was just a coincidence.

Still, Mile wondered, *what if it turned out that the person I chose to be my sacrificial lamb was actually my long-lost brother? No no no no no!* Mile shook her head wildly. *Don't even think about that!*

As the days went on, Mile's work continued steadily, with classroom lessons and training on the weekdays, money-earning and independent magic practice on the rest days, and sword training with Mavis and Veil in between.

Her bonds with her classmates, even those outside her party, began to deepen, and though their school wasn't a normal one, Mile soon found herself living a version of the normal student life she had always hoped for.

Even on the days when they trained fiercely, the other students thinking seriously of their futures, Mile saw it all as an enjoyable part of student life. The days passed in the blink of an eye, and soon, graduation was just around the corner.

One day near the end of their schooling, it was announced that they would be going out for some field training.

"...A class field trip?" Mile said.

"It's field training!" their instructor said. "What is this 'foldtripe' you're talking about?"

"Oh, like camp!"

"What are you even talking about?!"

They weren't going to be fighting ogres or anything. As many of the students were inexperienced hunters, they would be going out in search of orcs and goblins instead, in order for them to get accustomed to killing humanoid creatures. Without such preparation, there was a far higher chance of students dying in their first battle, surrounded only by their fellow rookie hunters rather than those with experience in the field.

On top of all that, field training would also give them the experience of camping in the wild.

Several days later, the students of the Hunters' Prep School found themselves in a forest about a half-day's walk from the capital. It was time for field training.

Each team—or rather, each party—would train together. As

usual, however, the teams had to be reorganized in order to address the imbalance of professions among the girls' parties. These rearrangements were left up to the students. As such things often happened when parties participated in large-scale operations, forming the parties themselves was considered good, practical experience.

While the intent was a general redistribution, complete disassembly of the existing parties would have been a waste of all the bonds the students had formed throughout their schooling. Therefore, the male students proposed that they only dissolve the girls' teams and redistribute their members among the boys' parties.

Of course, this plan dissolved the moment they rushed to extend invitations to the girls they hoped would join their parties.

"Wh-why don't you come with our team, Miley?"

"No, come with us!"

"No no, ours is definitely the best choice! There are four of us to look after you!"

"All of you shut up! Mile can serve as an advance guard for our party—we don't need any of you boys!"

"Huh? Miley's a magic user, isn't she? And just having you four girls in a party isn't really enough people."

Staring at the obstinate boys, Reina thought for second, then called to a boy standing toward the back. "Veil! Get over here with our party! If the girls from Team B join the rest of your party, they'll have another sword user on board, so they'll be fine without you. Team B, is that fine with you?"

"That's fine!!"

The four girls of Team B readily accepted, miffed at the boys of Teams 1 through 3, who had ignored them all and run straight to Team C Mile. Boys' Teams 4 and 6, as well as Team 5, Veil's team, had remained calm and unmoving—plus, there were some cute guys on Team 5, to boot.

"Way to go, Veil!"

Though they hadn't been able to snag Mile, the most coveted prize, the other boys of Team 5 got the chance to mingle with four cute girls, instead. It was a wise compromise.

"Now then," said one of the girls on Team A, "we'll divide up and join Teams 4 and 6!"

"What...?"

The five remaining girls on Team A shot the boys of Teams 1, 2, and 3 a cold look.

Team 1	*Boys: 5*
Team 2	*Boys: 5*
Team 3	*Boys: 5*
Team 4	*Boys: 4, Girls: 2*
Team 5	*Boys: 3, Girls: 4*
Team 6	*Boys: 4, Girls: 3*
Team C	*Boys: 1, Girls: 4*

"How did this happeeeeeeen?!?!" The boys of Teams 1 through 3 let loose a scream of frustration.

In truth, though, they had only themselves to blame, but from that moment until the day of their graduation, half the boys in the class looked upon Veil with jealous eyes.

"How did you end up with seven teams?" Elbert said, looking rather troubled. "I thought you were just going to shuffle the girls into the boys' teams for six parties. I only brought two extra hunters to chaperone..." Including Elbert, there were four instructors, so even with the other two hunters along, they were now one person short.

"It's fine. Mavis, your party will be all right without a guide, won't you?"

"Y-yeah..."

It was always Reina who called the shots, and among their classmates, Team C was known most frequently as "Reina's Crew." Still, as far as the instructors were concerned, Mavis was the leader.

And at that point, none of that really mattered, anyway.

"No problems here."

"Leave it to us!"

Reina and Mile gladly agreed. Ultimately, it just made things easier for them.

"Well then, I'll leave it to you!" Elbert said, trying not to let on how worried he truly was.

Deep in the forest, far from base camp...

"Starting today, I'm lifting the ban on using the magic I've taught you in front of others," Mile said. "We'll be graduating soon, and this magic is meant to be used in your life as hunters after graduation. It's about time to get some real practice.

"It would be strange if you could suddenly use this magic right after graduation, so if you start now and use it a little bit at a time in front of the rest of the class, then it will look like it's just the results of all our training. After all, you'll have to show your full power in the official exit exams.

"Now. Showing off your magic is one thing, but—You. Must. Not. Tell. Anyone. Else. How. To. Use. It... or share the fact that I was the one who taught you! No matter what, you must consider what you've learned to be a secret! Do I make myself clear?!"

At Mile's uncharacteristically serious expression, the four others nodded fiercely.

Slash!
Smack!
"Now me! My turn!"
"You guys..."
Pauline and Reina hunted the goblins gleefully, while Veil shied away.

He wasn't surprised by Reina's ferocity, as much as he wished he could be.

However, among their classmates, Pauline was known as a meek and mild-mannered magic user, specializing in healing and recovery. Amongst so many boisterous young women in their class, she was a breath of fresh air, a precious commodity not unlike Mile—or so she *had* been.

"Dance, water droplets, into a raging boil, grrrahh! DIIIIEEEEEEE!!!"

Mile collapsed onto a fallen tree in shock at Pauline's outburst, while Mavis slumped forward, as if her very soul had left her body.

By the time Mavis and company returned to base camp, most of the other teams had already arrived and were making preparations for dinner. Naturally, they were cooking their own meals, with the prey they had hunted themselves. In fact, sharing one's catch with other teams was forbidden. Those who weren't strong enough hunters would go to bed hungry. That was the hunters' way.

The students, unaccustomed to cooking, stumbled through their preparations.

"All right!"

While other teams put together nice little meals out of tree fruits they had gathered and the jackalopes they hunted in between exterminating goblins, Mile pulled an entire orc out of storage.

Shwack shwack shwack shwack shwack!

Mavis chopped the meat with lightning speed.

Bwoosh!

Reina roasted it with her fire magic.

"Soup's up!" Pauline called.

She had made a broth by pouring water into four bowls, along with gathered herbs, orc meat, and leafy greens, which she then boiled.

"Hey! What about mine?" asked Veil pitifully.

"Oh, I'm so sorry! It was only out of habit..."

Hurriedly, Pauline rustled up another portion.

"Grrahh!"

Blurb blurb...

Elbert watched them, slack-jawed.

"You all sure are handy..." he muttered.

CHAPTER 9 |

The Crimson Vow

O NE WEEK REMAINED until the graduation ceremony, or rather, the graduation assessment.

Mile was worried.

What would she do after graduation?

Would she be able to live carefree as a normal, average C-rank hunter in this country? With her storage magic, she could hunt and gather a great deal at once, so she wouldn't ever have to work particularly hard.

Six months had passed, and it didn't seem like anyone from her home country had a clue as to where she had disappeared to. She might never be able to go back, but at least it seemed like her troubles there were over.

With no real reason to wander elsewhere, Mile decided to remain in this country.

That much was fine, but she nonetheless had some worries.

I'll still have to go solo, won't I? If I travel with a party, eventually too much will be revealed.

It would hurt to part with the friends with whom she had grown so close, but each of them had their own circumstances and their own ambitions. Mavis and Pauline were close to their families, and she was sure that even Reina must have other friends and acquaintances. She couldn't burden them by clinging on forever.

The three of them accepted Mile, despite all her quirks. The thought of them ever rejecting her rendered Mile speechless and terrified.

Ultimately, Mile knew that where there were hellos, there were also goodbyes—just as in the beginning and end of her friendship with the Wonder Trio.

Someday, I'll surely be able to make more friends...

Her thoughts were optimistic, but her expression was dark.

"Where are we going to be stationed after graduation?"

"Huh???"

The three girls were returning to their room after dinner when they were blindsided—not for the first time—by Reina's words.

"Huh? What do you mean 'stationed'?"

"I mean where are we going to be based. As hunters."

"Huuhhhh???"

The three girls were still puzzled, but Reina continued. "Why are you so surprised? We're all going to be living as hunters after graduation, aren't we? Going solo is hard for a rookie hunter, so instead of ending up in a party full of strangers somewhere and getting used as a lackey, wouldn't it be better to party up with your bosom pals?

"Besides, none of you really have anywhere to go, do you? What I see here is a runaway, a fugitive, and an old geezer's concubine!"

"Eugh..."

Mavis, Mile, and Pauline were lost for words.

"B-but, I've got a mother and a younger brother..."

"Would they be glad to see you sold off for their own gain? Do you really think that would make them happy?"

"Er..."

"Right now, you're living well enough on your own. Shouldn't your family's number one concern be to make sure that you're happy?"

"..."

Pauline was silent.

After Pauline, Mile spoke up. "I-I'm, I'm... kind of a weirdo, though. All I'd do is cause trouble for you all..."

"........."

"And?" Reina broke the silence that followed Mile's words.

"Huh?"

"Go on!"

"No, well, I'm just saying that compared to you guys, I'm kind of weird, so I'd be nothing but a burden to you!"

"We already heard that. If you've got something else to say, then spit it out!"

"Huh?"

"..........."

"Well, we're going to have to stay at the cheaper inns for the foreseeable future," Mavis said, matter-of-factly. "Getting a four-person room shouldn't be too expensive, and it'll certainly be nicer than this place."

"B-but..." Mile tried to rebut her friend, but Reina wouldn't let her.

"Quiet! The matter is settled! Besides, you made us a promise on the day of the entrance ceremony!"

"Ah..."

That was when Mile remembered.

The conversation they had shared in that very room, six months ago.

"If you get any party invitations from here on out, just tell them, 'I already promised I'd be with my roommates.' And, if anyone tries to ask you on a date, tell them, 'I'm not interested right now. I want to focus on my training.' Got it?!"

"Y-yes, ma'am!"

"Th-that was a promise...?" Mile said. "I thought that was just a line to turn down the others' offers..."

"Enough of your excuses! It's already been settled!"

Silenced, Mile took a moment to reflect. She had striven with all her might to be normal, all so she could finally make friends. Now, trying to distance the dear friends she had made just so she could continue pretending to be normal... She would have been completely missing the point.

"Ha... Aha ha ha... Gnh..."

"Waaah..."

Seeing Mile giggling through tears, Pauline started to cry also.

Mavis patted them both on the shoulders.

"You see? As long as the red blood still flows through our veins, we will never betray our comrades! Our friendship is immortal!"

"Yeah!!!"

"I have a request."

Three days before the final assessment, after their afternoon lessons, Mile and company were called to the office of the principal, and head instructor, Elbert. When they arrived, they were shocked to see Elbert kneel before them.

"I'm begging you. The final assessment is in three days, and I need each of you to give it your all!"

"Huh...?"

Elbert proceeded to elaborate.

Six years ago, the Hunters' Prep School had been established on a trial basis, thanks to the efforts of Count Christopher, a legendary S-rank hunter turned noble.

Since its founding, many splendid hunters had emerged from the school's ranks, but their track record was still short, and they had yet to produce anyone of A-rank or greater. As long as the bulk of nobles didn't consider the program a waste of funding, and assuming it did well upon being thoroughly assessed, the school would be able to expand to full capacity. However, there was also the possibility that the budget would be cut, or withdrawn entirely...

"Normally, the selection exams for the class following yours should already have been completed by now," Elbert said. "However, as the next term's budget hasn't yet been finalized, they've been delayed. We haven't told the current prospective students, but at this rate, there's a chance that the school might not make it to the next term at all."

"I see..." said Reina, who seemed at least somewhat aware of the circumstances. "I did think it odd that there didn't seem to be any selection exams happening. The ones for our class were all finished before last year's final assessment..."

"I noticed that the facilities and equipment had yet to be refreshed, and I guessed it was something like that..." Pauline muttered.

Mile, who had bypassed the selection exam, and Mavis, who was generally oblivious to such matters, had not suspected a thing.

"Currently, under Count Christopher, this prep school came into being with the intention to allow hunters to bypass the minimum term requirement for promotion, instilling even those outside the school with the abilities necessary to reach higher levels. The eventual aim was to gain enough of a foothold to start changing the rules and regulations of the guild as a whole.

"It's very important that we not allow this place to be squashed."

With this, he looked at the four of them.

"As your opponents for the mock battles in the exit exams, we've requested the participation of a party that's at the very top of B-rank, nearly A-rank. Furthermore, there may be quite a crowd in addition to our patron, Count Christopher. The officials of the local guildhalls will come to see the results of the school's curriculum, while the guild masters themselves will be on hand to take a look at you rookies. Hunters will scout graduates for their parties. Nobles, wealthy folk, and commoners starved for entertainment, all love the spectacle and novelty. Most importantly, however, it's quite possible that the finance officials who hold our budget in their hands may be in attendance, perhaps even along with the king."

Elbert bowed his head. "I'm begging you, please show us your best at the assessment! I know you girls have been hiding your true potential, and it's easy to imagine that there must be a reason for that. Therefore, all of us instructors have pretended not to notice.

"However, even knowing this, I must implore you! Without this school, young people like you would have to waste precious years of their lives gathering herbs and hunting jackalopes. This school is an absolute necessity! We need you to help beat this into everyone's heads!

"I beg you! I don't want this school to disappear!" Elbert bowed so low that his forehead was on the desk. The four girls stood, gaping, for some time.

"Leave it to us!"

Two voices rang throughout the office, shocking Mile.

"How can one possibly refuse such a sincere request from the teacher who has cared for us?!" Reina said. "When this will have such an immense impact on the lives of all future hunters?! This school is vital for people like us. We *will* meet your expectations!"

"Besides," Mavis added, "this is a splendid chance to put our names out there. How could we run from that?! Please leave it to us!"

"...I beg you," the principal said again.

Seeing Elbert, who was usually so confident, with such a pitiful look, Mile decided, finally, to cooperate.

Thank goodness she had prepared a sacrificial lamb for just such an occasion...

And so, the day of the final assessment arrived.

It was held in a stadium near the palace, a spectacular, recently built state-of-the-art facility. Not only could it hold numerous guests, but it also employed strong barriers and protection magic, so as to avoid damages to the facilities or injuries to the viewers during magical battles.

"All of our preparations have paid off. Today, we'll see not only the finance officers, but also other influential nobles. Even their Majesties the king and queen, and their Highnesses the prince and princess will be in attendance. The countries' guilds will be well represented, as well.

"This year, when we were extending the invitations, we told them, 'We have some truly excellent rookies.' So please don't let us down!"

At Elbert's proclamation, Mavis and Reina swapped looks of exhilaration, while Pauline stood awed. Mile was white as a sheet.

In just a few short moments, the exit exam mock battles would begin. Their results would determine not only the fates of the graduates, but the fate of the Hunters' Prep School itself. The exit exam mock battles, called grad battles for short, weren't undertaken by all of the students. Only a handful were hand-selected by the instructors to participate. Typically, these were the students who had the abilities and characteristics to qualify as a C-rank hunter, the rank with which they would graduate if they did well. Even if the students selected didn't wish to participate, in many cases, they would be strongly encouraged to do so by the instructors.

Those who failed the exam, refused it, or were judged by the instructors to be underqualified to participate, graduated automatically at a D-rank.

Many of these students still strove to rise to C-rank relatively quickly, having met the minimum requirements through their training at the school. Even failing wasn't such a tragedy, as these students were only considered to be just a bit lacking. After all, anyone who was truly useless would have dropped out ages before.

This time, there had been forty exam hopefuls. The entire class. Since they had nothing to lose, the students had all figured that there was no harm in trying. Even before Elbert's request, Mile herself had hoped to participate in the exam. Being a D-rank would be inconvenient for a solo hunter, and so she had put in her application early on, before Reina had proposed that they form a party after graduation.

Of the forty students in their class, eighteen would be participating in the grad battles: the four from Mile's party; five swordsmen, including Veil; two spear users; three archers; and four magic users. Their opponents for the battle would be the B-rank party, the Roaring Mithrils, who had only six members—unusual for a group of their rank.

Parties of F to C-rank often had smaller numbers, four to seven people on average, but at B-rank and higher, you normally saw parties of ten members and up. Sometimes, there were even twenty or thirty hunters on a roster, so that if any member was injured or ill, they could still take on jobs, and the party could divide and conquer. In most of those cases, however, the parties often included people with lesser skill, as well as a handful with less-than-ideal personalities...

In the case of the Roaring Mithrils, however, their numbers were few but truly elite. Everyone in the party was an exceptionally skilled hunter. The group consisted of their leader, a greatsword wielder of about 40 years old; a skilled lancer of approximately the same age; a youngish swordsman in his mid-20s; and three mages, one older, one in his late 30s, and another closer to her late 20s. They lacked an archer, but with mages who were skilled in long-range attacks, the party had no need for one.

Finally, Elbert, the principal, announced the start of the exit exam mock battles. The test began.

In order to truly show off the test participants' skills, they had to face up against a party with a clear difference in raw power. For this purpose, the school typically requested a B-rank party. For them, the battle would be an easy job, as any hunter in the group could take on several students at once.

Since being able to work well with rookies was a necessary skill for any high-ranking hunter, the test takers would be facing only the younger members of the party, while the leader and the older mage would sit back and observe the participants' performance. Still, though they were young in comparison to their leader, the rest of the party members were still B-rank hunters, each with such strength that, in any other party, they would have been heavy hitters themselves.

The first several mock battles progressed smoothly. While the test takers didn't win the matches, thanks to their opponents, they were able to show off their strengths and come across as worthy fighters. Each had a satisfying battle. Of course, a great deal of this was thanks to their opponents' considerable skill and forethought; however, most of the participants didn't appear to notice this and seemed satisfied with their own display.

Finally, it was down to Mile's party and Veil.

Mile's group would be tested first, and Veil would be last.

Naturally, Elbert had arranged it this way, on Mile's request.

"You can do it, Pauline!"

"I know you can win! Keep your cool, and be careful!"

"The whims of fate can turn a battle. Just give it your all, and fight with no regrets."

The other three shouted words of encouragement as Pauline trembled from stress and nerves. Her timid nature had reared its head, and she couldn't seem to muster the will to continue.

"It's nice of you to say those things, but... I guess if I were a freak like you, Mavis, or if I had Reina's childish stubbornness, or maybe if I were as oblivious as Mile, then I wouldn't be so nervous..."

"Er..."

Mavis, Reina, and Mile had taken fatal blows before their matches even began.

"It's your turn now, is it, young lady? What are you trembling for? It'll be fine."

Pauline's opponent was Olga, a young magic user in her late 20s, who had already faced several other participants who specialized in utility and healing magic. She had the same magical specialties as Pauline. However, as a B-ranker, she could also wield a staff reasonably well in self-defense.

"P-please treat me kindly..."

"Of course. Are those girls over there your friends? They're all so little! If the prep school is letting in bitty things like that, I wonder if their standards have fallen..."

Clack!

"What's this? Are you trying to knock me out in your first blow? Maybe they should disqualify you..."

Crack!

"Well then, I suppose I'll let you take the first strike. Do as you like..."

"Shut the hell up, you flat-chested bitch!"

"Wh..."

Time seemed to freeze.

The acoustics of the stadium were designed to create a calculated reverberation so that spectators could hear the conversation between the fighters. Although quiet comments did not always reach the spectators' seats, Pauline's words echoed through the arena easily—which meant that, while the onlookers hadn't heard Olga's first utterance, which she'd made half to herself, Pauline's scream of rage had reached their ears. Quite easily.

"Wh-what did that girl just say?!"

Not only had Pauline just cursed at a B-rank hunter, her senior, but she had insulted the woman's body. It was an egregious jab.

Worse still was the fact that she had done so quite loudly, in front of the country's bigwigs, the leadership of numerous guilds, and a number of other spectators.

Their party's name was going to become famous—just not exactly for the reason they hoped.

Reina clutched her head. Mavis paled.

"Eugh... F-flat-chested..."

Behind them both, Mile was devastated.

"What's with this rookie?!"

"Has she no manners at all?"

Even among the spectators' seats, which had first fallen silent, a clamor now began to grow.

"It seems like she snapped. That's the only explanation," Reina started. "But Pauline's not the sort of person to lose her cool just because someone insults her. Do you think that woman was making fun of us? Now I guess we just have to wait and see whether Pauline can just shout back insults—or if she can back it up with some results."

Even Reina had been flustered, but she was quick to recover. Was it simply because of her own brashness or because she truly believed in her friend?

"You insulted my friends—you're going to regret that!" Pauline cried.

"Fl-flat-chested... flat-chested bitch..." The older woman was trembling with rage.

Fairly tall and slender, Olga was, in fact, quite a beauty. Combined with the fact that she was a B-rank hunter, this had made her rather popular in the past. However, she had yet to find herself a good man, and as the years went on, she felt more and more conscious of her lack of a partner.

Slapped in the face by Pauline's insult, Olga was reeling. "Flat-chested... Flat-chested..."

"Blaze, O heart of mine! Let my rage become the flames and the fire that burns before me! FIIIRE! BWAAAAAAAAAAAAALLL!!!"

A shuddering ball of flame, nearly a meter in diameter, appeared before Pauline, swiftly snapping Olga back to reality.

A fireball? Olga thought. *It's huge, but it doesn't look very cohesive. Of course, it's quite impressive that a specialist in utility magic can use an attack spell at all, but it can't possibly have much power...*

"GOOOOO!!!"

The fireball moved toward Olga, who shielded herself calmly. "Come to me, magic barrier, shield me from that fireball!"

The ball collided with Olga's conjured barrier; however, without sufficient power to destroy the shield, it simply washed over it.

Fire covered Olga's field of vision, but she was unhurt.

"With attack magic like that—*gwahh!*" Olga screamed in anguish as a sudden pain raked her left side.

When she looked to her left, she saw a staff, jammed between the gaps in her leathers.

The end of the staff withdrew and flew towards her again.

"You braaaat!" Ignoring the pain in her side, she pushed the staff off with all her might and in quick succession, swung her own weapon at her opponent's body and launched a kick at Pauline's stomach with her right leg.

Huff... Huff... Huff...

Olga quickly assessed her injury, and while the pain was great, it didn't appear to have broken any bones or ruptured internal organs. Even though the attack had been aimed at a gap, her leather armor had done its job well enough.

Struck by both the kick and the heavy staff blow, Pauline collapsed. Perhaps Olga had broken one of her bones.

Though Olga might be reprimanded later for using excessive force on a student, it had nonetheless been unseemly for that girl to speak as she had to a senior hunter. Olga's response had only been inevitable.

"Erase the pain and heal the wounds! High Heal!" As the healing magic began to wash her pain away, Olga let out a sigh. She glanced her opponent's way to find Pauline already on her feet again.

Pauline's face was twisted in pain, though, and her left arm was bent at an unnatural angle.

"How rude!" the girl said. "I fought so hard to surprise you with that blow, and you just shook it off with a single spell? Healing magic is so clever and useful, though... And with that in mind..." Pauline trailed off with a crooked grin, then said, "Numb the pain, restore the bones, join and mend them! Restore the tissue, repair the blood vessels, refresh the nerves! Mega Heal!"

"Wh-what is that?!" Olga said.

"Allow me to..." Pauline swung her left arm, which should have been completely shattered, leaving Olga and the spectators lost for words.

Silence fell over the stands again.

"H-how...?" Olga muttered.

Simply being able to use recovery magic and basic healing magic, as well as having decent self-defense skills, would be enough to see one comfortably recognized as a C-rank healing magic user. On top of that, though, Pauline could use attack magic—weak though it may have been. Nevertheless, she could swing her staff at full force. And there'd been that ridiculous healing spell, too!

Once, Olga had heard from a physician about the existence of a powerful healing magic—one that surpassed even her own "High Heal" spells. It had the power to mend shattered limbs in an instant and was far beyond what she herself would ever be able to achieve.

And that little girl had such an ability?

"Impossible..."

Ignoring Olga's muttering, Pauline started to chant another spell. "Burn, O heart of mine! Let my rage become the flames, and come to me, blazing fire!"

"Wh-what? The awkward fireball again? Do you really think I'm going to fall for your little smoke and mirror trick again?!" Olga screamed in rage. Combined with the healing magic she had just seen, she was certain the girl was trying to make a fool of her.

"Hm? Fireball? What are you talking about? What I used before was 'Fire Wall.' *This* is Fireball."

"Wh...?"

Pauline continued her spell, unconcerned with Olga. "Compress!"

"No way! Your only attack magic is that faulty spe..."

The fire shrank and split into two complete orbs. Olga cried out.

"Do you think I went through special training just to acquire that measly level of attack magic?" Pauline said. "Now, hammer of rage, bear down on the fool who insulted my companions! GOOOOOO!!!"

Ka-bwoosh!

Before she could react, the fire orbs clipped both of Olga's shoulders, and she flew backwards into the stone wall.

Olga sat slumped, her face blank.

"Round oveeeeer!"

As the end of the match was announced, Pauline turned on her heel and walked away.

"WHOAAAAAAAAA!!!"

There was a great roaring cheer from the stands. In reply, Pauline raised her right hand gently.

"So that's the 'amazing rookie' you mentioned then, is it?!" said the finance officer. "I would say that 'amazing' was an understatement! To tell the truth, I didn't believe you. I thought you were just exaggerating so that you could get your budget through. I'm sorry to have doubted you!"

Elbert was taken aback at the finance officer's candid apology.

Beside them, the prep school's benefactor, Count Christopher, was grinning happily.

"That is one impressive young lady!" said the king. "It's nearly unheard of to see such powerful healing magic, especially in combination with ingenuity and the ability to launch attack magic as well. In fact, she would make an excellent court magician. Which means this school is useful for scouting talent, after all. And this term has been particularly fruitful..."

Elbert made a strange face.

"Hm? What is it?"

Elbert answered, his expression troubled, "Um, well, there was something I heard this girl say earlier..."

"Oh? What was it, then?"

"She was laughing, but I think her exact words were, 'Ha ha! I'm only the weakest of the Four Sages!'"

"........"

"You did it!"

"You were wonderful! This is the start of a glorious future for our party!"

"That was amazing, Pauline!"

With Pauline's pre-match insults already far from their minds, the other three congratulated their friend on her victory.

Pauline sat down, red in the face, her expression still twisted. The tension that had built up as a result of her anger seemed to finally be fading, her sanity restored—or perhaps, she was suddenly recalling all the things she had said in front of that huge crowd, inspired by the flights of fancy born from Mile's bedtime stories.

"Well, Pauline did her best. You can't afford to lose, either!"

Mavis nodded at Reina's words, equipping herself with her practice sword and stepping out into the area where the mock battles were being held.

Then came the second hunter who would surely suffer at the hands of his own hubris—Mavis's opponent, a swordsman in his mid-twenties. At his age, normally, he would have still been well within C-rank. However, not only was he already a B-rank, he was one of the Roaring Mithrils. While he was still nowhere near the level of their leader, an A-rank hunter named Gren, the man had enough talent to be considered a true prodigy.

Moreover, he had a pompous manner and a pretty face, and he was popular with all the ladies in the capital, which surely played a role in making the Roaring Mithrils just a little more famous.

Yet no matter how young he was, there was still nearly a decade between him and the seventeen-year-old Mavis. That age difference was representative of the difference in practice and experience between the two sword users, as well—not to mention the discrepancies in physical build and power.

Their difference in real combat experience was perhaps the most notable. For Mavis, who never employed any kind of trick, the chance of winning against a sly hunter like this one was extremely slim.

However, such things didn't concern Mavis. She knew she just had to throw all her strength into the battle. Thus, with that in mind, she exchanged formalities with her opponent and drew her sword.

"I humbly accept your lessons," said Mavis.

"Sure," the swordsman replied, in the magnanimous words of a senior hunter. "Go ahead and give it all you've got."

"Special technique, 'Godspeed Blade,' attack!"

With that declaration, Mavis launched her offensive.

Whoosh!

"Whoa!"

Shing!

The swordsman blocked Mavis's lightning-fast attacks, his face panicked.

Clang clang clang clang clang clang clang clang clang!

Mavis was unrelenting, and as the swordsman continued to block her attacks, his expression grew dire.

"Guh! What is this?"

Facing a far fiercer battle than he expected, the swordsman answered each one of Mavis's sallies with rapid attacks of his own.

However, Mavis fielded these blows almost nonchalantly.

"Huh? Is this all...?" Mavis said. Lately, her only opponents had been Mile and Veil, as the other students were now loathe to go up against the three of them. As a result, her expectations had become somewhat skewed.

Thus, though she had come in with high expectations about the challenge of facing a B-rank hunter, she found that he was slower than Mile or even Veil. Was this truly her competition?

Unthinking, she muttered in disappointment. "Wh-what did...?"

Despite putting a real effort into his swings, the hunter was being crushed by a prep school graduate.

His pride in his B-rank status was shrinking to just an iota, and his face began to pale.

"Well then, let's try it from here..." Mavis muttered.

Thwack thwack thwack thwack thwack thwack thwack thwack thwack!

"Wh-whoa..." Though he had only narrowly managed to protect himself in the face of Mavis's attacks, the swordsman was finally getting used to her speed, which was gradually increasing. "Well, now that I'm finally warmed up, let's do this for real!"

"Wh-what...?" Mavis exclaimed, then pressed forward.

Blam blam blam blam blam blam blam blam blam!

Ka-shing!

"Gwahh!" The young swordsman took a blow directly to his left side and crumpled nearly in half.

"WHOOOOOOOAAAAAA!!!" An excited roar rose from the stands. The rookie had just felled a supposedly expert swordsman in a single blow!

Yet the test had only gone on for a short time, and there was no call announcing the end of the battle. The aim of the match wasn't to decide a victor, but to see the abilities of the test taker, so calling it too soon would defeat the purpose of the fight.

"Ugh..." the swordsman groaned. Though Mavis used only

a practice sword, it was no different from being struck with an iron bar. Things were not helped by the fact that the hunter wore leather, rather than metal, armor.

The swordsman mustered all his determination in order to stand, biting back the pain.

As he finally readied his sword again, Mavis spoke coolly.

"Currently, I'm using 'Godspeed Blade' at 1.2 times speed. Next up, I'll face you at 1.3 times."

"Wh-what...?"

Ka-slam!

"Gwahh!!"

Even in perfect physical condition, he couldn't have stood up to this expedited blade—in his current condition, there was no contest.

"Match oveeeeer!! Someone call a medic!"

The end of the match was finally declared, as it became clear that the swordsman wouldn't be returning to his feet without assistance.

Still unsatisfied by the battle, Mavis huffed, disappointed. "I still had two more levels..."

Then, amidst ear-splitting cheers, she left the stage.

"Wh-what was happening with that swordsman?! She was so fast I couldn't even see her blade!" The finance officer was enraptured. Count Christopher's eyes were wide as well.

"That was incredible! This girl must have been that 'amazing rookie'!" said the king.

"Lately, her favorite sentence has been, 'How come I'm the only one getting left behind?!'" Elbert replied, a strange expression on his face.

"My, she was rather splendid..." said the princess from behind them as her heart began to beat faster.

"Great work!" Reina called to Mavis as she moved to the center of the stadium, a daring grin spread across her face.

One of the Roaring Mithrils' magic users, a man in his late thirties, looked to the elderly mage, then to Gren—the sword-wielding party leader—with a troubled expression, but both of them were silent, impassive.

The magic user had confidence in his strength. Certainly, he was no match for Anselm the Dragonslayer, the old-timer who was their party's chief magic user. However, the difference between them boiled down to nothing more than a difference in experience. Anselm had lived and worked as a mage and hunter for nearly twice as long as he, so naturally his knowledge and technique were far superior. By the time the man reached Anselm's age, he would be just as strong or stronger. In fact, he was already stronger than the old-timer had been back in his thirties. Even now, had he fought with all his might, there was a chance that he could beat the now-enfeebled old man.

Still, the man, who was normally filled with such confidence, was trembling.

Somehow, members of the Roaring Mithrils, a party said to be on the verge of an A-rank promotion, had been bested by graduates of the Hunters' Prep School not once, but twice.

That was absolutely unforgivable. Who would ever nominate them for an A-rank at this rate? Who would even entrust their party with high-ranking jobs?

The more he thought about it, the more sure he became: there was no way that any B-rank hunter could possibly lose to a student. Yet they had. Twice in a row! It had to be a set-up—a plot by an enemy who wanted to drag the Roaring Mithrils through the mud and ruin their reputations.

The school had produced some strong rookies, clearly. But the notion that there might be more who were even stronger was ridiculous! However, what if that were true? What if, by some slim chance, he lost as well?

Was he really the right one for the task? Would it not be better for the old-timer, or even their leader, to handle this?

Was he really going to lose to a child in front of all these people? If that happened...

Steeling his troubled heart, the mage proceeded onto the field.

The girl was a combat magic specialist, so they kept some distance between themselves as they squared off.

"Looking forward to a good match," she called. "By the way, do you have any family?"

"...!!"

Why would she ask a thing like that?!

Was she already thinking about his survivors?!

Hopelessly intimidated, the mage lost all composure. Then again, his composure had probably already fled before he ever set foot on the field.

"O raging flames of the deep, consume my enemy and burn him to the ground! Hellfire!"

"Wh—you idiot! Stooooop!!" The scream came from the Roaring Mithrils' waiting area.

Their dismay was understandable. The spell was one that was

meant only to be used against high-level monsters. It was a fatal spell, and unless the caster purposely held back or stopped the spell before it ran its course, there would be no hope of survival.

It was a mighty spell, his most powerful and the fastest he could fire—and in a maelstrom of fear, unease, and agitation, he had just reflexively fired it straight at a young girl.

Though he had considerable ability, the mage, whom his elder party member still considered "half-baked," was naturally a backline fighter. His role was to fire off powerful attacks of magic from the back of the group. Thanks to his party's advance and mid-guard fighters, never once in his years of combat had he ever taken a direct attack.

He had almost never dealt with a magical attack, either. Save for elder dragons, monsters weren't particularly bright, and even monsters who could use magic tended to attack only the nearest enemy, meaning they hardly ever reached the back line. Besides, guarding against the magic wrought by monsters was a breeze for someone of his abilities.

Even when facing other humans in combat, serving as an escort or the like, it was rare to face magic users of particular skill. A person who was particularly skilled in magic, after all, had no need to waste their time on criminal acts and common banditry. Therefore, the magic user, who had been a part of high-ranking parties from an early age onward, had never been put in a truly life-threatening situation. As a result, he was relatively unprepared to come face to face with combat magic—his own specialty.

When he volunteered for this job, he had figured merely that it might be a good opportunity to train juniors. He hadn't thought that it would disintegrate into a situation that would cause the party's reputation to crumble—nor had he ever suspected that he himself would be put in a position where he might contribute to their ruin. Mentally unprepared, the mage's heart filled with fear and unease.

If she doesn't hold back or stop before she hits me...or if she makes a mistake due to some lack of skill and I'm struck with magic that powerful—or if she feigns a lack of skill and actually hits me with a perfectly aimed blow...

Wife and children aside, could he really stand to die a pointless death in this arena?!

At this thought, his mind went reflexively to the one attack spell he could use in an instant, the one that would never fail him. In moments, the little girl was surrounded by raging hellfire, her form obscured.

When the mage came to his senses and realized what he had done, he was stunned, but it was already too late. Until the flames burned themselves out, there was nothing he could do. The only thing left to worry about was whether or not any bones would remain to hand over to her loved ones.

"Ah, aah, aaaah..." The mage collapsed on the ground. The spectators, believing themselves to have witnessed the little girl's demise, were shocked into silence.

And then, the flames gradually subsided, revealing...

"Oh? Are we finished already?" Reina asked, cool as a cucumber.

"Wait, huh...?" the mage said.

"My specialty is fire magic," Reina explained, "but lately I've been getting pretty good with ice and protection magic too." She looked down at the mage, who was sitting on the ground, devoid of all will to fight, and muttered, "When people say that 'the best offense is a strong defense,' I suppose this is what they mean?"

Then, she began to chant a spell that would settle the battle once and for all. Indeed, it was the same spell that she had been attacked with: "O raging flames of the deep, consume my enemy and burn him to the ground! Hell—"

"Th-that's enough!! Match oveeeeeer!!!" The referee signaled the end of the fight.

Her face remained calm, but truthfully, Reina was a bit angry.

"Wh-what on earth was that?! What *happened* with the students this term?!" The finance officer did not conceal his amazement.

"I didn't catch the attack spell," said Count Christopher, "but it could've been a real catastrophe if it hadn't been stopped when it was. There's no doubt it would have struck, and... At any rate, that defense magic alone is more than ample indication of her abilities, so that should be enough for the test." Relief visible on his face.

Elbert was silent. Thought he had suspected that the four girls had hidden their abilities, he had never imagined the extent of their true powers.

"Th-that was amazing! Truly amazing!" said the king.

"Father, if I went to the prep school too, do you think I could become as strong as they are?"

The king turned to the bright-eyed prince and princess and patted them softly on the head, muttering, "Is this the dawning of a new era? Our world has been stagnant for so long..."

"Win."

That was Reina's message as she passed Mile, who grimaced.

As they watched Reina retreat and Mile take her place, the Roaring Mithrils began to quarrel.

"She's a magic user, so I should obviously be the one to fight!"

"No, look at her! She's definitely a swordsman! I'll fight!"

The oldest mage and the middle-aged lancer both argued their cases, explaining why they should be the next to take the field.

After listening for a while, Gren, the greatsword wielder, passed down his decision as the party leader.

"I will fight."

Now, Mile and Gren—the leader of the Roaring Mithrils—stood face to face in the center of the arena.

"What the hell are you guys?" he asked her.

"Huh? You mean us? We're just average graduates from the Hunters' Prep School, aren't we? Perhaps we're a bit of an anomaly..."

"How can you be 'average' if you're an anomaly?!"

Mile grinned at the man's straightforward response—after all, who *wouldn't* smile in the face of a quip like that? "Let me introduce you to Mile, the completely normal magic swordsman!"

"Who the hell is that?!"

"Oh, er, well I figured if I called myself that, it would catch on. That's good, isn't it? Being 'normal'..."

"That's not my question! Well, actually, I've got a question about that as well, but... What is this 'magic swordsman' business?! Are you a mage or a swordsman? Which is it?!"

"I guess you'll just have to fight me and find out!"

"Well then, let's start!"

And so, the battle began.

Blam bang thwack bang!

Sh-sh-sh-sh-sh-sh-sh-sh-shing!

After exchanging a number of fiercely powerful blows, Mile's high-speed assault began.

It was no longer possible to even hear separate strikes.

The volleys continued at such speed that the spectators couldn't see their blades, and, stunned and enthralled, they began to cheer.

"Well, this is getting fun. Mind if I go a little bit faster?" Mile asked.

"Y-you brat! You've been holding back?! Go for it, show me your best!"

"Okay!"

KLANG KLANG KLANG!

KA-KLANG KA-KLANG KA-KLANG!

It appeared that Gren had been holding back as well, and even with Mile's speed increased, it was clear they were equally matched. Gren's expression began to twist, but it wasn't from pain or discomfort.

Anyone who knew Gren would recognize the expression as one of his rare smiles.

"Ha."

"Bwa..."

"Ahahahahahahahaha!"

"Bwahahahahahahaha!"

"No way... The boss is smiling..."

Over in the waiting area, the Roaring Mithrils exchanged looks of shock.

"What is this that we're witnessing?" the finance officer muttered.

"The last dance between a demon and an angel?" It was the prince who answered him.

It certainly wasn't wrong to say that it looked as though the two were dancing.

The art of dance, and the art of war. There was an inextricable link between the two.

"Can you see their swords?" the king asked.

Elbert answered him with a soft, "No..."

The hands of Count Christopher, the legendary S-rank hunter, were shaking. "Elbert, can I...?"

"You mustn't, Count!"

It seemed he wanted to fight as well.

Though the spectators had begun cheering, they fell again into a hush. They didn't have time to chatter or shout.

If they took the time to do that, they wouldn't be able to engrave the battle into their memories. Surely, the details of this fight would be passed down again and again for ages to come...

Ka-snap!

"Oh..."

Unable to take the strain of such force, Mile's sword finally snapped. It was only a cheap thing meant for mock battle, so this was no surprise.

Mile lacked Gren's technique, and the burden of the sword wore on her. However, neither of them was satisfied.

"Want to change swords?" Gren offered. "You can use your own if you like."

Mile knew she couldn't possibly use her mystery blade here. "No, I'm fine."

Instead, she slowly drew the thumb and forefinger of her left hand over the remaining portion of her blade, stopping at the end of the space where the blade used to be.

"Special technique, 'Light Beam Blade'!" she said, and a blade of light appeared there, in the trail left by her fingers.

"What is *that*?!" Gren's shout echoed throughout the stadium.

"So, you're a swordsman who fights with a magic blade! That's what makes you a a magic swordsman."

"Huh? No, it's just that I can use magic, too..."

Smack!

"W-well, fine! Let's continue!"

"Okay!!"

Gren told himself that she couldn't possible have cast such a difficult spell silently, just by waving her hand. The audience, on the other hand, had been unable to hear their hushed conversation and hadn't realized that Mile had cast the spell without words.

And then, the fierce battle began to rage again, as Mile used high-speed moves, turned backflips, and maneuvered to her heart's content. With her full physical potential hidden and limits put on her godly strength, Mile was a fine opponent for Gren—though she was no expert swordsman.

"Clone Technique!" she cried.

"What is this mimicry?!"

Mile had tried to enact a copycat technique, running quick

laps between two points, but such things were not so simple in reality. All Gren had to do was swing his sword down in the middle of her path for an easy strike.

"Th-that's fighting dirty..."

"Be serious!" Gren retorted.

Mile stopped her maneuver and moved back into the fray. "Battering Blade!"

"Whoa! You've got a lot of power in that body—not *just* speed!"

Gren, blocking Mile's attack, sounded surprised at the amount of strength behind her swing.

What came next was one punishing blow after another. Mile's strength and speed made up for what she lacked in skill and technique, but with Gren's skill and experience, he stood up to her head-on.

No tricks were needed—this was a straightforward, all-out battle.

How fun! How exciting!

A grin of delight was plastered on Mile's face, the sort of smile that even a much older adult could understand. In her previous life, she had never taken part in any competitive sports, spending all her time on games, RPGs, and the like.

The fight was a time of bliss that she wished she could enjoy forever.

However, no matter what she did, it would have to come to an end soon.

Mile had lost herself in the moment, but the second it became clear that Gren was reaching his limit, his pace slowing, she came back to reality.

Crap! I did it agaaaain!!

Though she had planned to show off a bit from the start, she had never intended to go this far. Everything had its limits.

Her face paling, Mile asked Gren in a small voice, "Sorry, I have a bit of a situation. I need to lose. Could you beat me? Ah— but, painlessly! If you can!"

"Got it."

In Gren's decades as a hunter, he had seen a great deal. He quickly understood that Mile was subject to some peculiar circumstance, and that she'd gone further than she had meant. It seemed that he himself had become part of the problem, and as he'd certainly had more than enough fun, he didn't mind following through with her request.

"Hooah!" he grunted.

"Gwahh! You got meeee!!"

They were two peas in a pod.

A perfect pair.

The spectators were baffled to see such a brutal end to the elegant match, but soon, speculations began to spread throughout the stadium.

"There must have been some special circumstance."

"I bet she let him win out of deference to a senior hunter."

The jig was up.

Yet, standing in the middle of the grounds, Mile's performance was not yet complete.

"You may have won against me, but take heed! There is another, before whom we Four Sages are nothing but mere mice! Lord Veil, please avenge me!"

"Huuuhh?!?!"

At Mile's sudden declaration, both Gren, and Veil, over in the waiting area, let out cries of confusion.

"H-hey, kid..."

"Look it's complicated! Complicated!" she said.

"I-I see... Wh-what is this impertinence?! Who would dare stand up to me?!"

Seeing Mile's desperation, Gren had no choice but to play along.

"The boss is acting strange..."

The Roaring Mithrils were alternatively gaping, in a tizzy, and trying desperately to hold back laughter.

And then there was Veil, who emerged from the waiting area, his face grim.

"What's all this fooling around?"

"No, wait. There must be some reason for all this. Isn't that so, Elbert?" the king said, turning to the principal.

"That one, as well as the three girls before—they're all in this together."

"I see..." the king mused.

"Mile!" Elbert said to her, as she returned from the fighting grounds. "What the heck was that?! That should've been a total victory for you!"

"No no no! If I'd won the fight, I would've stood out way too much to be starting as a C-rank hunter. That's bad! Besides, it would have been awful to give that much of a blow to their reputation."

"W-well, I suppose that's true..."

Upon hearing this, and recalling what she herself had done earlier, Reina suddenly felt a bit guilty. Maybe she could have dialed things back slightly. The mage she had faced was still over in the waiting area, after all, huddled in a ball and mumbling feverishly.

Now, in the center of the stadium, beneath the watchful eyes of the audience, Gren and Veil faced off.

After Mile's words, Gren had no choice but to keep fighting. Just as Mile had anticipated.

"Are you conspiring with those guys, too?" Gren asked Veil.

"N-no! Please don't lump me in with them!"

"Sorry. My mistake." Gren's apology was sincere.

As long as the boy was just a normal student, it would not matter that Gren was already worn out from the previous battle.

"Shall we begin, then?" he asked. "Come at me!"

"Yes, sir!"

Clang clang clang clang clang clang clang clang!

"Wh...! You tricked me!!"

"I haven't tricked you!"

Gren was becoming rather short of breath. Though Veil's speed paled in comparison to Mile's, his technique was far superior, and he was at least as fast as Mavis, which was saying something. Gren, having already been more than satisfied by his fight with Mile, felt exhaustion beginning to set in, his will fading.

That was the moment when Veil attempted a different sort of attack.

"Air Bullet!"

"Wh—?!"

Air Bullet. That simple phrase carried all the image Veil needed for this simple wind spell.

Due to their difference in height and the fact that Veil had fired from below, the shockwave of compressed air caused Gren's stance to crumble.

His reflexes were already slow from fatigue, so when Veil's sword swung toward him, Gren's legs shook. Still, no matter how badly he lost his composure, he refused to be defeated so easily. But then...

"Magic Blade!"

With a sharp sound, the blade of Gren's sword fell to the ground, sliced clean off. In the moment after the shearing, the magic dissipated from Veil's sword, and it became once again a normal, blunt practice blade, which he used to strike Gren against the side.

"Guuh!"

"Match over!"

Gren, the A-rank hunter, the leader of the Roaring Mithrils, had just suffered a painful defeat.

However, despite his loss, the man in question was completely calm. He knew exactly why he lost and was confident that he would never repeat the same mistake in the future.

The one who was truly stunned was the victor, Veil.

"I-I won...? Against a B-rank hunter?"

"Oi, kid. If you think that victory was all your doing, you're going to end up dead somewhere. Got it?"

"Ah, y-yes sir. That's obvious... But, um, well..."

"Okay, then. And, well, a victory's still a victory. Rejoice today

and resolve to do even better tomorrow. In any case, our party may be B-rank, but I'm an A-rank. Remember that!"

"Y-yessir! Thank you very much, sir!"

Amidst scattered applause, Veil headed back to the waiting area, his arms and legs swinging stiffly.

Yeeeeeeess! It's all going according to plan!

Back in the waiting area, Mile was gloating.

She was over the moon with the success of her plan to have Veil go last so that the impression she herself had left was lessened.

If the name of Veil, the boy who had beat the leader of the B-rank party, the Roaring Mithrils, became known by all, then the fame of the others would likely be second to his. Even if she'd overdone it a bit, when her exploits were compared to the breaking news that one of the students undertaking the graduation exam had vanquished Gren, the leader of the Roaring Mithrils, news of Mile would be inconsequential.

It was the perfect plan.

"Oi, Mile, come here a minute!"

Mile, still gloating at the success of her scheme, was startled when Gren called to her from the center of the battlefield.

If someone keeps calling for you, then eventually, you have no choice but to respond. Moreover, if that someone keeps calling you by name, everyone else is sure to remember that name— despite the fact that, at that moment, Mile was supposed to be nothing but a no-name graduate.

With those thoughts in mind, she stepped back out onto the field.

"Wh-what is it?"

"You're going to join us!" Gren shouted to her. "Get your bags in order, and come back to our base!"

"Wh...?" Hearing Gren, the spectators began to stir.

A rookie hunter, fresh out of the Hunters' Prep School, had just been scouted by the Roaring Mithrils. It was a dream of a lifetime.

There were but a few S-rank hunters in the whole world. Therefore, an S-rank party was virtually impossible, which meant that the highest existing parties stood at A-rank. And now, a rookie hunter had just been scouted by the Roaring Mithrils, who were just on the verge of that A-rank.

Certainly, pitting this girl against Gren, an A-rank hunter, had been by no means a fair matchup.

Yet Mile had exhibited such power and speed—and in such a small package, too. Not only that, but—despite calling herself the "Magic Swordsman"—she hadn't used any magic in their fight. Yet, it wasn't that she *couldn't* use it. It was that she *hadn't*—except for once, right in the middle of the fight. If she had used powerful magic, the fight would have been much easier. But perhaps she hadn't used magic because she wished to battle Gren with her sword alone.

She had to be quite the big shot to be playing around with an A-rank hunter.

Beyond all that, she was still only twelve years old. The more she learned as she grew older, the more capable she would become. With further practice and experience, Gren could only imagine what kind of monster she would grow into...

An A-rank? As if she would stop at such a piddling rank as that.

An S-rank? Was there really no higher rank available?

The legendary Christopher, the God of Blades, had risen from a commoner to a noble, and then to a count—but perhaps she would go even higher.

Perhaps they had all just witnessed the genesis of a new heroic legend. He was surely not the only person imagining such a future for her.

What kind of heroic feats would this little girl show them in the years to come?

Would she exterminate the dragons? Conquer the demon king?

With eyes full of hope, the people watched, straining their ears for the little girl's—no, the future hero's—enthusiastic reply.

"I refuse."

"...Huh?"

Surely, everyone's ears were playing tricks on them.

Gren, the spectators, the king and finance officer, Count Christopher, Elbert, the foreign guild members—everyone.

"I have a prior engagement."

At these words, Mile snapped her fingers, and three figures emerged from the waiting area: Reina, Mavis, and Pauline. They flocked around her.

"We were born at different times, in different places—"

"And though we may not share the same blood—"

"We are allies who walk the same road!"

"Even if our paths should part in the future—"

"As long as the blood flows red through our veins—"

"Our friendship is immortal!!!!"

"We are four joined down to our very souls! And our name is—"

"The Crimson Vow!!!!"

BOOOOOOM!!

As the four of them struck a pose, Mile conjured a magical explosion, a puff of four-colored smoke that burst behind them.

They had practiced lines and poses in preparation for a moment such as this, urged on by Mavis and her addiction to Mile's stories—even though Mile herself had never thought that they would ever actually make such a debut.

"O... oh."

Gren was left slack-jawed.

How else could he possibly react?

"I am afraid I must refuse," Mile repeated. "However, if our paths should again cross someday, I hope we can still be allies at that time."

With Mile's words as their signal, the four girls returned to the waiting area. They pushed past the throngs of nobles and scouts to make their way out of the stadium. In the space they left behind, several students were setting up some tables and chairs in front of an enormous pile of packages.

Atop the hastily assembled tables, they pulled from their boxes an array of sample products, which they set on top, along with a banner:

Crimson Vow Figures: 1 for 3 Silver, 4-Piece Set for 1 Gold

Displayed before them, the spectators saw miniature figures of Mile and company, just shy of twenty centimeters tall, just like the action figures one might see on Earth. There were versions garbed in both hunters' gear and casual clothes. There were 1,000 pieces in total.

"Come and get your Crimson Vow figures, just three silver each, with a half-gold discount if you buy the full set! How about one of these as a souvenir?!"

"Give me that one! I need Miss Mile!"

"Both versions of Miss Reina for me!"

"I'd like two each of Lady Mavis!"

"I want Pauline to abuse me!"

They sold out in no time.

Three days earlier, the evening after Elbert's special request, Mile had been doing a bit of end-of-term tidying up when she took inventory of her belongings inside the storage space and the loot box. She was making sure she returned anything she had been lent by the school.

"Huh? This is...?"

As Mile looked over the things she had pulled from her loot box, the other three drew nearer.

"What is that?"

"It's so cute!"

"Did you make that, Mile?"

It was the wooden figure that Mile had carved so long ago, killing time in the carriage on her way from her childhood home to Eckland Academy.

"I like the style. It looks like there should be a whole set."

"It really is nice. I bet you could sell it—don't you?"

"..."

As Mavis and Reina praised the figure, Pauline cut in.

"Can I borrow it, Mile?"

"Huhh???"

With Pauline in charge, things moved swiftly.

By the end of the night, she had spoken to all twenty of the students who weren't undergoing the graduation exam and gathered some candidates. They started a mass production team, with Mile's carved figure as a prototype.

Though the magic users were in charge of the figure production, they were assisted by those with artistic talent. Including those who handled the finishing touches and packaging, twelve students in total worked hard throughout the night. Because their plans would have no effect on the examination, they didn't speak to the test takers about what they were working on, but news spread via the magic users, and several more decided to participate.

"Miss Pauline, is this really all right?"

"He told us to crush it, didn't he? At the final assessment? So, it's fine!

"We're going to need all sorts of money after graduation. We need to buy equipment, and until work picks up, we'll need savings to tide us over. And of course, we can set some aside in case any of us gets injured or sick…

"Those who graduate at a D-rank are going to be in even more dire straits than we are. I'm sure any bit of money would be a huge help for them… Who are we to let such a lucrative chance pass us by—for our sake and theirs?!"

"W-well, we put you in charge, so I guess I can't complain. Just don't work them too hard…"

In the end, they sold all 1,000 pieces. With the full-set discounts, they garnered 2,800 silver pieces in total. From that, they paid each of the 18 participants 100 silver each and kept the remaining 1,000 pieces for their party.

In terms of Japanese money, they had made about 1,000,000 yen. A very large sum.

Even for the other participants, to start out their new lives after graduation with 100 silver already in their pockets meant a great deal. Everyone thanked the girls, and those who had declined to help, not thinking that they would actually turn a profit, regretted it deeply. However, what was done was done.

It was not long before the term "magic models" came into use in their world.

"I wonder if we'll be able to maintain the school's current budget?"

After Mile and the others left, Elbert remained in the stadium's special conference room with the king and officials.

Though he was usually full of confidence, before the king and other nobles, he lacked even a fraction of his usual presence, especially when it came to bringing up the topic of money.

"Hm? Maintain the current budget? What kind of nonsense is this?"

"W-well, I was just..." At the finance officer's reply, Elbert prepared to make his case. However...

"We couldn't possibly leave the budget as it is. We'll need to increase it—exponentially! Wouldn't you say, your Majesty?"

"Oh, yes! Most certainly. Furthermore, wasn't there a proposal several months ago to transition the prep school from a trial to official status? Please re-file it so we may examine the matter again. And we might need to request an audience with the foreign hunters' guilds sometime in the near future. I'd like to consult them on various topics and suggestions, as well.

"Count Christopher, could we rely on you for a few more matters?"

"Yes, certainly!"

Beside Count Christopher, whose eyes were shining with mirth, Elbert stood, mouth wide open.

"To think that such gems as those youngsters were hidden away in this very town. If we can uncover even more like them, then the school's budget would be a small price to pay for such riches."

At the king's hopeful words, Elbert became a bit worried.

"U-um, well, those girls were a bit of a special case... To find students like them every term would be..."

"You don't think I know that?! But if we can prevent even one genius from slipping through the cracks every decade, then that's enough. Furthermore, even if they aren't at that level, that hardly means that future graduates won't flourish! Cultivating talent takes time. Don't make such a fuss."

"You are so wise!" Elbert said. "Forgive me!"

Truly, they had been blessed with a fine king.

"And also," the king went on, "since the students attend tuition-free, don't you think we should ask them to stay in this country for a few years at minimum? They could do their duty to improve our nation, while making all sorts of connections that will keep them from wanting to leave!"

Truly, they had been blessed with a shrewd king, as well.

In the stands, everyone had gone home—except for one man, sitting silently, and a woman, who was shaking him by the shoulders.

It was the master of a certain region's guildhall, who had traveled eight days to get to the capital, along with his fellow traveler, the clerk Laura. They hadn't come to watch the graduation exam specifically, but rather, delayed some ordinary business so that their stay in the capital would coincide with the matches.

"…"

"Master, we need to go now!"

"…"

"Master!"

It was some time before the guild master was able to move again.

Not long after the day of the exam, Veil was hesitating. Normally, he would have started out his career as a hunter at a low D-rank, but thanks to that girl, he was debuting at a C-rank, accompanied by a magnificent fanfare.

To be known as "the man who defeated Gren" meant quite a lot.

In reality, he had done little more than topple a giant who was already teetering, but as the rumors spread, Veil became known as something of a superhuman figure. A number of influential people within the country, as well as guild members in positions of power, had been present at the event. Though it was clear to them that the girl was far more impressive, for those who only had heard the rumors, it seemed that the girl had put up a good fight and lost—while the boy, who had defeated Gren in the blink of an eye, was the one who was truly amazing.

Because of this, though he was unable to join any party as a full-time member, Veil received a number of invitations to join various groups for short-term engagements. Situations often arose where party members were injured, or a party lacked combat strength and needed back-up. As a result, he received a fairly decent number of these requests. Due to the fact that he always completed his work reliably, his reputation began to grow.

With just a bit more experience, he would be able to achieve his goal of becoming a party leader himself, creating opportunities for the orphans to work as low-ranking hunters. The F-rank kids could work as porters, carrying the spoils and the E-rank kids could be trained into D-ranks—at which point, a whole new world of possibilities would open up...

And then there was that girl who had granted him the means to make those dreams for the future come true, who was bright and cheerful, who was honest and cute and strong—and who had been kind to Veil.

He wanted to see her. But if they met, what would he say? Would he thank her? Again? He had already done as much at their graduation. They both lived in the capital, so there was a chance that they would run into each other sooner or later, but just as much of a chance that they wouldn't. That said, he *did* know the inn in which the girls had made their headquarters, which meant he could see her whenever he chose.

However...

It's too soon for that, Veil thought.

It was true. It was too soon.

Turning back the clock slightly, to a particular room in a certain inn, several days after the graduation exam...

"Well, anyway, I think this inn should serve as a good base. We've got a nice, big four-person room, and meals aside, we can get it for a discounted rate of three gold a month. A humble place like this is the perfect starting point. This is where our legend begins!"

As Reina spoke, the three others nodded.

"If we eat only the minimum amount," she went on, "that should cost us two gold a month. And even if we're a little indulgent, it shouldn't be more than three. That's already more than half of the almost ten gold we got from the figures. We also need to factor in replacing Mavis's half-broken sword, as well as emergency savings. We don't know when one of us is going to end up injured or sick, after all. And though we do have Pauline's healing magic, it's better to be safe than sorry.

"So, our budget's at its limit. In other words, we'll need to earn at least five gold pieces each month to cover the next month's expenses. And of course, if we want to buy new clothing or shop for any other things, we'll need a bit more.

"Speaking practically, we also need to save up to buy some new equipment—and on top of that, it would be nice to have a feast on our birthdays. Therefore, my goal is ten gold a month or more.

"If we earn anything significantly beyond that, we can relocate to an inn that has its own bath. For four girls, having only a wash basin to wipe off is less than ideal!"

Mavis and Pauline nodded again.

As for Mile, she said, "Wouldn't it be more convenient to wash ourselves with warm water magic when we go out hunting and eliminate any day-to-day sweat and dirt from our bodies and clothes with cleaning magic?"

"A-ah..."

"Ah?"

"YOU JERK!! If you know that kind of magic, then why didn't you teach it to us soooooooooner?! I did notice back at the dorm that you never seemed to take a bath... I guess you were just keeping your tricks to yourself!!!"

Thus began operations for the C-rank hunting party, the Crimson Vow—and Mile's life as a normal C-rank hunter.

"Those students really were amazing... We ought to consider a system like that, where talented individuals can be promoted in a short time, for the benefit of our own country," said the master of a certain country's capital guildhall, as his carriage rambled back along the road to his land's royal capital.

Inside his luggage, stowed away in the carriage, was a full four-piece set of figures that resembled a particular group of very talented girls.

Thusly laden, the carriage pressed on to the royal capital of a certain country, home to Eckland and Ardleigh Academies.

Adele's MAGNIFICENT ACADEMY LIFE

STORY 1 |

DIY Underwear

I T HAD BEEN SEVERAL WEEKS since the start of term at Eckland Academy.

Adele was a fairly resilient girl, but there was one thing that she was finding that she simply could not bear.

It was her underclothes. Or, as they were called, her "drawers."

As one might surmise, "drawers" were the only undergarments available for women in her world. Unfortunately, they were stiff and much too hot. And of course, when she donned trousers over them for physical fitness and martial arts training and then started moving around, they only got even sweatier. There had to be something she could do about this...

And so, she purchased a towel. It was a perfectly normal towel, just shy of thirty centimeters in width and eighty centimeters in length. Nonetheless, she was sure that she could make something of it.

Making underpants was simple enough, she knew. Surely she could manage to sew some.

Adele's face glowed with intention as she attached thread to the four corners of the towel. Next, she put the cloth against her skin. *All right. That feels good,* she thought, then pinned it around the left and right sides of her waist and tried tying the threads.

Slip.

It was only natural that towel had slipped down—the threads only held around her thighs, as they weren't tightened at her waist. Because she didn't have any elastic, her new garment lacked structural integrity.

She decided to try a new method. She draped the towel behind her and pulled the threads of the short end around the front of her waist and tied them there. Then, she pulled the towel up between her legs. However, when she pulled the cloth up to her waist, there was a lot left over.

Hmm... If I don't tie the threads first, then I can tie them from the inside at the front of my waist, right?

She tried it and the result felt just right.

Whoa! Adele thought. *I made the perfect pair of underwear! I must be a genius. They're easy to wear and amazingly comfortable. I bet if I sold them I could make a fortune!*

Of course, Adele had no idea that there was already a garment of exactly the same construction, known as fundoshi—a garment had been worn in the distant past, in her previous world. Even in her own, current world, such a thing was already worn by men as an undergarment...

Okay, but having all this extra stuff hanging down in the front isn't very cute... And if I wore pants over them, that would just be another place to get sweaty. That's better!

Adele cut the towel shorter and retied the threads, then tried on her new garment once more.

This is it!

She determined it was best to let the towel drape in the back, then pull that part around to the front and wrap the threads sewn at the towel's corners around her waist to tie them.

I did it! They're cheap, simple, non-sweaty, and comfortable to boot! My days of purchasing expensive "drawers" are over!

Gloating, Adele embroidered a little design onto her home-made underwear and felt quite pleased with herself.

The following day, after lunch, and before physical training...

The girls began changing from their uniforms into their gym clothes in the locker room.

As Marcela began to undress, her eyes suddenly stopped on Adele, changing beside her.

"Wh...?!"

What Marcela saw was Adele, her upper garments removed, about to step into her gym trousers...and wearing her homemade underpants.

"A-a-aaaaaah, Miss Adele!!!" Marcela shouted, red in the face.

Their classmates turned to see what was going on.

"Wh... wh-wh-wh-what are you wearing?! What on earth are those?!?!"

"Oh, these? I made them myself! They're great, aren't they?! They aren't itchy, or sweaty, and they're super easy to make! If you all like, I'll make some for every—"

Marcela, who had been in the process of unbuttoning her blouse, buttoned it back up. She handed Adele her skirt, then grabbed her by the collar.

"Huh? Why are we putting our uniforms back o... H-hey, Miss Marcela, where are we...?"

With Adele keeping her strength limited to that of a normal girl, even a slight young lady like Marcela could easily drag her along.

"U-um, but we have training now! Wh-where are we...?"

Marcela shot Adele a terrifying look and walked faster, until they'd left the others far behind.

"Where are Marcela and Adele?" Burgess asked.

"They're off having a special lesson about decency, modesty, and common sense," Monika said.

From her reply, Burgess could surmise the circumstances. "I'm marking Marcela as absent."

In the end, the two didn't return until afternoon classes were over.

Adele's MAGNIFICENT ACADEMY LIFE

STORY 2 |

DIY Natto

I WISH I HAD SOME JAPANESE FOOD, Adele thought one day. However, she didn't want to eat any fancy, high-class cooking.

All she wanted were simple dishes: miso soup and natto and sashimi on rice.

If she traveled to a seaside town, she might be able to eat fresh fish, but she would still have no wasabi or soy sauce.

"Well, I can't worry about what I don't have, so I'll have to try to make do! Plus, if I use a few cooking hacks, maybe I can save money!"

Adele had read many books in her previous life, including one on fermented foods.

"I'm definitely going to need some soy sauce, so I'll get soybeans, wheat, brine, yeast germ... Yeast germ?"

She had no idea what yeast germ even was nor where to get her hands on it. She probably wouldn't even know it if she saw it. She wasn't even sure it would be visible to the naked eye.

"Well, that's a no, then. Maybe I'll start with miso instead! As far as I remember, the only things you need to make miso are soybeans, salt, yeast... Never mind!"

Things were not going well. That little thing called yeast was standing in the way of all Adele's ambitions.

"Natto, then! Natto is just soybeans and natto-kin... That I know!"

Thankfully, natto-kin were something that she did have some knowledge of. They were a variety of bacteria often found on rice stalks. When subjected to high heat such as boiling, all other varieties of bacteria died off, leaving only the natto-kin behind.

She would have to wash and boil the soybeans, then mix in the bacteria. That seemed simple enough. Even if she failed, she could just keep experimenting and try it again. And, when she *did* finally succeed, she could make a lot, and store it in her loot box...

Proliferating bacterial weaponry is strictly prohibited.

"Huh?"

Proliferating bacterial weaponry is strictly prohibited. Bypassing this restriction requires at least a level seven authorization.

Adele froze as the nanomachine voice pierced her eardrums.

"Huh? No, um—it's just natto, a food!"

Proliferating bacterial weaponry is strictly prohibited.

The nanomachines, which had always seemed fairly friendly, now sounded harsh and cold. Adele was speechless.

"Wh-what do you meeeeeeean?!"

And so, Adele's Japanese cooking scheme was vanquished in a matter of moments.

Adele's MAGNIFICENT ACADEMY LIFE

STORY 3 |

Wicked Girl

O NE DAY, DURING LUNCH, a boy burst into the Class A classroom.

"Which of you is Adele?"

Whoa...

The students were quiet under the boy's glare.

"Um, I'm Adele..." she said, speaking up.

"Hm, you then?" He had a pompous air and scrutinized Adele rudely.

"All right. I'm going to make you my woman!"

Whaaaaaaaat?!?!

The students hid their faces in their hands.

Adele's response was immediate. "I refuse."

"Wh-what?! Do you have any idea who I am?!"

"No. I'm not very good with faces, so..."

This much was true. Even in her previous life, she had always struggled to remember faces, even though she could recall names perfectly—as well as the date and time she had met someone, and what they had talked about. Faces were a no-go, and to be honest, that shortcoming troubled Adele greatly.

"I am Chester von Closson, the third son of Viscount Closson, of Class C!"

"Ah. Well then, what business do you have with me?"

"I just told you! I'm going to make you my woman!"

"But I already declined, didn't I? If there are no other items, then I need to go ahead and prepare for afternoon lessons, so..."

The boy was enraged. "I'm telling you, I am the third son of Viscount Closson! I'm not one of you peasants or low-ranking swine! How dare you speak to me that way!"

Adele was not impressed by these words. "Oh? But everyone as this school is equal, aren't they? Regardless of status? Didn't you hear about this at orientation?

"Furthermore, this is a school for commoners and lesser nobles, as well as the fourth or younger sons and daughters of barons and the like. The third son of a wealthy viscount attending classes here, and not Ardleigh Academy, isn't really something to boast about, is it?"

WHOOOOAAAAA!

Adele's classmates were blown away by her honesty. Chester was petrified.

"Anyway, what on earth do you mean by 'I'll make you my woman'?!" she went on. "I am my own person. I am no one's possession. And whatever could you mean by 'make you'? You'll do this without my will or consent? Honestly...!"

Just then, someone clutched Adele's arm. She turned to see Marcela, quickly shaking her head back and forth.

The boy from Class C, named Chester, had been standing stock still, unmoving, for some time.

As it was nearly time for afternoon lessons to start, Marcela began to fret, but it seemed as though someone had alerted Chester's Class C peers, and a pair arrived to drag the still-frozen boy from the classroom.

As they left, Adele gave the two a bright smile, and said, "Thank you so much."

"I-It's no big deal!" they replied. "If you have any more problems, just call on us!"

Adele hadn't forgotten about Japanese politeness. Or was it feminine wiles that she was recalling instead?

"Ugh! That 'make you my woman' thing was ridiculous. He's probably just mimicking something that he heard from his father or older brother," said Marcela. "I suppose he thought that if he could snag Adele, the gem of Class A, it would be a boon for his reputation. I wouldn't worry over it."

"All right..." Adele said and nodded sincerely, thankful for Marcela's advice.

During lunch the following day, Chester stopped by the Class A classroom once again.

"Adele, let's go shopping together on tomorrow's rest day!" he said.

The class watched, worried. If a fellow classmate had extended a normal-seeming invitation to her, Adele wouldn't have responded rudely. She wanted friends after all, both female and male.

The thought of hanging out with a boy wasn't totally foreign to Adele—she was, after all, accustomed to the idea of girls who were slightly boyish and full of energy, always playing soccer and baseball with the boys. Just like in the *Tomboy Secchi* series she'd read in her previous life...

However.

"I refuse."

"Huh? Why...?"

Chester's face was filled with disbelief. He had been turned down again, despite the fact that someone must have bestowed some wisdom upon him since the previous afternoon—judging by the proper invitation he had issued this time, at least.

"It's not that I'm not flattered to receive your invitation," she told him. "However, I can't afford to give up my free school lunch and eat out—nor do I have the money to buy unnecessary things. Plus, I already have plans for tomorrow..."

That she was flattered to receive the invitation was all that Chester needed to hear.

"I can pay for your lunch! How about next week?!"

"Unfortunately, I have plans then, as well..."

"Then how about the week after next?!"

"Unfortunately, I have plans then, as well..."

"Then how about the week after the week after next?!"

"Unfortunately, I have plans then, as well..."

"Then when the heck *are* you going to be free?!" Chester's voice rose to an understandably frustrated cry.

Was she still only messing with him, despite the fact that this time, he'd said all the right things?

"Um, I work at a shop on every rest day. I don't receive an allowance, so if I don't work, I can't afford ink or paper or new clothes or soap or *anything*."

"Uh..."

"So that's how it is. I can't go hang out with anyone, no matter who they are. I'm very sorry..."

She couldn't hang out with anyone after school either, since the dorms had a curfew. Furthermore, Adele had no intention of skipping her free dinner.

Chester sulked his way back to his own classroom.

As for Adele's classmates, well—from the moment Chester had arrived, they had been watching with concern—not for her, but for Chester.

Then came the following rest day.

Adele was working the bakery counter as usual when, just after midday, a single customer entered.

"So, you're here."

"Um, oh. Chester... right?" Adele said.

"Do you still not remember me?!"

That customer was, in fact, Chester.

"It's time to go hang out!" he said.

"Oh, okay. Go ahead. I'll see you later!"

"You're coming, too!" he said. "Do you really think I came all this way just to tell you that I'm going to hang out?!"

"Huh? Did you not?"

Chester slammed both hands on the counter. "Just come with me already!"

"But I have to mind the shop..."

"Just make that old couple over there do it!"

"No. Those two are customers—they don't work here..."

Even Chester could see that it would be futile to try to make customers work in the shop, so he stood silently for a short while, thinking.

"All right, then. I'll buy everything."

"Huh?"

"I'm going to buy all the bread you have left. Then there'll be no need for you to mind the shop, will there?"

"Wh-what are you...?"

"Smart, isn't it?" he said.

"It's nonsense!"

"Huh?" Chester was taken aback at Adele's sudden rage.

"This shop is open for all the people who need bread on the rest days, but you want to leave it empty?! You'll buy all the bread just to drag me out? What a foolish deed—and a stupid plan of action!"

"S-sorry..." Seeing Adele, whom he had always thought so cool and composed, suddenly angry, Chester was shocked and quickly apologized. It seemed that he was at least an honest boy.

"Well, how about half, then?"

"Huh?" Chester stared, unsure of what he was being asked.

"I'm saying, how about you buy just half the bread?"

"S-sure..."

Faced with Adele's suggestion and her bright smile, Chester unthinkingly agreed.

"How did this happen...?"

Chester plodded back down the road to the dorm, his arms overflowing with bread and a dark cloud hanging over him. Still, perhaps it had been a small price to pay for the privilege of seeing Adele smile at him for the first time.

The corners of his mouth lifted, just a little.

"Well, Grandpa, what should we do about that one?"

"I think the girlie's got it covered."

"Reckon so..."

The old timers in the bakery were part of an informal Secret Service who stopped by the bakery to protect Adele from bad men. Apparently, they had deemed that Chester was not a threat.

In the future, when Chester stopped by the Class A classroom again, Adele's classmates were no longer concerned. They had also deemed him harmless.

Even if his attempts at flirtation were futile, it was fine if he just talked to Adele a bit, as long as he didn't make her mad at him.

While Adele would happily chat casually with both her class-mates and students from other classes, it was clear that she had no intention of taking on a boyfriend, future life partner, or even prospective *business* partner at this point.

Her classmates decided that Adele was simply too young to be thinking of romance, not realizing the real reason for her standoffishness. Mentally, Adele was more than eighteen years old, after all—thus, to her, all of her classmates were far too young to be recipients of her romantic interest.

This, of course, included a certain younger son of a viscount, who was vying desperately for her affections.

Though she had no interest in romantic associations with boys, if they spoke to her, she would happily converse, and would gladly hang out with them at lunch and after school. When she wasn't hanging out with Marcela and the girls, at least.

Even while working at the shop, when boys spoke to her, she would offer them a friendly smile.

As time proceeded, the number of boys who got the wrong impression grew.

Thus, once again, the old woman at the shop muttered, "Hoo hoo hoo, you're a wicked girl, Miss Adele..."

Afterword

NICE TO MEET YOU, everyone. My name is FUNA.

I first registered with the story-sharing site *Shousetsuka ni Narou* (*Let's Be Novelists*) some months ago, to further the dream I've had since elementary school of becoming a novelist. Honestly, I never truly thought that I would see that dream come true.

Well, it's a lie to say that I didn't expect for it to happen at all—but it was a bit like feeling, "Wouldn't it be great to win the lottery?" and certainly didn't seem like a realistic expectation.

This book's publication comes not even four short months after the day I received that fateful e-mail from the publishers.

So, it's not Marci's "One-Week Maid Story," but a "Four-Month Novelist Story."

At the time, the serialization of this story had barely begun, and so, when I received the e-mail, I thought it was in regard to one of my previous works, which had already finished serialization. But no—they meant my new one! When the publisher approached me, there was hardly enough content to fill even a single volume, and although one portion had been published, I didn't even know the overall direction of the story as a whole. I tried to persuade them over and over again to rethink this, saying, "Well, but, I don't think this is going to be a school story. She leaves school pretty quickly," and asking, "Are you really sure it's alright to make a decision like this so soon?" They told me it didn't matter.

Because I'm still an amateur, when it came time for publishing, there were a lot of typos, grammatical errors, and other mistakes, so everyone on the *Shousetsuka ni Narou* site was an enormous help to me. I especially want to thank Mirumiru-san, who was so professional that I still wonder whether they proofread for a living, for their exceptional guidance.

I first began serialization of this story about two months after I began posting on *Shousetsuka ni Narou*. It is my third posted work.

I worked on my first two serials simultaneously, so the process for those basically consisted of me more or less hastily spilling out ideas I'd had for a long time onto the page via the keyboard. This story I wrote at more of a leisurely pace, taking my time to relax, enjoy the process, and draw a bit more on my strengths.

The main character, in her previous life, was the sort of person who was good at studying but had hardly any acquaintances and knew nothing of the world. Therefore, she was a good girl who was bad at reading people.

Thus, this is the story of a quick-thinking main character who hopes that, once she's reincarnated, she'll be able to live life to the fullest. She wants to make friends and do whatever she pleases, so that she can die without regrets. Because she has no knowledge of her new world, and never knew much about how to deal with people or the world in general in her previous life, she thinks that as long as she can be an unremarkable, completely normal, average girl—passing her days peacefully and happily while saving up for her eventual retirement—then things should turn out fine.

So that she can live her new life in indulgent, blissful ignorance, even now she strives to be the sort of person who is still a completely normal, average C-rank hunter. This, despite being berated with insults like "I can't believe you were ever intelligent in your previous life," or "Is your intellect the average of a flea's back in that world?" Volume 1 marks the end of the Academy—Hunters' Prep School Arc, so from here on out, our protagonist will begin her new life as a rookie hunter. As plainly and ordinarily as possible.

Yes, she'll be trying her very best not to become an S-rank hunter.

I've been a bit lost as to what sort of title I should give myself from here on out—like "writer," or "storyteller"—but when I really think about it, I've realized that there's no reason to be so lost. I've been able to write because of everyone on the *Let's Be Novelists* site, so it only makes sense to call myself a "novelist," doesn't it...?

Still, even if I call myself a novelist, the future is hard to see. Will other volumes come out? Or will my career end with this single release? Whenever I wonder, "How far will I make it from here on out?" I remember a quote from the protagonist of a manga that I like:

"I wonder how far I'll make it from here on out."
"Where will you go?"
"Anywhere. As far as I can reach!"

Finally, to the editor, who reached out to me after finding my work among the hundreds of thousands of stories posted on *Shousetsuka ni Narou*; to Akata Itsuki, the illustrator; to Yamakami Yoichi, the cover designer; to everyone involved in the proofreading, editing, printing, binding, distribution, and selling of this book; to all the reviewers on *Shousetsuka ni Narou* who gave me their impressions, guidance, suggestions, and advice; and most of all, to everyone who's read my stories, both in print and online—I thank you all from the bottom of my heart.

Thank you for everything up till now and from here on out.

— FUNA

Didn't I Say
to Make My Abilities
Average **in the**
Next Life?!

AFTERWORD?

I JUST FELT LIKE DRAWING THESE, SO I DID THEM ON MY OWN WITHOUT CONSULTING ANYONE. THIS IS MISATO-CHAN BEFORE HER REINCARNATION INTO MILE.

BEFORE (UNOFFICIAL)
KURIHARA MISATO
AGE 18

I WONDER IF THIS WILL MAKE IT INTO THE BOOK? I HOPE IT DOES. ALSO, WHAT DO YOU THINK ABOUT CONDENSING THE TITLE, *"DIDN'T I SAY TO MAKE MY ABILITIES AVERAGE?!"* TO *"ABILAVERAGE!"* FOR SHORT?

AFTER
~~ADELE VON ASCHAM~~
MILE AGE 12

ITSUKI
AKATA

FUNA

Pleased to meet you! My name is FUNA. The publication of this volume marks the story's commercial debut, as well as my debut as an author. Follow along as a young girl tries her best to live in a fantastical world—the sort of world only these things called "books" can give us a glimpse into!

Itsuki Akata

It's been a long time since I've gotten to illustrate a fantasy work. All of these characters are absolutely adorable, though, so I had a lot of fun! I really hope you enjoy the drawings, too!

Didn't I Say
to Make My Abilities
Average in the
Next Life?! ──